Suns and Secrets at Blackberry Beach

HOLLY MARTIN

CHAPTER ONE

Fern drove over the hill in her sunshine-yellow VW van and smiled as the twinkling blue waves came into view. For someone who had never even seen the sea until she was fourteen, it was this view of the three beaches that made up Apple Hill Bay that she'd seen first and it always made her smile. This was home now and despite the fact she had lived with her best friend Ettie for the last few years in the next seaside town of White Cliff Bay, Apple Hill Bay always would be home for her. And now she was living here again since Ettie had got married and moved out of the flat they'd shared together. It was good to be back.

She drove down into the valley and parked the van near to the tunnel that led to Blackberry Beach, one of the three beaches that made up Apple Hill Bay.

She was so excited to be working here today. After Fern had painted murals on the bedroom and garden walls for a few people in town, her mum, Carrie, had persuaded her to set herself up as a mural artist and today was her first official day for her small business, The Big Picture.

She loved painting, it didn't matter what it was; animals, dinosaurs, superheroes, Disney princesses, she loved it all. For years it had been her escape but she'd never thought she'd make a living out of it.

She could put this job on her newly developed website that her brother Theo had set up for her. And everyone in the town of Apple Hill Bay and other local towns and villages would see her work whenever they came to Blackberry Beach so she might get more commissions that way. There was only one tiny problem with this commission. Well, two actually. The first being that she might not get paid. She supposed the increased visibility and exposure would be a good thing for a new business but exposure didn't pay the bills.

It was part of the reason why she had got this gig: no serious artist would ever work for free so only a few people had applied for the job. Councillor Bishop had whittled it down to two people out of a handful of applications. Which was the second part of the problem. Fern would be competing against someone else for the prize money of five thousand pounds. She would be painting the left half of the tunnel and Fletcher Harrison, whoever he was, would be painting the right half. The public would choose their favourite by putting tokens in boxes next to the mural they liked the best and the winner of the Great Mural Painting Competition would be announced on Friday and would win the money.

She was determined to win. Not because of the money, although she couldn't deny that five thousand pounds would be gratefully received, but being able to put the 'Winner of the Great Mural Painting competition' on her website would feel like a wonderful accolade. Admittedly, the competition

2

was between two people, so not actually that 'Great' after all, but not everyone would know that. Other businesses might employ her based on winning.

Fern had looked into Fletcher Harrison as soon as she'd heard she'd be competing against him. She couldn't find anything to say he had an art background. He had a website selling furniture and jewellery made from bits of wood but there was nothing to indicate he had experience with painting. Carpentry and art didn't necessarily feel like a good mix. Creating something beautiful out of wood didn't mean he could paint. She was kind of hoping he was only in this for the money and his artistic skills would be somewhat limited.

She loaded up her trolley with her paints, brushes and other tools and started walking down the tunnel. The tunnel to the beach had been built in Victorian times to transport limestone to the nearby kilns although the locals had called it Smuggler's Tunnel to make it sound more mysterious than it was. It was a long tunnel that wound its way through the heart of the cliff. There were several sections and corners, which just added to the mystery and intrigue of it, as if she was walking into a different world, but she had made this journey many times and she knew it came out onto a beautiful little cove. The tunnel and therefore the beach was closed for today and Tuesday while they completed their paintings so they wouldn't be disturbed.

She and Fletcher would be painting the last section that led out onto the beach. She had come down the night before ready to paint her base coat of white only to find that both sides of the tunnel had already been painted white, probably in preparation for the competition.

Fern turned the last corner to see a huge bear of a man

3

already hard at work painting the walls. And, to her annoyance, he was painting on her side of the tunnel.

'You're painting the wrong side,' Fern said as she approached.

He turned to face her, the sunlight catching his gentle grey eyes, his face lighting up in a warm smile. 'Ah you must be Fern Lucas.' He held out a giant paw of a hand. 'I'm Fletcher Harrison.'

She hadn't totally appreciated how big he was until she'd got up close but he must be nearly seven foot tall. She was five foot three and he seemed to be almost two foot taller than her. He was broad too, like he would have trouble walking through doors. He almost completely filled the tunnel he was so big. He had muscles everywhere. Even his thighs were thick like treetrunks. He was beautiful, not in a catwalk model kind of way but in that rough, rugged way that she supposed some women would like. But not her, definitely not her. She didn't do relationships at all.

So she was annoyed that when she took his hand to shake, she felt something inside her that felt like desire and need but was probably just a bit of indigestion or heartburn. She definitely didn't *need* a man like Fletcher Harrison. Or any man actually. Especially not a man who couldn't follow instructions.

'Pleased to meet you. But you're painting the wrong side.'

She felt like she needed to focus on that rather than what her heart and stomach were doing at being in such close proximity to him. And to her frustration she realised she was still holding his hand like some lovesick teenager meeting her idol. She quickly removed it.

To her surprise, he'd clearly felt something when they'd

touched too. His eyes were dark with a sudden need that hadn't been there before.

He cleared his throat and looked away down towards the beach. 'I don't think I am. Councillor Bishop said we were painting the first section nearest to the beach. She said I was painting the right-hand side. From the beach, this side is the right side.'

'I'm painting the left side, but obviously that means the left side as you approach it from the car park. That's how you would see it first. You'd have to come down the tunnel to the beach and then go back again into the tunnel to call the side you're painting the right side. That doesn't make sense.'

Fletcher shrugged. 'Oh well, it doesn't really matter, does it? We both have half a tunnel to paint, it doesn't matter who goes where. I'm looking forward to working with you.'

He had such a laid-back, chilled-out vibe about him, as if nothing could ever bother him. It was quite endearing. And in the face of it she felt some of her frustration seep away.

'Except we're not really working with each other, we're supposed to be competing against one another,' Fern said.

'Yes, well, I don't think it was supposed to be a fight to the death.'

She smiled, feeling all the fight fall out of her. 'Sorry, I think we got off on the wrong foot. I've started a new business painting murals and this is my first official job. I really want to make a good impression to help build my business up from the ground. I thought winning would be a great accolade to add to my website. So I came down here nervous and excited and…' she trailed off.

'Ready to fight to the death,' Fletcher said.

She smirked. 'Something like that.'

He rubbed his hand across his stubble and she had an

overwhelming desire to do the same, wondering if it would be soft or spiky.

'Well if you insist on a duel, we need to pick a method I stand a chance of winning with. I've never even held a pistol or a sword and if it came down to a bare-knuckle fight, I've never raised my fists to anyone, I wouldn't even know how to punch someone. Whereas you've come down here with this big steely attitude, I reckon you could fell someone in one punch.'

Fern laughed at the thought of beating him in a fist fight. He was rock solid, it would be like starting a fight with a concrete wall.

'How about nunchucks?' she asked.

He burst out laughing and it was loud and rich and warm. It filled her up from the inside.

'Now this is getting serious. But the proper etiquette for a duel is for the person challenged to choose the weapon and fortunately I have just the thing at home. Will you meet me here at sunset and we can resolve it once and for all?'

She couldn't help smiling. There was something so infectiously cheerful about him, she felt happier just standing near him.

'OK, but I warn you, I'll be bringing my savage dog with me. You make a wrong move and he'll lick you to death,' Fern said,

'I'll take that into consideration.'

'In the meantime I have a competition to win so I'm going to start painting.' She glanced over his shoulder at what he'd already painted and smiled to see a comical-looking crab walking along the sea bed with large bulbous eyes and its claws held aloft as he tried to defend himself against a menacing-looking shark. The style was very cartoony but it was obvious Fletcher had a lot more skill than she'd hoped he would. 'This is really good.'

He shrugged. 'I always used to doodle stuff when I was a kid, I used to make my own comics and sell them to the kids at school.'

'Is that what you do now, as well as your carpentry?'

'No, I'm not an artist, I don't do anything like this any more, apart from for fun. I just need the money to help fund my own business. But should I be flattered that you looked me up?'

'I wanted to see who I was up against, but I didn't see anything arty in what I found, so I was hoping for an easy win. Now I can see I'm going to have to win this duel tonight so I can nobble the competition.'

He grinned. 'I looked you up too. Your paintings are amazing. I don't think you have too much to worry about in me. I might have to resort to underhand tactics in the duel.'

She stared at him, smiling like an idiot. What was going on here?

'I should...' she gestured to the wall behind her.

He nodded. 'Yes, me too. I'd start from the beach end if I were you, the wall that end is still a bit tacky from when I painted it yesterday.'

She frowned in confusion. 'You painted it white, for me?'

'Well, I was here painting my side white, it made sense just to paint the whole thing.'

'Thank you, that's really kind. You're not really cut out for this competing-against-each-other, fighting-to-the-death scenario, are you?'

'Not really. I'm more the helping-someone-out kind of person.'

'Damn it.'

'What?'

'I wasn't expecting you to be so nice.'

'Oh, just you wait for the duel. I can be really mean.'

She smiled. 'I look forward to it.'

She made herself turn away and start work but, when she glanced back, he was still watching her as if she was a puzzle he was trying to solve. He quickly looked away and carried on working on his shark.

She tried to stamp down on the butterflies fluttering like mad in her stomach, tried to trap them all in a jar and slam down the lid, but they refused to cooperate.

Fletcher stepped back to inspect his work. It was looking good so far but there was still a ton left to do. His stomach growled in protest. He checked the time and realised it was already past two. He was always like this when he was busy working on a project. Time would get away from him as he fully immersed himself in his work. Normally it was some wooden furniture which captured his attention and his imagination, so it was fun to do something different for a change.

'Would you like to join me for some lunch?' he said, grabbing his bag of food.

'Oh, I'm not really that hungry and I should probably get on,' Fern gestured to the wall that had transformed under her hand over the last few hours. She had painted the golden sands of a beach and already added a seagull sneaking up on a man eating chips. She was in the middle of painting a fantastic towering sandcastle that had turrets and flags flying from the top. It was amazing.

Her stomach gurgling betrayed her.

'You have to eat something,' Fletcher said. 'And we have the beach completely to ourselves as the tunnel is closed, seems a shame to waste such an opportunity. And it's a beautiful day.'

She turned to look at him and her smile just warmed him. He'd never really been a sucker for a smile, but there was something wonderful about Fern Lucas that had got under his skin and was seeping into his soul. She had certainly captured his attention too. She was dressed in dungarees and a t-shirt that had little ducks on it and, with her blonde hair in plaited pigtails, she looked cute. She had been singing and dancing along to music from her phone all morning and it was so damned endearing that he wanted to sweep her up in his arms and dance with her.

'Go on then. But just a quick lunch.'

She grabbed her bag and they walked down the steps from the tunnel onto the beach. It was beautifully deserted, making them feel like the only people in the world.

They sat down on the golden sand, staring out over the turquoise water. The sea was flat calm today, like a millpond.

'So you're starting a mural painting business. That sounds fantastic. What made you want to do that?' Fletcher said.

Fern looked at him in surprise, her packet of sandwiches open on her lap. 'You know, most people, when I tell them I'm going to be painting murals for a living, say things like, oh that's a nice hobby or will it pay the bills or when are you going to get a proper job.'

Fletcher pulled a face. 'I restore and make furniture out of unwanted and unloved household items that have been thrown away. I'm not in any position to judge. And then to make it worse I teach people my skills so I'm passing on that

9

dream job to others too. Honestly, we spend so much of our lives at work, we have to find something that makes us happy. It takes bravery to shun the conventional nine-to-five job of working in a bank or a shop to pursue something you love. I admire that.'

She smiled and took a bite from her sandwich.

'To answer your question, I've always loved painting,' she said when she'd finished her mouthful. 'It was an escape for me when I was a child.'

He watched her, wondering what she'd had to escape from. She saw the look and gave a sad smile. 'I grew up in foster care, so it wasn't exactly a happy childhood.'

He studied her. 'That must have been so hard for you.'

She looked at him again. 'You seem to always know the right thing to say. I don't talk about this a lot. Every time I tell someone, the first thing they always say is, what happened to your parents and that's a question I don't like to answer. So I end up just saying something like they couldn't look after me rather than the truth, which makes people's eyes light up because they've got a juicy bit of salacious gossip.'

'Gossip doesn't interest me and I'm not trying to win brownie points by saying the right thing. I don't need to know what happened to your parents, unless you want to tell me. My first thought was how lonely it must have been for you growing up without someone to love you.'

She stared at him with wide eyes. 'It was hard. Incredibly so.'

She looked out over the sea and Fletcher didn't expect her to share any more but he found himself reaching out and taking her hand. She glanced down at their joined hands and he wondered if he'd overstepped a boundary. He didn't know her and here they were sitting alone on the beach holding hands. He was about to remove his hand when she started talking again.

'I never knew my dad. I don't even know his name. Angela, my birth mum, preferred drink and taking drugs to looking after me. I'd be shipped off to foster care for a few weeks then back to her then back into the system again, a different foster home, a different family. I don't actually remember a time when I wasn't in foster care, I think she'd always looked out for herself rather than me. And I know addiction is a horrible thing and it's hard to break the cycle but, from what I remember of her, she never even tried. And I think for me that was the hardest part, that I wasn't enough to make her want to stop. She had lots of different boyfriends, well men that were always hanging around, and some of them were violent with her. I think in the end the authorities decided it was safer for me to be put in foster care permanently.'

She took another bite of her sandwich and he felt like she was playing for time.

'She was supposed to maintain contact, we should have had supervised visits once a week. She didn't even want to do that. She was there for a few, missed a lot of them and then disappeared for a while. I'd heard she was working up in Blackpool and then she was caught stealing money from her employer, quite a significant amount that had built up over many months, so she served some time in prison and then went to Italy after that. I've not seen her or spoken to her since I was seven. I have no idea where she is or what she is doing and I have no desire to.'

Fern was silent for a moment then shook her head as if to clear it. 'I don't know why I told you that, I don't… it's not

11

something I really talk about. I'm sorry. We've just met and I've just dumped all this on you.'

'You don't need to apologise.'

'I kind of do. You simply asked about my mural painting business and I unleashed a whole ton of baggage. But I suppose, in some weird way, she is part of this. I don't have too many memories of her and none of them are good, but I do remember I loved to paint, even as a little child, and I told her I was going to be a famous painter one day and people would pay me thousands of pounds for my paintings. She laughed and told me my paintings weren't worth anything. Now, with a wiser head on my shoulders, I have no desire for fame or fortune but I am determined to make a success of this business to prove her wrong.'

Fletcher watched her, carefully. 'To prove *you* have worth,' he said, softly.

She looked at him again and let out a heavy breath. 'Well, that's very astute. It's silly, isn't it? I haven't seen or spoken to the woman in twenty-two years. I have a wonderful mum now, Carrie adopted me when I was fourteen and she is everything you would ever want in a mum and more. Exuberant, completely over the top with her love for me, generous, kind, I love her so much. Carrie gave me a family, having already adopted my two brothers a few years before. I was loved for the first time in my life and by three people, I will always be so grateful for that. And Angela probably hasn't given me a single thought. But, while I have no desire to ever see her again, I do think of her often. I wonder why I wasn't enough.' She blew out a breath that made her blonde fringe flop up. 'Jesus, this is a heavy conversation. Let's talk about something else, tell me about you.'

'You are enough,' Fletcher said. 'And you should never feel that you have to prove that, to anyone.'

She looked at him and then down at their joined hands. 'Well I didn't expect this when I came to work this morning.'

She deliberately let go of his hand so she could have a drink. Once she'd finished she didn't return her hand to his.

He sensed she needed a subject change. 'So have you always worked doing something arty?'

'No, it was always my dream to be an artist but I never thought I could make a living out of it. Probably thanks to Angela I didn't think I was good enough. I went down the boring, conventional route of employment instead. I've had lots of jobs actually, I worked as a waitress, sold double glazing, even worked at the local plastic factory in the next town. But then I fell into selling foreign currency at the nearby airport and it was easy and good money and mind-numbingly boring. But it meant I could afford to get a flat with my best friend Ettie. I always did art as a sideline though. I have my Etsy shop, have done for years, selling landscapes and pet portraits. I paint stones and vases and mugs too, but I was only ever making a tiny amount from that. Then the company I worked for at the airport folded, redundancies were made, Ettie moved out to be with her new husband and I was left jobless and unable to pay the rent on my flat alone.'

She offered him a crisp from her packet and he took one.

'My mum, Carrie, is building that new holiday resort above Strawberry Sands, The Little Beach Hut Hotel, where guests can stay in the beach huts. She already has ten up and running as guest accommodation and now work has started on another thirty. She said I could stay in one of them for a while to save some money. Carrie has always been my biggest supporter and she encouraged me to use this time to find a way to make my art pay. I put some posters around town and put some posts out on the town forum asking if anyone wanted a mural painted on their bedroom walls. I painted a fairy garden on one bedroom, dragons on another, and soon I had quite a few people asking me to paint in their houses and gardens too. I could see this could be a thing. My mum persuaded me to set up a business doing it, she said now was the time to pursue what I love. And here I am.'

'It sounds like Carrie is far more the reason you're doing this than Angela is,' Fletcher said.

Fern grinned. 'Oh, a hundred percent she is. It's because of Carrie's love, support and encouragement that I believed in myself enough to start my business and I'm determined to make it work for her too and for me. I've had quite a bit of interest too. I've submitted some designs to Apple Hill School as they're looking for someone to paint the nursery and the children's ward of the hospital has been in touch. I've even submitted designs to paint the bedrooms of a boutique hotel. Carrie wants me to paint the inside of all the new beach huts she's building as part of her resort and I start that as soon as I'm finished here. I think a lot of people will want what I offer, it's just about getting the word out now.'

'Have you thought about Facebook advertising, targeting local areas? You could have a slide show of what you've painted so far, offer some kind of discount just to build your portfolio.'

'That's a good idea. I hadn't thought of that.' She finished the last bite of her sandwich and threw the crust to a nearby seagull who caught it before it even hit the ground. 'What about you, you've heard my entire life history. What's your story?'

Fletcher thought back over his life and the dark part he

would definitely skate over. He was all for sharing but he didn't want her to think badly of him. He was not the person he'd been in the past but she still didn't need to know *everything* about him.

'I was born and raised in the next town of White Cliff Bay.'

'Oh, I was just living there for the last three years but I'm back here now.'

'Where did you live?'

'In a little block of flats overlooking Silver Cove.'

'Ah, I loved surfing there. I lived near the lifeboat station on the other side of town.'

'I know it. Sorry, go on, you were telling me about your past,' Fern said.

'I guess my childhood was relatively normal by today's standards. I have an older sister, Lara. Our parents didn't marry until I was eight but as far as I could tell they were very much in love before then. Afterwards they hated each other, they were always screaming and shouting at each other. Dad was hardly ever there and they ended up divorcing two years later. The rest of our childhood was spent between their two houses, seeing Dad half the week, seeing Mum the other half. Both of them insulting the other whenever we were with them. It wasn't great but a lot of my friends' parents were divorcing too so I wasn't exactly alone.'

He took a bite of his sandwich before carrying on. 'I wasn't particularly academic at school, but I loved woodwork. That was something I could excel at. Went on to study it at college. I was quite lucky in that my parents supported that rather than pushing me to do something more conventional. Dad said the world would always need carpenters. I worked in Tenerife for a bit but then came back to White

Cliff Bay when...' he paused as he reworded the part of his past he'd rather forget '...when a friend needed some help. Stayed there for a while and ended up doing an apprenticeship at the White Cliff Bay Furniture Company, took welding courses, metalwork courses, worked for various different companies around the UK making things out of wood and metal, lived in London for a bit and Yorkshire, and now I'm back here running my own business too.'

'Tell me about your company. It sounds fascinating.'

He loved the way she turned her body to face him as if she was really interested in what he had to say. He studied her, the way the sunlight caught the gold flecks in her green eyes, the smile on her lips that was just for him. There was something so damned likeable about Fern Lucas.

He cleared his throat. 'We make new things from old. I'll make a lamp from an old sewing machine or a table from a cartwheel, or I'll just take a broken chest of drawers and make it beautiful again. I love making stuff out of antique or vintage pieces especially, bringing old things back to life. I even make some jewellery with the leftover pieces of wood: rings, pendants and bracelets, that kind of thing. I teach others too, normally people who haven't had the opportunity to learn such skills. Some of the people I've taught have now become the teachers themselves. We received a community grant a few years ago and we moved into much bigger premises and the mentors were able to take home a small monthly salary too. But we don't always have a lot of money for new tools. If I win this competition, I'm going to use the money for some new welding equipment.'

'Wait, your company, it's called ReLoved, isn't it?'

He smiled in surprise. 'Yes, it is.'

'I know all about you. I've been following your story for

16

some time. You were the man that helped George off the streets. I read about it in the local paper – how he would often sleep outside your little shed and you'd invite him in to have coffee with you every day. Then you started teaching him different carpentry skills and soon he was making and selling his own furniture. Now he works teaching others the skills he learned from you. What you do up there is wonderful. I've thought about coming up there and learning a new skill myself but I know it's not for people like me, it's for the homeless or the kids from poorer backgrounds. But it just sounds like such a positive environment.'

'It is and you'd be very welcome. I love teaching people, regardless of their background.'

'I might just do that then. What an amazing thing to be a part of.'

She was looking at him as if he was some kind of hero.

He shook his head. 'I never intended to be this… pillar of the community. I was just making and selling furniture, chatting to George every day. He asked me to show him how to do some woodwork and I was happy to do it and I loved to see him working on his own projects. Then one day he brought one of his friends along and I started teaching him too. One of my old school friends, Max, he's a policeman, he said there were some kids around town that were always getting into trouble and he wondered whether, if they had some place to go where they could use their skills and have something positive to pour their energies into, it might keep them out of trouble. So I started teaching them too. One of them, Leo, has turned out to be this incredible artist, he makes animal hybrids out of rubbish that he collects on the beaches. People heard about what we were doing and it grew from there.'

'But you must be so proud of what you've achieved.'

'I'm proud of what all the mentors are doing.'

Fern smiled and shook her head. 'But it all started with you.'

'I think you're probably overselling my part in this. It took on a life of its own.'

'Well I think you're amazing.' She glanced at her watch. 'We better get back.'

She threw all her rubbish back into her bag and stood up. He stood up too but as he turned back towards the tunnel she snagged his arm.

'I know this is going to sound weird, but when I read the article about you and George I swore if I ever met you I would give you a big hug. I've chatted to George for years, and I always wanted to help him but, beyond buying him a sandwich or a coffee every time I went down into the town, or buying a jumper and some blankets from the charity shops for him, there wasn't a lot I could do. But you did something wonderful. I saw him a few months ago and he said he had his own place now, a little one-bedroom flat he's renting. You gave him that. And I know you'd like to dismiss the part you've played but I'd like to say thank you. Would it be OK if I gave you a hug, a no-strings-attached, completely platonic hug?'

Fletcher stood frozen in place. He wanted to say that wasn't necessary as he didn't feel like he deserved thanks for any of that but he also really wanted to hug her. He nodded, knowing he was going to hell because if he hugged her it definitely wasn't going to be platonic for him.

She stepped forward and wrapped her arms around him, resting her head on his chest. He slid his hands around her back. Her sweet coconut smell surrounded him and the warmth of her body against his was heaven. Christ this felt too good. And he didn't understand why. He wasn't short of female attention. It hadn't been so long since he'd been with a woman for him to be having such a strong reaction to a simple friendly hug. His heart was hammering in his chest and to his surprise he could feel hers thundering too.

She pulled back slightly to look up at him and he could see her eyes were dark with desire.

All thought and reason went straight out of his head and he found himself cupping her face and bending his head to kiss her. She closed her eyes, leaning up towards him, but before he could kiss her she suddenly pulled back out of his arms and took a few steps back.

'God, I'm so sorry,' Fletcher said, pushing his hands through his hair. 'You made it very clear that the hug was completely platonic and I tried to make it into something more. I don't know what came over me. I'm so sorry, I misread the signals and—'

He stopped as she moved back towards him, reaching up to cup his face.

'You didn't misread the signals. Please don't apologise or think you did anything wrong. I wanted you to kiss me too. I just...'

She let him go, stepping back again.

He frowned. 'Do you have a boyfriend?'

'No, definitely not. Actually my last relationship ended a few weeks ago after I caught him in bed with someone else. I've had a bad run of men over the years. A lot of them have cheated on me. One of them stole from me and one even hit me. And I've realised I'm really bad at picking men or just really bad at relationships so I'm on a bit of a detox for a while. No relationships, no men.'

19

He nodded. 'I totally get it. I don't do relationships either. Not any more.' He'd never had a proper relationship with anyone, not since Lauren – well, not even then.

She stared at him. 'So we're in agreement then. This thing between us. This almost kiss. It's not going to happen. We're better off not going down that path.'

He couldn't help feeling disappointed about that but he knew she was right. 'Absolutely. I agree one hundred percent.'

She nodded. 'So just friends then.'

'Yes, definitely.'

They continued to stare at each other until she took a step back. 'We should go back to work.'

'You go ahead. I'll just…'

She nodded and went back inside the tunnel.

He took a few minutes to get his breathing under control and to clear his head and then followed her back inside the tunnel. She had her headphones on and was singing away, deliberately not looking at him. He picked up his brush and carried on painting.

CHAPTER TWO

Fern pulled out her headphones and looked at the picture of the Bernese mountain dog she'd painted lolloping across the sand. As Blackberry Beach was dog friendly, it made sense to have a dog playing in her beach scene so why not immortalise her own dog Bones? She smiled at the big inane grin on Bones's face, which she'd captured perfectly.

She stepped back to look at the whole mural, but her legs hit something hard behind her and suddenly she was toppling over backwards, as she slid, bum first, legs in the air, over the other side of the thing she'd hit and landed with a splat in a tray of paint.

She realised to her horror the thing had been Fletcher, on his hands and knees as he painted the bottom of his mural. Even more embarrassing, one of her legs was still wrapped around his neck.

'Are you OK?' Fletcher said.

'Oh my god, I'm so sorry.' Fern tried to get up and remove her leg from his neck at the same time but the cute buttons at the bottom of her dungarees legs were caught on the collar of his shirt. As she floundered around trying to free herself she managed to knee him in the face.

'Ooof,' Fletcher said.

'Sorry, I'm stuck.'

'So I see.'

He reached round the back of his neck to try to free her, running his hand up her bare ankle as he tried to find where they were joined.

'What were you doing sneaking around behind me anyway?' Fern said.

'I was hardly sneaking. You moved to where I was working, not the other way round,' Fletcher said.

He knelt up. She let out a yelp as he took her with him. Now her head was resting in his lap as she dangled upside down.

'Sorry,' Fletcher said.

'Stop moving.'

'I'm trying to free you.'

'You're making it worse.'

'I'm not sure this can get much worse, my face is in your crotch.'

She stopped struggling and burst out laughing. 'So much for my let's just be friends speech.'

He smiled. 'Are you hurt?'

'No, just my pride, although this isn't particularly comfortable.'

'Here, let me take my shirt off.'

'Oh sure, that's one way to improve the sexual tension between us,' Fern said.

He grinned and took it off anyway, sliding it straight over his head which released her from hanging around his neck but made her slither to the floor.

And she was right because there was his chest in all its glorious loveliness. His skin was a gorgeous golden brown, probably from working outside in the recent heat. He was muscular, with the faint lines of a six-pack showing at the top of his shorts, and there was a gorgeous smattering of hair across his chest and down to his belly button. Her eyes were drawn to an impressive dragon tattoo and she had an overwhelming desire to trace the scales across his skin.

He tried to free the shirt from the bottom of her dungarees but it was caught up pretty bad. And as she lay there on the floor of the tunnel, him kneeling between her legs as he leaned over her completely bare-chested, she almost laughed. In terms of sexual tension, this was definitely making it worse.

He finally freed her leg and glanced over at her and she smirked when he clearly realised their inappropriate position as well.

He scrambled up and offered out a hand to help her up but, in his haste to put an end to this awkwardness, he pulled her up too hard and she almost slammed into his chest, face first. She burst out laughing and he did too.

'God I'm sorry.'

'You're fine.'

She looked up at him and he moved his hand to the back of her head, which was such a sweet intimate gesture, the laughter died on her lips.

'You have paint in your hair,' Fletcher said. He looked down at her and realised how he was holding her and quickly stepped back. 'Christ, I'm really making things worse today. I'm not normally this disrespectful around women. I don't normally touch them or try to kiss them without their permission.'

'I don't think you're disrespectful at all. I think you're rather lovely, which makes the whole no-men, no-relationships thing a lot harder than I thought. So on that note, I'm going to go before I throw caution to the wind and kiss you.'

He nodded. 'Good idea. I'm a terrible kisser anyway, so you're really not missing out on much.'

She laughed. 'Good to know. How are you in bed?'

'Awful.' He held up his little finger and she burst out laughing.

'Well, this is helpful.'

'Now we've completely taken sex off the table, will I see you tonight at sunset for our duel?'

'I'll be there. I never back down from a fight.'

'I'll see you later then.'

She smiled and quickly packed up her things, ignoring that he was watching her the whole time. She gave him a wave and headed back up the tunnel.

She shook her head. He was going to be impossible to work with tomorrow.

She got back to her van and used a towel to mop up as much paint off her bum as possible. She always went home covered in paint but never to this extent. Giving up on an impossible job, she got in the van and drove off.

She parked her van in the car park of The Little Beach Hut Hotel, which had the reception area on one side and her best friend Orla's café, Seahorses, on the other.

Seahorses was there to serve breakfast and lunch to the guests of The Little Beach Hut Hotel but also to provide drinks and food to the many hikers and ramblers who crossed over the surrounding cliffs and hills. The café would be closing for the day soon but there was still time to grab a coffee.

She stepped inside and smiled to see her best friend Ettie sitting at the counter chatting to Orla. The café was largely empty.

'Hey, how was the honeymoon?' Fern said, giving Ettie a hug and a kiss before leaning over the counter to do the same to Orla.

'Wonderful,' giggled Ettie. 'Although we didn't actually see a lot of Zakynthos. But we did get to see a lot of the hotel room.'

Fern smiled. Tom and Ettie were head over heels in love with each other and had not been able to keep their hands off each other since their relationship started. Fern had never had that, she'd never been in love, never had someone who wanted sex from her so badly he'd come home from work at lunch just so he could have his wicked way with her. She'd never had someone love her so completely and utterly that they wanted forever with her. She didn't know whether she ever would. She was so happy for her friend that she had found her happy ever after with Tom but she couldn't help feeling a tiny bit jealous. She wanted what they had, a marriage, forever with her soul mate, the whole fairytale.

As a child she'd always dreamed of getting married. She'd never had a conventional childhood. She'd almost never celebrated her birthday, had several crappy Christmases. She'd never gone on a family day out to a zoo or theme park, never gone on holiday anywhere. She'd missed out on so much that other children took completely for granted. So she'd always wanted a little bit of normality and for her it was a wedding that she'd fantasised about. Growing up, she had loved anything to do with weddings. She'd seen the films, read the books and she'd imagined what her own wedding was going to be like, the dress, the reception, the ceremony, the flowers, she'd pictured it all. And although she'd grown up a lot since she'd had those childhood dreams, part of the fairytale she'd always wanted had been getting married, someone loving her enough to want forever with her.

But she'd been hurt too many times in the past and she was wary of getting her heart stamped on again.

'Hey, how was your first day painting the tunnel?' Orla said. Fern loved her Irish accent, it was so soft and lilting, she could listen to it all day.

Ettie pulled out a stool for her so she could sit next to her.

'Good, except...' Fern looked around but the old man in the corner was busy reading his paper. 'What do you two know about Fletcher Harrison?'

'Oh, he's a friend of Tom's. I don't know him that well as I've only met him a few times but, from what I know of him, he's really lovely, a gentle soul.'

'But he didn't come to your wedding.' Fern definitely would have remembered him had he been there.

'It was his mum's sixtieth birthday party so he couldn't. He gave us the most beautiful wedding gift though. This gorgeous wooden loveseat for the garden with our names entwined and carved on the top.'

'That's very generous,' Fern said.

'He owns ReLoved on the other side of the hill,' Orla said. 'It's kind of a carpentry, furniture-building school but it's also a bit of a community project, teaching those that wouldn't have had the opportunity to learn those skills.'

'Yeah, I've heard all about the good work they do up at ReLoved but I don't know a lot about the man himself other than he's probably the most gorgeous man I've ever set eyes on and also the most lovely,' Fern said. 'And he's funny and laid-back and easy to talk to. We've clicked in a way I've never felt before.'

Damn. He had got under her skin.

Ettie's eyes lit up. 'Oh my god, you like him.'

'He's painting the tunnel with you, isn't he?' Orla said.

'Yeah. We've spent the day together today and...' Fern let out a heavy sigh at saying it out loud. 'And I really like him.'

Ettie clapped her hands together excitedly. 'This is brilliant. And he likes you?'

Fern nodded. 'We almost kissed.'

'After one day!' Ettie squealed.

'I know and I've told him things I've never told any other man before, stuff about my birth mum and being in foster care. I have no idea why I spilled my whole life story to him, but he was just so bloody nice about it.'

'Why are you frowning like this is a bad thing?' Orla said. 'By all accounts he's a lovely man.'

'I'm just really bad at relationships. They never last – they either fizzle out before they start or the men turn out to be dickheads. In the last year I've dated Jon who had a secret wife, Blake who stole money from me, Wes who had a different girlfriend for every day of the week, Jacob who had some horrible kinky fetishes, and lastly Will who I literally walked in on while he was shagging his next-door neighbour and who asked me if I wanted to join them. After that, I decided no more men. I need a break from bad relationships for a while because it always makes me feel a little bit deflated, like maybe there must be something wrong with me and I don't ever want to think like that.'

'I totally get that,' Ettie said. 'But, as the old adage says, sometimes you have to kiss a lot of frogs to find your prince.

27

I really don't think giving up on men is the answer. Just maybe be a bit more selective.'

'It's hard to be selective as they don't reveal their true colours on the first date. I didn't know these men were shit-heads when I started dating them.'

'Of course you didn't. I'm just saying sometimes your heart just knows. I've never seen you light up like you did when you talked about Fletcher. Maybe it's worth the risk.'

'He says he doesn't do relationships either, that doesn't sound like the kind of man who is looking for any kind of commitment.'

'Maybe he's had some bad experiences too,' Orla said.

'Maybe you can heal each other,' Ettie said, excitedly, seeing the fairytale where there probably wasn't one.

Just then the door opened and Fern smiled to see her mum Carrie and brother Shay walk in. Shay had been in charge of all the building and decorating of the new guest beach huts and he'd become quite the fixture around Orla's café. She'd long thought that Shay had a bit of a thing for Orla. She wasn't entirely sure it was reciprocated though.

Out of Carrie's three adopted children, Shay was the one that looked most like his mum, with his dark hair. Carrie's was long and wavy but with one curl of pure silver near the front which had come about after a car accident. Fern had offered to dye her silver forelock bright blue or pink to make it really stand out in a dramatic way, but Carrie was happy with it as it was.

Fern gave a subtle warning shake of the head to her friends and they both nodded. She couldn't possibly talk about Fletcher in front of her mum – any sniff of something romantic and Carrie would be buying a wedding hat and marching Fern off down the local wedding dress shop. She was desperate to have some grandchildren and it didn't look like Fern's brothers, Shay and Theo, would be making that dream come true any time soon for her either.

Shay was holding the door for someone and, after a few seconds, Bones bounded through, a big grin on his face.

As soon as he saw her, he charged across the café towards her. Fern quickly got down off her stool to greet him.

'Hello you beautiful bear,' Fern said, squatting down and bracing herself against the counter for the onslaught of fifty kilos of dog throwing himself at her. 'Did you enjoy your day with Uncle Shay?'

'He was absolutely fine,' Shay said. 'We went for a long walk along the clifftops, and then he pretty much snoozed for the rest of the day outside Starfish Cottage where I've been working.'

All the beach huts were named after different sea animals and in two days Fern would start painting murals of each sea creature inside the huts. She was kind of dreading painting Starfish Cottage, because although the starfish – or sea stars, to use their proper name – were pretty and came in various different shapes and colours, they didn't have much personality like the dolphins, seals and sea birds. Unless she took a leaf out of Fletcher's book and made them cartoony. Maybe the starfish with googly eyes and smiley faces could be having some kind of party on the sea bed. She could imagine them jiving and dancing with each other, linking arms as they boogied among the seaweed and shells. She would sketch out a quick design when she got home and see if Carrie and Shay approved. They were her clients after all, even if they were family.

'How was your day painting?' Carrie asked.

'Really good. I got a lot done and I've sketched out the

rest of the design using chalk,' Fern said, deliberately not mentioning her rather lovely painting partner.

'And you're competing against Fletcher Harrison, aren't you?' Shay said.

Fern nodded vaguely. 'Yep.'

She busied herself with stroking Bones.

'Oh, he's a lovely man,' Carrie said. 'What he does up there for ReLoved is wonderful but I've bumped into him a few times and he's such a gentleman too. So kind and gentle.'

'I've played rugby with him a few times and, apart from the fact that he's an absolute demon on the field, he's definitely one of the good guys,' Shay said.

'See!' Ettie said, then clamped her hand over her mouth.

Carrie looked between the two of them. 'What's going on?'

'Nothing,' Fern said. 'I was just asking about him because he seems very quiet, keeping himself to himself, focussed on his art. I wondered if these guys knew anything about him.'

'Why? Are you interested?' Carrie said, her eyes lighting up.

'No, of course not. Man detox, remember. And I don't know anything about him to be interested in him. I was just curious, that's all. I better go, I need a shower and my dinner and I'm out tonight with a friend, so I must dash.'

Fern whistled for Bones and gave them all a wave before she hurried out, hoping she hadn't made it too obvious she'd just run away. She turned back to close the door behind her to find they were all watching her suspiciously. Yep, definitely too obvious.

~

Carrie finished sending an email and stood up to make a cup of tea. The launch of The Little Beach Hut Hotel was taking a lot of organising. Councillor Bishop had suggested they had a traditional funfair with all the rides so it was something everyone could enjoy instead of making it too formal. Carrie had thought that was a lovely idea. There was going to be a ghost train, helter-skelter, carousel, dodgems and many other attractions. That part of it was all sorted, it was the rest that was taking so much time: the fireworks, the food stalls, the entertainers like the stilt walkers and fire breathers, the car parking, and even the toilets. With all of Councillor Bishop's brilliant ideas for the launch, it had been left to Carrie to organise it all.

The Little Beach Hut Hotel had come about quite by accident. After inheriting the land from her grandad a few years before, she'd had no idea what to do with it. He had done nothing with it in all the years he'd owned it apart from fighting off developers who wanted to build houses and big hotels on it as it was in such a prime position overlooking Strawberry Sands. He'd wanted everyone in the town of Apple Hill Bay to be able to enjoy the view. Carrie had honoured that by opening a public path over the top of the cliff and providing plenty of benches.

The only thing her grandad had built on the land was a small row of beach huts which he'd rented out to the tourists in the summer. But by the time Carrie had inherited the land, the huts needed a lot of work. She'd renovated them, painting them in bright colours, and rented them out by the day or week. But the question that everyone asked was if they could stay there. So she'd built a much bigger hut with a lounge, kitchen and upstairs bedroom.

It had been a hit and had sold out over the summer

months within a few days of her advertising it on the website. So she'd built nine more and they'd sold out too. In the last six months she'd built thirty more with planning permission for another twenty further down the line.

Fortunately, with the land inheritance had come some money and, while she could have used that to buy herself a big house with a pool or squandered it on fast cars or luxury holidays, instead she'd employed people of the town to make it into a proper resort. Plumbing and electricity for the huts had been the biggest obstacle to overcome. She'd paid carpenters to build the huts and decorators to paint them. She'd hired local companies to lay proper paths and steps between the huts and gardeners to landscape the land with flower beds, wild flower patches and an abundance of trees. She was really proud of what she'd achieved. She only hoped her grandad would have been proud of it too.

She glanced out the window to see Antonio Garcia walking up her garden path and she rolled her eyes. He lived on the opposite side of the bay to The Little Beach Hut Hotel and, as his was the only house on this side of the town apart from hers, he was the one person whose view had been altered by the arrival of all Carrie's beach huts. Ever since she'd put in planning permission for the huts, he had been over here complaining about one thing or another practically every day. Well, it had started off as once a week but it had become a lot more frequent lately. It was a shame that he liked to complain so much, because the man was incredibly sexy. He had the gorgeous Mediterranean glow of his Spanish parents, dark, curly hair, and a lovely smile, which she only saw on very rare occasions. She'd be lying if she said she didn't enjoy their little chats, despite his moaning.

She opened the door. 'Good morning Antonio. What lovely things do you have to say to me this morning?'

'You've planted leylandii,' Antonio said, storming past her into the house.

'Very observant. So you know your plants. I have a pesky bush growing at the back of my garden. It's uncontrollable and I've thought about pulling it out but the bees love it and we need to help the bees. What do you think it is?' She pointed to the bush that was growing tall and straggly at an incredible rate near her garden shed. It had little blooms of purple flowers hanging off it.

Antonio came to stand next to her to see what she was pointing at and his wonderful scent wafted over her. He smelled of fresh lemons on a summer's day.

'That's a buddleia. It's a weed. You should get rid of it. They grow so quick they can be massively detrimental to the other plants.'

'Ah thank you. I'll do that then.'

'If you want to help the bees, I'd plant some hollyhocks or foxgloves or even some lavender, the bees love them. Lupins are good too.'

'Perfect, thank you, I'll keep that in mind. Cup of tea?'

'Yes please. No sugar.'

He sat down at the kitchen table as she prepared his tea with a spoonful of sugar to sweeten him up. She did this with every cup of tea she made him and saw him wince every time he took a drink. It gave her a small sense of revenge for all the moaning.

'It's a beautiful day, isn't it?' Carrie said.

'Don't think you can distract me from the leylandii.'

'I was kind of hoping I could. Why do you have a problem with my leylandii?'

'Do you know they grow at a rate of over one metre every year?'

'Well that's good, I wanted some trees that would grow quickly. We need to offer some shade and a bank of trees will encourage all kinds of wildlife. I didn't want some little feeble saplings that would take thirty years before they turn into a tree.'

'If they grow too tall, they'll ruin the view.'

'Whose view? Don't tell me they'll ruin your view because you live one and a half miles away as the crow flies. I've checked. You'd have to use a telescope to look at my leylandii.'

'But if I'm walking over the hills here, I don't want big bushy trees ruining my view of Apple Hill Bay.'

'But you have plenty of hills over your side of the bay to enjoy the view from, you only come round this side to cause trouble.' She plonked his cup of tea down in front of him, probably a bit too hard as it sloshed over the side. He took a sip and winced from the taste of the sugar but surprisingly, despite being such a big complainer, he never moaned about the sugar in his tea. Maybe he was too polite for that.

'I enjoy coming round this side for a walk, I just utilise my time wisely and coincide my walks with our *lovely* chats,' Antonio said.

'And I look forward to them so much,' Carrie said, dryly.

He actually had the audacity to smirk as he drank his tea.

'Besides,' Carrie went on. 'The leylandii are down near the beach. We're two hundred feet high up here, my trees are not going to grow sixty metres tall to ruin the view from up here. And if they do I can always have them cut back.'

Antonio grunted his displeasure and took another swig of tea.

'And while you're complaining about my bushes, you should know I've also planted some box hedges. When they grow a bit bigger, I've found a topiary expert in the town and he's going to come up here and cut them into the shapes of different sea animals. I'm sure you'll hate that too.'

He huffed out a noise that could only be described as pompous. He took another drink. 'I suppose that will look quite interesting actually. The kids will like it.'

She let out a little gasp. 'Was that actually a compliment?'

He finished his drink and stood up to leave. 'Never.'

He gave her a little wave and walked out the kitchen door.

Infuriating man. It was such a shame he was so damned sexy.

CHAPTER THREE

Fern stood on the deck of her little beach hut looking out over the spectacular view. Her bright purple beach hut was in a prime position overlooking Strawberry Sands. Apple Hill Bay was a deep horseshoe-shaped bay made up of three beautiful beaches: Strawberry Sands was a long strip of golden sands directly under The Little Beach Hut Hotel, while in the middle of the bay was Blackberry Beach where she'd spent the day, and on the far side was Cranberry Cove. The actual town of Apple Hill, where most of the shops and houses were, was on the other side of the cliffs in a little harbour so the views on this side were green and beautifully rugged. She could look out on this view forever and never get bored of it.

Fern loved her little beach hut, she loved how compact it was, the tiny kitchen that led into the lounge and the small dining table that sat in front of the French doors that opened onto the decking. Upstairs on a mezzanine level was her bedroom and the bathroom. The size of it would annoy some people if they had to live in it full time but for Fern it was perfect.

She saw movement out the corner of her eye and smiled to see her brother Theo jogging along the hill towards her. He'd jog in this direction most nights and would always stop for a quick chat before he carried on his way. She disappeared inside to get him a glass of apple juice and smiled when she heard him greeting Bones as if talking to a little child. Theo was a very successful CEO who seemingly sat in stuffy important business meetings all day but when he spoke to or played with Bones he was like a big kid.

She took their drinks out onto the decking and offered him a glass.

He took it in one hand and gave her a one-armed hug with the other. 'How was your day painting the tunnel?'

She couldn't help the smile erupting on her face as she thought about her day with Fletcher. 'It was good.'

'God, look at that smile. I envy you so much.'

'What do you mean?'

'You're doing something you love and starting a business where you get to do that all day. I miss that.'

'Theo, you did exactly that a year ago. You created a computer program where people could send in photos of their pets and you made their pets into characters in their own book. And then it went viral and now you have more Instagram followers than David Beckham and NASA. Pet Protagonist is huge, everyone has heard about it. You should be incredibly proud of what you've achieved.'

'I am, it's amazing. I never expected it to go that far. I just hoped to make enough to survive and now...' he trailed off.

'Your company is worth millions.'

'But I have a whole team of people now who produce the

books for me, I have a marketing team, an accounts team, a team of artists, story writers and computer programmers. I don't get to do any of the fun stuff any more. I used to produce each book myself from beginning to end, I would do all the marketing and everything and I loved it all. But now I sit in meetings all day and I've lost the joy.'

'Can you not do something to get it back? You're in charge up there in that big shiny office, can you not claw back some of the control?'

'I think it's gone too far for that. So yeah, I do envy you. Doing what you love as a job is hugely important. Work takes up so much of our lives. I want your new company to be a big success for you but don't let it become too big. Don't become this big conglomerate company painting murals in offices across the world while you sit in a big fancy office directing it all. That's not you.'

'That's not you either. A stuffy businessman is not the teenage boy who used to get so much pleasure and excitement out of building computer programs and games. If this isn't bringing you joy, why not employ someone to do all the boring stuff for you and you can do something else?'

He took a long swig of his drink, then swirled the rest around his glass as if the juice was a fine wine and he was letting it breathe. 'Maybe you're right.' He downed the rest of his drink. 'And maybe I should stop being so bloody ungrateful. How many small businesses would kill to be in my position a year after they launched, how many businesses go under and I'm moaning about it not being fun any more. I have over fifty people working for me and now we're expanding overseas there will be more. These people rely on this company for their income. Maybe I just need to grow up and face the fact that I'm not a little boy playing with his computer any more. Sorry, it's just been a stressful day.' He put the glass down on the table. 'Thanks for the drink, and the ear.' He glanced down at her dress. 'You off out?'

'Just meeting a friend.'

He nodded and gave her a kiss on the cheek. 'Have a good night.'

And with that he ran off across the hills. She watched him go, wondering what she would do if she was in his position. She hated to see him miserable.

She glanced at her watch, knowing she would have to leave soon. She took a sip of her drink and sighed. She had agreed to go to the duel with Fletcher but now she was doubting her decision. It had seemed something silly that would definitely draw the lines of friendship in the sand but she didn't need any more alone time with Fletcher than she had to. All day she had been aware of his proximity, and kept catching his eye as they moved around the tunnel. When she'd hugged him she'd been adamant that it didn't mean anything, but she couldn't deny how good it had felt to be held in his arms. When she heard his heart hammering against his chest she'd realised it meant as much to him as it did to her. It had taken every ounce of willpower to walk away because she damned well wanted to go back and finish that kiss.

And if she wanted to draw the lines of friendship why the hell was she going to a deserted beach at sunset with him? It couldn't be any more romantic. But as she didn't have any way of contacting him to tell him she wasn't coming, and she didn't want to stand him up, she knew she would have to go and just be really super strict with herself.

She whistled for Bones and he scrambled to his feet, excited to be going out.

They climbed in the van and she fastened Bones's car harness before winding down the windows so he could stick his head out, tongue lolling in the wind. She drove down into the valley trying her best to keep her bloody butterflies in check. They had no place fluttering wildly inside her. She was going to have some fun with a new friend, it was as simple as that.

She pulled up in the car park and let Bones out. He'd been to Blackberry Beach many times so he dragged her straight to the tunnel, lolloping through it, tail in the air, big grin on his face. She'd keep him on the lead until the end of the tunnel as she didn't want him standing in the paints that were probably still left out.

She reached the end of the tunnel and could see that Fletcher was waiting for her on the beach. The sun was just disappearing into the water, leaving behind beautiful clouds of plum and cranberry which were painting the sea in vivid colours. It was beautiful and even more so because they had the beach completely to themselves.

She released Bones and, as he leapt down the steps, she watched to see Fletcher's reaction to her beloved best friend. She'd always thought you could tell a lot about a person by their relationship with dogs. Her last boyfriend had largely been indifferent to Bones, which had been a bit off-putting to say the least.

Fletcher's face lit up at seeing Bones bounding towards him and knelt down to greet her oversized puppy. Bones barrelled into him, which would have sent any normal person flying but Fletcher was huge enough to withstand the force of a fifty-kilo dog. Bones loved meeting people and when they walked through town it would take two or three times longer than if she was alone as Bones wanted to say hello to everyone or everyone wanted to say hello to him. Having a giant breed dog always got a lot of attention. Fletcher stroked under his chin, his chest, and then laughed as Bones turned round and sat on him so Fletcher could continue stroking him more thoroughly. Fletcher was happy to oblige.

Fern went down to join them. Fletcher had the biggest grin on his face at meeting her dog, while Bones had a matching one at making a new best friend.

'He's brilliant, what's his name?' Fletcher said.

'This is Bones. He's eighteen months old.'

'Only a puppy and he's huge like a horse.'

'Yeah, he's pretty much full-grown now though, he won't get much bigger.'

Bones got up and bounded off down the beach and, as they were alone with no one else for Bones to harass and no way off the beach, she let him go.

'So I have the weapons for our duel,' Fletcher said, indicating the blanket that was covering a few lumps. She made a move towards them but he snagged her hand, sending goosebumps up her arm at his touch.

'There's no shame in backing out of this duel, no one needs to know,' Fletcher said, seriously.

'I'd know.'

'I was afraid you'd say that. So a fight to the death it is.'

He moved over to the blanket and lifted it to show two hand-held water pistols and a huge Super Soaker. She laughed.

'Last chance to back out,' Fletcher said.

'No way.'

'Right then. You can choose the two small ones or the big one,' Fletcher said. 'Neither of them are currently loaded.'

Fern quickly grabbed the Super Soaker. 'What are the rules of the duel?'

'Whoever is the wettest after five minutes is the loser,' Fletcher said.

'That's it, nothing else?'

Fletcher shrugged.

'OK, let's do this.'

Fletcher took his phone out and started a timer. 'Five minutes starting from now.'

They both ran down to the water's edge and Fletcher dunked both of his pistols into the sea at the same time, Fern looked at her Super Soaker, and tried to work out how to fill it. It had a big green water tank on the top so that had to be the thing that was filled with water, but there didn't appear to be any hole. She looked underneath, round the sides, nothing.

Fletcher stepped back from the sea and started squirting her with both pistols. Fern squealed with laughter as the cold water penetrated her clothes.

'I haven't filled mine yet,' Fern said.

'The five minutes includes filling time,' Fletcher said, relentlessly squirting her all over.

He stepped back to the water and quickly refilled and started squirting her again.

'How do I get water in it?' Fern squealed.

'You have to unscrew the tank.'

Fern spent a few moments trying to figure out how to do that all while Fletcher was squirting her. It was getting in her hair, her eyes, all over her clothes. Finally she managed to unscrew the tank, pulled it away from the Super Soaker and dunked it under the sea while Fletcher went back for a third refill. He was done before her tank was even half filled. But now she'd got the tank off, she might as well fill it to the top. He started soaking her again as she finished filling the tank and clumsily reattached it to the water pistol. She turned to shoot it at him, pressing the trigger, but nothing happened.

'Why won't it work?' she laughed.

Fletcher smiled and carried on soaking her. Currently he didn't have a single drop of water on him. She turned and started trying to flick the water on him with the water pistol, scooping it out of the sea and tossing it in his direction, but that only succeeded in getting a light spray on his t-shirt, certainly not enough to soak him.

As he went back to refill his pistols again, she turned and ran up the beach towards where Bones was playing near a little stream that was coming from the cliffs into the sea. If she could just buy herself some time to work out the water pistol she could unleash a torrent of water on Fletcher.

As she ran she noticed the pump at the bottom of the Super Soaker and tried to slide it backwards and forwards but she could hear Fletcher close behind her and needed to get some distance between them. She increased her speed, running flat out along the beach, but as she looked over her shoulder, she laughed to see he was gaining on her. Suddenly the ground disappeared beneath her feet and she stumbled head first into the stream – which she realised, as she face-planted the sand and the water covered her head, was a lot deeper than she'd first thought. Water gushed up her nose and down her throat and she pushed herself up, gasping for air and choking.

Suddenly she was scooped up out of the water into Fletcher's arms as she wheezed and spluttered all over him, trying to catch her breath. Her eyes were streaming, water pouring out of her nose.

'Jesus,' Fletcher muttered as he knelt down, sitting her in his lap as he rubbed her back. 'You're OK, just try to breathe.'

Fern took a few breaths, trying to clear her lungs, and the choking and spluttering subsided. Her breath was still heavy and she leaned her head against his shoulder for a moment. The alarm on Fletcher's phone suddenly went off to let them know the five minutes were up.

'I think you won that one,' Fern said, weakly.

'I'm so sorry.'

'Don't be. I was having fun before I fell over. That's not your fault, I should have looked where I was going.'

Bones came bounding over to see if she was OK and, after slobbering all over her face, he lolloped off again, clearly satisfied she was.

She realised her hand was wrapped tightly around Fletcher's t-shirt and she quickly let it go. He didn't seem in any rush to let her go though, and as she didn't quite have the strength to stand up yet she was quite happy to sit here like this, in his arms.

Although if she wanted to put a nail in the coffin of their sexual tension, she'd probably done that with her coughing, spluttering and wheezing all over him. That was definitely not an attractive look.

She glanced up at him and saw he was watching her with concern. He gently swept her hair from her face. 'Come on, let's get you warm.'

She climbed off his lap and he helped her up, before getting up himself. They started walking back up the beach but, without the warmth of his body against hers, she found herself shivering at the feel of her cold wet clothes against her skin. Fletcher noticed and immediately wrapped an arm around her shoulders, pulling her against him as they walked. It felt too nice for her to protest.

'I brought some spare clothes,' Fletcher said. 'I guessed that one or both of us would get wet, although I didn't imagine we'd get as wet as you did.'

'I was already soaked before I fell over. You knew what you were doing when you offered me that bloody Super Soaker.'

He smiled. 'It's not my first rodeo. I have two nephews who are a lot sneakier than I am. You have to be cunning with them around.'

They reached his stuff and Fletcher let go of her to get some clothes out of his bag. He passed her a towel and what looked like a massive jumper and a pair of jogging bottoms.

'There's a cave at the back you could get changed in,' Fletcher gestured to the cliffs. 'I'll get a fire going.'

She hesitated for a moment. It made more sense for her to just go home and get showered and changed but for some reason she wanted to stay. She smiled as she looked at Fletcher. Not some reason, one reason.

She took the clothes and went off to the cave to change. What was she doing? She wanted to avoid romantic moments with him yet she was about to sit by a fire with him on a deserted beach at sunset. She rolled her eyes.

She stripped off down to her underwear and was just debating taking that off as well when Fletcher appeared in the cave entrance with his hand clamped firmly over his eyes.

'Sorry, I just thought, the jogging bottoms will probably be too big. You could wear my boxers instead. They're clean, I promise.' Fletcher held out a pair of black shorts, the tight kind that left very little to the imagination.

She stepped forward to take it. 'Thank you.'

He moved away and she watched him gathering driftwood from the back of the beach and making a pile for the fire. God he made her smile so much. She couldn't leave now, even if she wanted to.

She quickly finished undressing, dried herself off and pulled on his boxer shorts. They were still quite loose but they probably wouldn't fall down any time soon like the jogging bottoms would. She tugged his huge jumper on over her head and smiled when it came down to her knees. It was a beautiful teal colour, like the sea, and made from the softest wool. It also smelled distinctly of him, which was heavenly. He smelled of wood, probably from his days working with it, and there was something so manly and rugged about this scent mixed with a little bit of a citrus tang. If they could bottle this scent, they'd make an absolute fortune.

She stepped out the cave and Fletcher looked at her, his eyes casting down to her bare legs before he quickly looked away, focussing on lighting the fire. Bones was mooching nearby and he bounded over when he saw her, sniffing her as he took in this new scent too. Happy it was still her, he flopped down by the fire.

She moved closer to the fire as small flames licked the wood. She could see Fletcher had laid out some blankets and there was a bag of marshmallows and some long kebab sticks for roasting them. He even had a bowl of fresh water for Bones, which made her smile. He'd clearly planned this to be something a lot more than just a duel.

She sat down next to the fire and he moved to drape another blanket around her shoulders, although now she was dry, the heat from the fire was warming her nicely. The sun was no more than a sliver of gold lying on top of the sea as it disappeared under the horizon. The night seemed to be chasing it across the heavens as the sky turned a beautiful peacock blue.

'I thought we'd need the fire to warm ourselves up after and, if we're going to have a fire, we can't not have marshmallows,' Fletcher said.

'Do you normally provide such a hospitable service to those you duel with?' Fern said.

'I'll let you know a little secret. You're my first duel.'

Fern laughed. 'I can tell.'

'I'm offended. Are you not happy with my duelling abilities?'

She held up the blanket and gestured to the fire and the marshmallows. 'It doesn't really set the tone for a fight to the death.'

He nodded and sat down next to her. 'Fair point. I actually thought we could watch the meteor shower. If you like that sort of thing.'

She let out a little gasp. 'There's a meteor shower?'

'The Lyrids meteor shower which is part of Thatcher's Comet. Its peak is tonight and the meteors will be quite low in the sky so we stand a really good chance of seeing them.'

'Oh how wonderful, I can't wait to see them.'

The last sliver of sun disappeared, leaving them in a rose-gold twilight. It was beautiful and couldn't be any more romantic.

'I have to say, after our talk about just being friends, you've gone to a lot of trouble for a romantic night.'

'I don't think I can take any credit for the meteor shower or the beautiful sunset or the deserted beach,' Fletcher said.

Her cheeks flushed with embarrassment. She was seeing

romance where there wasn't any. This was clearly just two new friends watching a meteor shower together.

'I'm not saying I haven't totally capitalised on the romance of it all though.'

She looked at him, hope blooming in her heart.

'I've never been good at following the rules. But all this doesn't come with any expectation. I just wanted to make the effort for you.'

She found herself extraordinarily pleased by this. No one had ever made this much effort for her before. And she suddenly realised what had been missing from all of her other relationships, not just the ones that had ended with her swearing off men for life but the ones that had simply fizzled out as well. It was romance. It was big romantic gestures like this. It was someone putting the effort in, purely to make her smile. Maybe she had spent far too much time reading romance novels with the heroes going above and beyond for their women and it had given her unrealistic expectations of what a relationship should be. But growing up completely without love had made her dream of the fairytale where one day some man would fall so in love with her he would want to do nice things like this for her, and most importantly he would want forever. And it didn't matter if this thing with Fletcher led nowhere – although now she was really hoping it would, because tonight had shown her that she should never settle for ordinary.

Fletcher was lying on his back staring at the inky canopy above him. It was a crystal clear night with not a single cloud tarnishing the view. Thousands of stars peppered the sky

48

making the backdrop for the meteors look spectacular. They were lying on the sand next to the fire, cuddled up under blankets. Fletcher had even wrapped one around Bones which Fern had found amusing, given that his thick fur coat was designed for snowy mountains.

Tonight had been perfect. He hadn't known what to expect when he'd seen there was a meteor shower on that night. He'd hoped for a few shooting stars to impress her but there'd been loads, all ripping through the ebony sky in a vast array of colours. Some were only there for a few seconds, others took a longer, slower journey across the heavens. It was beautiful.

But that wasn't what had made the night so perfect. When they'd spotted the first meteor, Fern had grabbed his hand and she hadn't let it go since. It made him smile so damned much.

There was something so wonderfully intimate about holding hands while they looked at the stars. He couldn't remember the last time he'd held hands with anyone but he was enjoying himself immensely. There had been quite a few women in his life but he'd never done anything like this with any of them, nor had he wanted to. Spending the night together had always meant sexually, but he'd never been so happy to just lie next to a woman and enjoy being with her.

He thought about that for a moment. He had actively avoided serious relationships all his life and he knew that was partly because he never wanted to let anyone down. Not again. But this was different to anything else he'd ever experienced and maybe he could make it work.

He glanced over at Fern as another shooting star ripped through the sky above them and watched her face light up in awe. She was so endearing.

'Do you know anything about the stars?' she said.

'You mean constellations? A few. I know the Plough or the Big Dipper, which is part of Ursa Major, the Great Bear,' Fletcher said, pointing to what looked like a big saucepan in the sky. 'And Leo is quite a good one to spot as, unlike its counterparts, the shape of Leo does look like it could be a lion lying down.' He pointed it out, describing which stars belonged to that constellation.

'Yes, I can see it,' Fern said, excitedly. 'I know Orion, the Hunter. If you can find the three stars in a short row, that's his belt. The rest of it is quite easy to find after that.'

Fletcher pulled out his phone and swiped the screen a few times. 'I do actually have a star app. You just point it at the area of the sky you want to know more about and it tells you the names of all the stars and constellations at that point.' He held it up to the sky and waited for a few seconds for it to update. 'Oh look, that's Aquarius above us.'

Fern shuffled over, resting her head on his shoulder so she could see too. 'Oh wow, that's really cool. Look, there's Leo as you said and right next to it is Cancer. Doesn't really look like a crab though.' She put her hand on his to guide the phone around. 'Some of these I've never even heard of. Camelopardalis, what's that?'

'A giraffe apparently.'

'Oh, my grandad would have loved this app,' Fern said, still moving his hand and phone around to look at all the constellations. 'God, I haven't thought about him in years.'

Fletcher put the phone down. 'Carrie's dad?'

'No, Angela's. He died when I was seven. Being with him was the only time in my childhood I really felt loved. We'd sit out in his garden on sun loungers and watch the stars and he'd point out various constellations. If ever there was an eclipse or a comet or a rare astrological event, he would know about it and we'd stay up most of the night watching it. He always made sure I was covered in hundreds of blankets and gave me a hot water bottle to hug too, which he'd keep topped up throughout the night. Plus there was always snacks. Our midnight feast. He used to bake slices of apple with peanut butter. They tasted amazing. And every morning after we'd spent a night under the stars, he'd make these chocolate chip muffins. We'd eat them hot from the oven when the chocolate chips were still melty and gooey. They were small, almost bitesize, so we didn't think we were being too unhealthy by eating them but then we'd end up eating four or five. God, those were some happy memories I'd forgotten about. I didn't see him that often as he lived somewhere else, but my mum would send me to stay with him as often as she could, especially when I'd come back from staying in foster care for a little while. But he wasn't well so my visits became less and less frequent and then he died. I do remember feeling so lost when he passed away, like a light had gone out.'

'I'm so sorry. That must have been so much harder to lose him when you didn't have anyone else.'

'Yeah,' she said, softly.

Fletcher put an arm round her shoulders and pulled her tighter against his chest. He drew the blankets up over them both and then wrapped his other arm round her. She moved her hand to his chest.

They lay in silence for a while.

'Do you want to go home soon or do you want to stay here for the rest of the night?'

Her hand tightened on his shirt. 'I'd like to stay.'

He smiled. 'That's fine by me.'

CHAPTER FOUR

Fern woke as the first whispers of sunlight kissed her face. She opened her eyes. The fire had long since gone out, and there was a definite early morning chill that came from the sun not having warmed up the day yet, but she was cosy in Fletcher's arms, her head on his chest as she listened to the steady rhythm of his heart.

Bones was lying on the blanket Fletcher had wrapped around him the night before, snoring softly. He would be awake soon, demanding his breakfast, but she was going to make the most of this quiet lull.

The sun was a shimmering gold as it peeped its head above the horizon, casting a glittery blanket across the waves.

This was so unexpected for her. She'd arrived at work the day before determined to win and now she'd spent the night wrapped in her competitor's arms. Fletcher Harrison was a man she could very easily fall for. He was just so damned lovely.

She looked up at him and realised he was awake too, looking out on the waves.

'It's beautiful, isn't it.'

He looked down at her and smiled. 'I can't think of a more perfect way to wake up in the morning.'

She smiled. She so wanted to reach up and kiss him but she felt like she had to guard her heart. 'Why are you single? You said you don't do relationships, why is that?'

He sighed. 'I'd love to tell you that I've never found the right woman but I think it's probably something more than that.'

She waited to see if there was more of an explanation but, judging from Fletcher's face, he really didn't want to go into it.

He was silent for a moment but then he spoke. 'I think I'm just not good at relationships. My parents divorced after constant fighting. My grandad on my dad's side had multiple affairs before my nan finally left him. My grandmother on my mum's side walked out on her husband one day and never came back. Several aunts and uncles have divorced too for various reasons and I don't feel I have any good role models for a great relationship. I've had quite a few one-night stands where the expectations were very clear on both sides and sometimes I've dated a few women for a couple of nights but I've ended it before it got serious. I've never wanted more.'

Fern looked back over the waves. It didn't fill her with a lot of hope if she started dating him but there was something between them that made her want to explore it. She had never had this connection with anyone before, especially not this quickly. She refused to believe all this effort was purely to get her into bed for a one-night stand.

He stroked her hair and she looked back at him again. 'So if something was to happen between us, it would just be sex?'

He frowned. 'I really like you. I have never been so happy to just be with someone before. I'd really like to know you more, and I don't mean sexually, but I don't want to promise something I can't deliver. You've had some crappy relationships with men who haven't treated you right and you've ended up getting hurt. I don't want to do anything to hurt you.'

There was a big part of her that wanted to say to hell with it, why not have some fun with Fletcher and see where it went. And if it didn't go anywhere, where was the harm, she was walking into it with her eyes wide open. But the part of her that had always wanted the fairytale knew she wasn't going to get that with Fletcher so what was the point of pursuing it?

They lay there for a while, his arms around her. She couldn't pretend they hadn't already crossed some line between them. This was way beyond friendly and they both knew that. But she could stop now, she didn't have to take it any further.

Although she didn't have to make any decisions right at this moment. She had the rest of the day painting the tunnel with Fletcher to enjoy.

Bones stretched and let out a massive yawn, looking at her expectantly.

Fern reluctantly sat up. 'I should get back and feed him and grab a shower but I'll bring him back down here in a bit so he can hang out with us for the day if that's OK?'

'Sure, and I'll grab some breakfast things for us.'

'Sounds good.'

~

Fern stopped at Seahorses on the way back to Blackberry Beach to pick up some coffee for her and Fletcher. The local WI rambling group were in there before they started their weekly coastal walk but thankfully it appeared they had all been served and were just standing around drinking their coffee and eating their cakes before their amble around the bay.

Fern went to the counter and Bones sat next to her, licking his lips in the hope of getting some morsels.

'Morning, gorgeous. Two coffees please,' Fern said to Orla when she came to serve her.

Orla set about making them. 'Your man was just in here.'

Fern smiled. 'I don't think he's my man.'

'Well he certainly had a big dreamy smile on his face as if he was thinking about someone.'

This made her heart leap. 'He was probably just looking forward to his breakfast. Who can refuse your delicious bacon rolls.'

'Well when it was very clear he was buying for two, I did suggest that if he was trying to impress someone with breakfast, then my bacon rolls normally go down a treat and that my best friend Fern loves them. He soon bought them after that. Why is he trying to impress you with breakfast?'

Fern looked around but the WI were too busy putting the world to rights to worry about her.

'We spent the night together last night,' Fern whispered but then quickly clarified when she saw Orla's eyes light up. 'Not like that. It wasn't sex, we haven't even kissed, but there was a meteor shower and we stayed on the beach watching it and we did have a cuddle and I ended up sleeping in his arms under the stars.'

'Oh my god, this sounds very romantic. Ettie would love this. So are you two dating or…'

'I have no idea what this is. We're not dating, I can't call it that. He doesn't do relationships and has a history of one-night stands and I've never done that before.'

'Before? Are you thinking of doing it now?' Orla said.

Fern chewed on one of her fingernails. She couldn't deny that the thought had crossed her mind. Well she didn't want just one night with Fletcher. She imagined that would be like eating the most incredible cake she'd ever tasted and then never getting the chance to eat it again. But she knew that if she did get involved with him one night would be all it was, maybe two, but it was never going to be the thing she had been searching for almost her entire life. It was never going to be love, the fairytale marriage, the big happy ever after. Though maybe that was OK. Maybe she didn't need to enter every relationship looking for forever. If she knew she wasn't going to get it, she couldn't be disappointed. The only thing she knew for sure was that if she walked away from Fletcher without exploring this wonderful connection between them she would end up regretting it for the rest of her life.

'Oh my god, you are,' Orla said, reading her face. 'Oh honey. I don't want to see you getting hurt.'

'I don't want to get hurt either but he makes me want to throw all my caution out the window. I don't know. It feels like we have something special and I want to see where this goes.'

'And if it doesn't go anywhere after that one-night stand?'

Fern smiled. 'Well, at least I would have had a lot of fun finding out.'

Orla grinned. 'As long as you can separate your feelings from this, why the hell not.'

Fern took her coffees and after Orla had given Bones a bit of watermelon she waved goodbye and they walked off towards Blackberry Beach.

She could separate her feelings from this. She was sure she could. Although she knew her heart was a fragile thing, she simply wouldn't engage it.

She started walking through the tunnel, suddenly doubting herself. Was it best to just keep away from Fletcher Harrison? She could finish the painting and then she never needed to see him again. Well, she was sure she'd bump into him in Apple Hill Bay, it was small enough, but he was generally working on the other side of town and she would be busy with her painting business. If they did see each other, they could politely pass the time of day. Nothing had happened between them so it didn't need to be awkward.

Bones excitedly dragged her through the tunnel, as if he knew he was seeing Fletcher again and couldn't wait. Or maybe he was just excited to be going to the beach.

She reached the end and Fletcher was standing at the top of the steps that led to the beach, leaning over the railings as he stared at the sea.

He turned when he heard them approach and his smile spread across his face. Although she wasn't sure if it was for her or her beloved dog.

He bent down to stroke Bones, who slammed into him in excitement and then turned round so Fletcher could scratch his bum. Happy that he had been suitably stroked, Bones bounded off onto the beach, barking at the waves and chasing the seagulls that were chilling out in the early morning sun.

'Hey,' Fletcher said.

'Hi,' Fern said.

She couldn't help smiling at him, feeling like she was a schoolgirl with a silly crush.

'I got you a coffee,' she said, putting the two cups down on the ground.

'Oh thanks. I got a few bits for breakfast, your bacon rolls are over there, but I also got you these.'

He handed her a bag and she peered inside to see it was filled with tiny chocolate chip muffins. She swallowed a lump in her throat.

'They are probably nowhere near as nice as the ones your grandad used to make, and they're not particularly warm so not gooey and melty, but I thought you should have chocolate chip muffins after a night of stargazing.'

She looked at him and knew right then and there she was done for.

She reached up to stroke his face and then leaned up to kiss him. He stalled in surprise for a second before he wrapped his arms around her and kissed her back. The spark between them was instant, igniting a fire inside her. The taste of him was magnificent and she shifted closer to his body, wanting more of him. The feel of his hard body against hers, his hands around her back, his hot mouth on her lips, gave her such a kick of need for him. She felt the kiss change to something more and suddenly he lifted her. She wrapped her legs around him as he moved her back against the wall of the tunnel. The feel of him between her legs made her moan softly against his lips. His hands were at her waist and when he slid his thumbs under the fabric of her t-shirt, trailing them softly against the warm skin above her waistband, she gasped. She was in heaven. This was the hottest first kiss of her entire life and she suddenly wanted so much more. But just as she felt like the kiss might lead there, he pulled back gently, leaning his forehead against hers, his breath heavy on her lips.

She caught her breath, wrapping her hands around his neck, stroking his hair. 'You lied.'

'What?'

'You said you were an awful kisser. Now I'm worried about when we have sex. You kiss me like that for our first kiss, I don't think I will survive the first time we make love.'

His breath was still heavy as he stared at her. '*When* we have sex?'

'After a kiss like that, it feels like a foregone conclusion.'

'Well if I'm honest, it was only a sheer amount of willpower that stopped our first kiss from ending up there.'

The thought of that made her stomach clench with need.

'Why did you stop?'

'Because you deserve more for our first time together than a quick shag against the wall of a tunnel. And also because I didn't buy those muffins with the hope that you would kiss me, I just wanted to do something nice for you.'

'Well I kissed you because you are so bloody nice. Although I wasn't expecting the kiss to be that heated. You sure as hell know what you're doing when it comes to a first kiss. No wonder all those women jumped into bed with you if you kiss like that.'

'I've never kissed anyone like that before, what we have is something different,' Fletcher said.

She stared at him. She didn't dare to acknowledge that this was different. She felt it was too, but knew that believing it was something special would give her false hope.

'I should check on Bones,' Fern said. 'And then I need to finish my paintings.'

Fletcher nodded and gave her another brief kiss but this one was more gentle, slower, not as passionate and needful, but just as loving. Then he pulled back and slowly lowered her legs to the floor.

She leaned against the tunnel wall for a moment as her legs were still wobbly and he held her, searching her eyes. 'Are you OK?'

She knew he wasn't just asking if she was OK to stand but also whether she was OK about the kiss, that she didn't regret it. But there was no way she could regret a kiss like that. She stroked his face and nodded.

He stepped back and she adjusted her clothing before stepping out the tunnel onto the beach, taking a cooling breath of air.

Bones wasn't too far away, digging a hole as if trying to find Australia. She poured him a bowl of water from the bottle in her bag and left it at the top of the steps. She called for him and he came bounding over to her, big grin on his sand-covered face. He took a long drink and then flopped down in the shade at the top of the steps. After the walk from her beach hut, he would probably flake out there for the next few hours.

She turned back to the tunnel. Fletcher was already busy painting so she moved to look at her side of the tunnel. This morning she was going to do an ice cream van with a large queue of people and this afternoon she was going to paint a Punch and Judy show being watched by a group of children on the sand. And that would be it. Her time in the tunnel with Fletcher would be over and she felt sad about that. She picked up the bag of muffins that had dropped to the floor during the best kiss of her life and took a bite of one.

She glanced over at Fletcher, still feeling that kiss on her lips. There was no way she could separate her emotions from whatever this was between them. She thought she could but there was something about Fletcher that had already buried itself deep inside her. She wanted so much more from him. For the first time in forever, she felt really excited about a relationship and she didn't even know if she would have one with him. It could be over before it even began.

He realised he was being watched and he looked over at her, a smile spreading across his face. She couldn't help smiling too.

She quickly glanced at what he was painting and was delighted to see a fat puffer fish with a puffed-out body and cheeks, eyes bulging comically as if the fish had blown himself up a little bit too much.

'You've very good at this,' Fern said.

'Thank you. It's just a bit of fun. My nephews love them. I painted their bedroom walls for their birthdays and they were over the moon. But I don't know if the adults in the town would like it. It's definitely not in the same league as your wonderful pictures.'

'Oh, mine are realistic enough, but yours have a lovely charm. The kids are going to love your pictures. They're funny and cute.'

'Are you worried about losing out to me?' Fletcher teased.

'Not any more. If you win, which I'm sure you will, it will be very much deserved.'

'What about the accolade of being Apple Hill Bay's Great

Mural Painting Competition winner, or whatever they're calling it?'

'I don't need it. I'll put photos of the mural on my website and it will be a great addition to my portfolio regardless of if I win or not.'

'We can split the winnings,' Fletcher said.

'Absolutely not. I actually want you to win because that money will really help ReLoved.'

'That's really sweet of you but it's only fair that we both get paid for our work. Two and a half thousand pounds will be more than enough to buy some more welding gear for us.'

'But imagine what you could buy for five. I entered this competition knowing I might not get paid, just so I could add it to my gallery and portfolio and for more people to see my work. I don't need to win. Besides, I feel like I'm getting more out of this experience than I ever bargained for.'

He frowned in confusion for a second then smiled. 'Me too. A whole lot more.'

She felt her heart leap as they stood there staring at each other.

'I should…' she gestured to her wall.

He nodded and turned back to his puffer fish, humming happily to himself.

She picked up her chalk to start drawing her ice cream van. He made her happy too.

Carrie had just finished washing up when she saw Antonio walking up to her house. He was quite a way off but he was clearly annoyed about something. She let out a little sigh and flicked the kettle on. She made two cups of tea and put them on the table.

She opened the kitchen door just as he raised his fist to knock. He quickly lowered his hand. He looked grumpy, as always, but he carried that brooding, grumpy look so sexily.

'What bee is in your bonnet today?'

'Are you really having a badger-feeding station up here?'

She stepped back to let him in and he sat down at the table.

'How can you possibly have a problem with badgers? They're cute and fluffy. And baby badgers. There's nothing cuter than a baby badger. Even you with your grumpiness can't hate badgers.'

'I don't hate them. I have a badger sett at the bottom of my garden. I enjoy watching them. But I don't feed them.'

'Well that's your prerogative. Over here on this side of the bay we like to encourage wildlife. I ordered some hollyhocks and foxgloves by the way, just as you said, to help encourage the bees and butterflies. Or should I not be feeding them either?'

'That's entirely different. We need bees and butterflies for pollination. Most of our fruits and vegetables rely on pollination to fertilise and grow, even the crops our livestock eat need to be pollinated. The world would be very hungry without bees.'

'I'm pretty sure we need badgers too. In the past we've hunted beavers to extinction and it has ruined the ecosystem so much that they've had to reintroduce them again. What if the same can be said of badgers?'

'Look, I'm not saying we need to get rid of badgers, I'm saying they are a wild animal and should not be reliant on us for food. They have to fend for themselves.'

'Antonio Garcia, I've been to your house when I first wanted to discuss the plans with you. You have bird tables and bird feeders everywhere, those little fat balls hanging off the trees, nuts out for the squirrels. Saucers of water and fruits out for the hedgehogs. How is what I'm doing any different?'

He took a long swig of his tea and gave an obligatory shudder at the taste of the sugar. 'I think it's different. You don't want a wild animal to use you as their only way to get food. They should be independent. What I'm doing is merely supplementing their normal food.'

'That's exactly what I'm doing. And these badgers have been fed by my grandad since before we were born. Rightly or wrongly they have come to expect it.'

'I don't think these badgers were fed by your grandad, that would make them sixty or seventy years old and I'm pretty sure they don't live that long.'

'You're so pedantic. You know full well I mean different generations of badgers. The badgers here now would have been brought here by their parents, and they will bring their own children too. And it's not every day. I only feed them twice a week. All I'm doing with the feeding station is making it more of an official thing. We've built a hide near to where I normally put food out. Our guests from The Little Beach Hut Hotel can come to the hide twice a week and watch the badgers eat the food I've put out for them. Many people that live in the big cities have probably never seen one. This is a great way to introduce people to the wildlife that's around here and let them get up close without scaring the animals. It's an educational experience.'

'I think it would be more educational to teach people the reasons why we don't feed wildlife.'

'Oh yes, they'll be queuing up round the block for that talk.'

And there was that infuriating smirk again, which he tried to hide behind his mug of tea.

'OK, maybe I am being a bit hypocritical when I happily feed my birds every day, I didn't think about it like that.'

She blinked in surprise. 'Are you actually backing down from this fight?'

'I think it's more like agreeing to disagree.'

She laughed. 'Men can never admit when they're wrong.'

He stood up to leave. 'I'm never wrong, just… misguided.'

'I think that boils down to the same thing.'

He gave her a wave and left and she couldn't help smiling as he walked away.

CHAPTER FIVE

'I think we should celebrate,' Fletcher said as he and Fern sat on their own private beach together eating their lunch.

Fern took another bite of her sandwich and then gave Bones the corner of the crust. She leaned back on her elbows looking out over the sun-drenched waves. There was something about having the beach completely to themselves which just made everything feel so much more romantic. It was like they were in their own private bubble here, shutting out the rest of the world so it was just the two of them. They'd walked up the beach together holding hands before lunch so Bones could have a run around and it was as if they were a proper couple who had been together for years. It simultaneously filled her with joy and worry at the same time, because if this was the beginning of the fairytale what happened when the clock struck midnight and the dream came to a sudden end?

Fletcher leaned back too, wrapping an arm around her and pulling her onto his chest. She smiled. Maybe she should just enjoy the dream while it lasted rather than worrying about the end.

She reached up and kissed him again and felt him smile against her lips as he kissed her back. This time it was much slower and more gentle than the first passionate kiss and it made her come alive. He kissed her like it meant something to him, like he wanted so much more too, and she decided she would believe in it rather than doubt it.

Suddenly she remembered what he'd said and she pulled away slightly.

'Celebrate what?'

He paused as he regathered his thoughts. 'Umm, we should celebrate that we've finished the tunnel and make the most of having the beach to ourselves for one more night. And one more incredible sunrise.'

'You want to spend the night on the beach again?'

He nodded, stroking her hair. Her heart leapt at the thought because now they seemed to be kissing so easily, if they spent the night under the stars, would there be more? They'd both spoken about how they wanted that.

'And what would we be doing as part of the celebration?' Fern asked, fingering the button on his shirt.

'Well, we could have a picnic, some wine, some music and there'll definitely be a lot more of this.' Fletcher lifted her chin gently and kissed her again. Her heart roared in her chest. How could a simple kiss make it feel like there were fireworks going off inside her? She'd never had a kiss feel like this before. And the butterflies were taking flight, letting her know this was something wonderful.

She pulled back slightly. 'How much more?'

His eyes darkened with need for her and that gave her such a thrill.

'However much or as little as you like. From my point of view, I'd just like to spend another night with you. I'm more than happy to talk and eat and dance and hold you in my arms when we go to sleep. There are no expectations for tonight. This isn't me setting up a big romantic evening so you want to jump into bed with me. Whatever you want from tonight is fine by me.'

She stroked his face. 'You're very sweet.'

She looked at him. He was the loveliest man she'd ever met and no matter what happened tonight she had to make sure she didn't fall in love with him.

Fletcher finished lighting the candles inside the storm lanterns and stood back to check it all looked OK. For some reason he felt like tonight mattered and he wanted to make sure everything was right.

He turned at movement at the entrance to the tunnel and smiled when he saw Bones come bounding towards him as if they were best friends. Dogs made friends very easily. They just sniffed each other's bums and were friends for life. They didn't need candles or flowers to impress each other. To be fair, Fern probably didn't need that either. She'd been perfectly happy with a bag of marshmallows and a few blankets the night before. But he felt like he wanted to make the effort tonight.

He bent down to greet his new furry friend, realising Bones had a ball attached to a rope in his mouth, but he didn't seem like he wanted to give it up any time soon as Fletcher had a brief tug of war with him. He saw more movement out the corner of his eye and glanced up to see Fern reach the end of the tunnel. Bones and his ball were quickly forgotten. She looked incredible in a pretty blue dress with dolphins on it and little sequins that were catching the light of the setting sun.

He grabbed the bunch of wildflowers he'd picked for her, a collection of yellow and blue which somehow seemed appropriate for her as she reminded him of a summer's day. He went to meet her at the bottom of the steps and saw her eyes taking in all his efforts.

'Wow, you've really gone to a lot of trouble. I thought we might just have a glass of wine and a ham sandwich. I wasn't expecting a proper date.'

He frowned and looked back at the candles and the food laid out on the blankets. Was this a date? He supposed it was. He'd never done anything like this before but he'd also never dated anyone before so he had no real idea what that looked like.

'Sorry, I didn't mean to presume this is a date,' Fern said. 'It's just with the flowers and candles—'

He took her hand. 'It's a date.'

The smile spread across her face and he knew he'd said the right thing. He handed her the flowers and kissed her on the cheek and her smile grew.

She leaned up and kissed him full on the mouth and god if the taste of her wasn't the most magnificent thing he'd ever experienced. He stroked her cheeks, relishing in the feel of her soft skin. He'd never believed in love at first sight, he wasn't even sure he believed in love at all. He'd seen too many bitter and angry divorces for him to believe that forever kind of love really existed. But there was something going on here that made him excited to see where it led and, while he didn't think it was love, there was definitely an attraction so strong it went way beyond anything he'd ever felt before.

The kiss changed to something more needful. He moved his hands down to her waist, holding her tighter against him, and then she pulled back slightly, looking up at him with darkened eyes.

'Are you sure this is a date?' she said, her breath heavy.

He frowned in confusion and nodded.

'That's a shame because I never sleep with someone on the first date.'

He laughed. 'So if it wasn't a date we'd be having crazy hot sex right now on the sand?'

She gave a shrug. 'I guess we'll never know but, now we're officially on a date, you have to impress me, wow me with your romancing skills. Spending the whole night trying to get me to play hide the sausage is not going to cut it.'

He burst out laughing. 'That's absolutely fine. Sausages are off the menu.'

As they walked across the sand, he was surprised by how fine he was about it. Every woman he'd ever slept with, it had purely been about sex and, while he couldn't deny he wanted that with Fern, he was more than happy spending the night just chatting and kissing. He didn't need it to be more than that.

They walked over to the picnic blanket where Bones was already sniffing at some of the treats.

'Will you dance with me?' Fletcher said.

'What?'

'Have you never danced on a date before?'

'I've never danced with a man ever. My dancing extends to feet moving from side to side and swinging my arms around in my drunken clubbing days.'

'You can't go too far wrong with a slow dance,' Fletcher said, retrieving his phone from his pocket. Swiping across the screen a few times, he started playing Ed Sheeran's 'Thinking Out Loud'.

He watched her uncertainty about dancing melting away.

'I love this song.'

He put the phone down and came back to her. He took both hands, placing one of them on his shoulder and lifting the other slightly to the side, and then rested his hand on her hip in the classic ballroom dancing position. He started moving them slowly around.

She was staring at him, partly in awe and partly as if she didn't know what to make of it.

'I didn't envisage this when I came here tonight,' Fern said. 'I didn't envisage any of this. You're clearly a master at this dating malarkey.'

'Honestly, my experience with women is normally meeting a woman in a bar and then going back to her place for sex. I know that makes me sound shitty but a proper relationship has never been on my radar. I've never done the dating thing and I've never done anything like this. So if I'm doing well it's only because I like you so damned much.'

He loved the smile on her face. She moved closer to him, holding his hand against his chest and sliding her other round his neck, which took some doing as she was a lot shorter than he was. He moved his hand round her lower back, loving the feel of her warm body against his.

'You're doing very well and I'm not just saying that because I like you so much too.'

They continued moving around.

'Why do you always go to the woman's place?' Fern asked.

He wasn't expecting that question. He chewed his lip as

he thought how to answer it without coming across like a dick. 'I live on a canal boat, it's very small but that gets a whole lot smaller when there's someone else there.'

'You mean someone else there that you don't really want there.'

He looked down at her. 'When I sleep with a woman, we both know it's nothing more than sex. If the sex is really good we might meet up for more sex but that's it. Generally I leave once we've had sex. I'm not running out of there while we're still catching our breath, throwing my clothes on as I run down the street, I'm not a complete arsehole, and I'm not counting down the seconds until I think it's polite for me to hotfoot it out of there either, but I don't spend the night. I've never been one for sleeping in the same bed as a woman or cuddling, so no, I don't really want a woman in my space after sex.'

'You cuddled me last night, all night.'

He stroked her hair. 'It seems I'm throwing every rule out of the window when it comes to you.'

She smiled and put her head back on his chest.

'So you've really never had a serious relationship before, with anyone?'

'Nope, never.' Was that a lie? It didn't feel like it was. His mind went straight to Lauren and he wondered if he should tell Fern about her. On paper, it ticked all the boxes for a serious relationship but in reality it had been far from that. Fern didn't need to know about her. It was in the past and didn't impact on their relationship now. And if Fern knew what a complete and utter arsehole he had been to Lauren she wouldn't want anything more to do with him. He decided to change the subject. 'Are you up for a bit of an unconventional slow dance?'

She looked back up. 'I'm not doing the floss or any of those other weird dance trends.'

'No need. But we both might find this a bit easier.' He picked her up so she was head height with him. She wrapped her legs around him and her arms around his neck as he continued to move slowly to the music.

'This is much better,' she said, leaning her forehead against his.

It was also a lot more intimate staring into each other's eyes as he moved around. She was stroking his hair at the back of his neck and it felt amazing. He leaned forward and captured her mouth with his and she instantly responded. Kissing had always been nice with other women but this was insanely good and he had no idea why. Desire and need erupted in him in ways he'd never felt before.

He was vaguely aware of the music changing and suddenly he could hear 'I Want It That Way' by the Backstreet Boys. He cringed, he had a recollection that the Ed Sheeran song had been part of a list of greatest number ones. Hopefully she wouldn't notice. Although that hope died when she giggled and snorted against his lips.

'Are you a fan of the Backstreet Boys?'

'Damn it, I was doing so well with our date, now all my credibility has gone out the window.'

'You'd have to do a lot worse than the Backstreet Boys to put me off. But shall we go and eat, I'm starving.'

He carefully put her down as she was singing along to the tune, which he quickly turned off before something else embarrassing started playing too.

He opened up the picnic hamper and pulled out some pâté, a baguette, cheeses and crackers, some meats, olives and grapes.

'This looks wonderful thank you, you've gone to so much trouble.'

'You're very welcome. I felt like we definitely needed to celebrate the completion of our brilliant tunnel. Your side looks amazing and you should be proud of what you've achieved. Whatever happens, whoever wins on Friday, I want you to know I've had the best time painting the tunnel with you.'

'I have too.' Fern frowned, picking up a sliver of ham and passing it to Bones, who quickly snaffled it up before ambling off a little way to dig a hole.

She sat down and Fletcher sat down next to her. 'Why are you frowning?'

'I'm just wondering what happens after tonight.'

'What do you mean?'

'The tunnel is painted, you'll be going back to ReLoved, I'll be starting work painting the new beach huts at The Little Beach Hut Hotel. Where does that leave us? If there is an us.'

'I want to see you again,' Fletcher said, without hesitation, although he was surprised to hear those words come out of his mouth. All of this was so new to him: dating and romantic moments, being in a relationship – if that's what he had with Fern – but he knew he wasn't ready to walk away from this just yet. 'Actually I go to a pub quiz with my friends every Thursday. If you don't think it's too soon to meet my mates, I'd love to have you along. One of the boys has started bringing his wife so you won't be the only woman there.'

She smiled. 'I would love that. I can bring my gift of knowing useless movie trivia. I also have a fairly good geographical knowledge if it's questions like what's the longest river in the world or the largest lake or capital cities.

I had to revise a whole list of those kind of facts for my GCSEs and for some reason some of it has stuck.'

'Perfect. We almost never win but it's good fun trying. There's a team that almost always win and they're particularly smug about it. We always try to beat them if we can.'

'Excellent. I like the challenge.'

They started eating the food, watching the sun sink beneath the waves.

'So you didn't grow up around here?' Fletcher said.

'No, actually I grew up just outside the Cotswolds, but I was moved around a lot because I was in foster care. They try to keep you in the same school but it wasn't always possible. I went to Carrie when I was thirteen and I was just fourteen when the adoption finally came through. Shortly after that Carrie moved me and my brothers down here. She was born and raised in Apple Hill Bay but moved away when she was older. Her grandad still lived down here, he owned the land that The Little Beach Hut Hotel is now on and Carrie's farmhouse. He wasn't well so she wanted to be closer to him to help him when he needed it. When I moved down here that was the first time I'd seen the sea and I knew then that, whatever happened in my life, I always wanted to live close to the sea.'

'I know what you mean. I grew up with the sea on my doorstep. I'd go to the beach every day and I always took it completely for granted but I never realised how important it was to me until I left. The sea is my home now. Wherever I am in the world, I want to be close to it. Sometimes, I bring a book down here and sit and read just to get my sea fix.'

'I do that too sometimes. I bring Bones down here for his walks most days. He loves the sea too. And if there's time I'll bring a book to read and we'll just chill out on the beach for a bit.'

'What books do you read?'

'I read cosy mysteries and autobiographies. I loved Michelle Obama's one. I've read a few fantasy books, I like paranormal books like stories about ghosts or fairies. I read a lot of romance books so there's a bit of a crossover with paranormal romance. What about you?'

'Oh a mix, autobiographies too, crime, espionage. And I also read cosy mysteries which I know is not the norm for a rufty-tufty man like me but I'm more interested in how they did the crime than the gore. I read sci-fi, fantasy – any books with dragons in, I'm there. I've always loved dragons. I read a lot of historical stuff too. I find history fascinating.'

He watched her as the sun caught her hair and thought he probably found Fern Lucas far more fascinating than any book he'd ever read.

Fern had never felt so completely and utterly happy as she did right now. They'd chatted, ate, walked along the moonlit shore and played with Bones. They'd also kissed a lot and now she was cuddled up against Fletcher's chest. For a man who didn't do cuddling he seemed surprisingly content to lie here with her in his arms.

Bones was fast asleep, half lying in the hole he'd proudly dug for himself. The half-purring half-snoring noises he was making made her smile. He seemed perfectly content too.

'Do you want to stay here the night or do you want to go home?' Fletcher said, playing with her fingers, stroking them, running his fingers up and down them.

She looked up at him. 'What do you want to do? Cuddling and spending the night with a woman is not really your thing.'

'Right now, I feel like I could stay with you like this forever.'

She smiled, her heart melting for him. She leaned up and kissed him and, after a few moments' kissing, Fletcher wrapped his arms around her and shifted her further up his body so he could kiss her more comfortably, but the feel of his hard chest against hers sent sparks of desire shooting through her body. She wanted to be with him tonight and she didn't even care if it was only for one night. She wanted romance in her life and making love to this wonderful man by candlelight, under a blanket of stars, couldn't be any more romantic.

She moved slightly off him so they were lying on their sides, kissing each other, and started undoing the buttons on his shirt. He didn't even seem to notice as he was too busy kissing her, stroking her arms. It wasn't until she slipped her hands inside the shirt to stroke his chest did he suddenly realise. He moaned softly against her lips and the fact that she could have such an effect on him made her feel so powerful. She moved her hand lower towards the waistband of his shorts and slid her hand inside, gasping against his lips when she realised how much he wanted this too. She wrapped her hand around him and the noise he made was pure animal.

He caught her hand and pinned it above her head. 'I don't need to be any more turned on than I am. I want you so much right now. But I don't want you to do something you'll later regret.'

She stroked his face with her other hand. 'I think my only

regret will be if I don't do this with you.'

He stared at her for a moment and then he kissed her hard.

He moved back so he was kneeling between her legs and gently started rolling her dress up, following it with his mouth as he kissed his way back up her body. He kissed her on the mouth as he pulled the dress over her head. Her bra was the next thing to go so the only thing she was wearing was her knickers, whereas frustratingly he was almost still fully clothed.

He kissed her shoulder, trailing his mouth down her arm, and she was surprised by how intimate it felt when he placed slow loving kisses across her wrist and up over her palm. He was adoring her body and she'd never had a man do that before. He started working his way up the arm and she stroked the back of his head. The smile he gave her sent those butterflies fluttering madly again. She really bloody liked this man and if she wasn't careful she could easily fall in love with him.

He moved his mouth across her breast, making her heart leap and her stomach clench with need.

'Is this OK?' Fletcher said.

'It's more than OK, don't stop.'

'You need to tell me if I do something you don't like.'

'I will, I promise, but right now I can't think of a single thing that you could do that I won't like.'

He trailed his hot tongue across her nipple and she arched off the blanket. She ached for him but he was clearly in no rush. He placed a long lingering kiss right over her heart.

She didn't know what to do with this. She'd expected sex with Fletcher to be fast and passionate. She hadn't expected it to be slow and gentle. She hadn't expected that he would make love to her.

He kissed his way very slowly down her body, slowly inching down her knickers and kissing down her inner thigh as he slid them off. He kissed her ankles and started kissing very slowly back up the inside of her other leg. She whimpered with need as he reached the top of her legs but after giving a very brief kiss right there where she needed him he carried on kissing back up the body.

Christ she was going to die from a sheer desperation to be with him. Never ever had a man taken so much time with her body before, making her pleasure such a priority.

He kissed her on the mouth and it was so hot and needful she wondered how he could possibly hold himself back. She pushed his shirt off his shoulders, desperate to feel his skin. The candlelight flickered over his flesh, painting him with gold. She dragged his shorts off his bum and he wriggled out of them.

He moved his hand between her legs and that feeling that had been building in the pit of her stomach exploded out of her almost as soon as he touched her there. He captured her moans on his lips. But he knew exactly what he was doing with his hands and no sooner had those feelings started to ebb away they started to build again, her stomach tightening with need, every part of her igniting in fireworks until she snatched her mouth from his so she could shout out his name as that feeling ripped through her again.

Her body was still buzzing when he dealt with the condom and leaned over her, kissing her briefly before very slowly sliding inside her. He watched her face making sure she was OK and she wrapped her arms and legs around him, arching up to take him.

But he didn't start moving, he just stared down at her with such adoration in his eyes.

'I've never had this before,' Fletcher said.

'What?'

'I don't know, this is different. It feels like it's... more.'

She didn't dare ask how much more. She couldn't let herself believe in the fairytale, not with Fletcher. Instead she reached up and kissed him.

He started moving slowly against her, and amazingly that feeling began to build again, that need for him was bubbling over. He started moving faster, taking her higher and higher, but when he pulled back from their kiss to look at her, it was the look of love from him that sent her roaring over the edge.

CHAPTER SIX

Fern woke up in the morning as Fletcher stroked her hair. She was surprisingly warm and cosy. It had got a bit chilly in the night and he'd given her his jumper to wear and he'd pulled on a t-shirt and they were wrapped in several blankets. She felt like she could stay there forever. She looked up at him and smiled.

'Hey,' Fern said.

'Hi, how are you feeling this morning?'

'I feel amazing, how about you?'

He grinned. 'I do too, I just didn't want you waking this morning with any regret for last night.'

'There's no way I could regret last night. Look, I know you don't do relationships but, for however long this thing lasts between us until you're done with me, I will never regret being with you.'

He frowned and then bent his head and kissed her.

She sat up and straddled him and he sat up too, cupping her face and kissing her. God she was never going to get enough of this man.

He pulled off the jumper she was wearing and the cool spring breeze brushed across her skin. Fletcher kissed her neck and her shoulder and then stopped.

'Umm... it appears we have an audience,' he gestured behind her.

She looked round and burst out laughing to see Bones sitting a few feet away staring at them intently, his head cocked on one side as if confused.

'I feel like he's judging us.'

She laughed. 'He won't tell anyone what we get up to.'

'No, but we might traumatise him if we take this any further.'

Fern grabbed Bones's ball on a rope and threw it down the beach. The dog went bounding after it but a few seconds later he brought it back to them, whipping his head around so the rope hit both Fern and Fletcher in the face at the same time. Fortunately it wasn't hard but the mood of the moment had well and truly gone. Fern climbed off Fletcher, laughing, and grabbed the end of the rope, having a tug of war with Bones.

Suddenly Fletcher bundled her in a blanket, covering her body completely.

'I can hear voices coming down the tunnel,' he said, wrestling another blanket around his waist.

'But the tunnel is closed until ten this morning.'

'They're probably coming to take advantage of the empty beach just like us.'

'Hopefully not just like us, or it's about to get awkward.'

But as two men appeared at the top of the steps with their surfboards, Fern realised it was about to get a whole lot more awkward.

'Oh, that's my friend Theo and I think that's his brother,' Fletcher said.

'Your friend Theo is *my* brother Theo.'

Fletcher's head whipped around to look at her in alarm. 'What?'

'Yep. And that's my other brother Shay.'

Theo and Shay stopped at the top of the steps when they saw they had company but they quickly realised who the company was and what was, or at least had been, going on.

Bones bounded over to greet his uncles and they both greeted him with lots of strokes before they started making their way over to where Fern and Fletcher were sitting.

'Oh god, they're coming over,' Fern said.

'This is not how I'd like to meet your family for the first time,' Fletcher said.

'You already know Theo.'

'Yes but that was before he caught me... hiding the sausage with his little sister.'

She snorted.

Theo and Shay stopped a few feet away. 'Well this is interesting,' Theo said.

'You know the tunnel is closed until ten,' Fern said, suddenly finding the whole thing hilarious as she peeped out from the top of the blanket. Fletcher was desperately trying to keep his blanket closed around his waist. There was literally no point in trying to pretend she hadn't spent the night having the best sex of her entire life. Well, they probably didn't need that detail.

'You can't judge us for breaking the rules when you're here too,' Shay said.

'We never left after we finished painting the tunnel.

There was a meteor shower so we spent the night watching it,' Fern said innocently. Although that had been the first night they'd spent on the beach, it didn't feel like a total lie.

'Naked?' Theo said, his mouth twitching in a smile, the affection he had for her clear in his eyes.

'Well, it got a bit hot.'

Theo turned to Fletcher. 'This is a little weird, my friend shagging my little sister.'

'Theo!' Fern said. 'It's absolutely none of your business who I sleep with.'

'Yeah, I don't want to know those details,' Shay said.

'Shagging makes it sound like it was something meaningless and it absolutely wasn't that. It was something special,' Fletcher said. 'And I didn't know she was your sister but it wouldn't have made any difference. I'm crazy about her and I'm not going to apologise for that.'

Fern couldn't help the huge smile that spread across her face. His words made her feel warm inside.

Theo glanced at Fern and then back at Fletcher. 'I was going to say that's good enough for me but, even if it wasn't, that smile definitely is. Come on Shay, we've got waves to catch.'

With that her brothers ran off into the sea and were riding the waves a few moments later.

'I'm sorry about them,' Fern said.

'Don't be, they're just looking out for you.'

'I liked what you said.'

'And I meant it.'

She smiled and leaned over to kiss him, not caring if her brothers were watching.

~

Fern stood at the top of the tunnel kissing Fletcher. She didn't want to say goodbye to him. It had felt like they'd been in a bubble the last two days with it just being them on the beach. It had felt weird this morning suddenly having Theo and Shay there, not just because she and Fletcher had been half naked and they were her brothers, but because for forty-eight hours the beach had been her private space with Fletcher and suddenly that privacy and intimacy had been shattered.

And now their time in the tunnel was over and they'd already had sex with each other, how much more would Fletcher want to see of her? She was quite surprised to get an invite to the pub quiz tomorrow night as that didn't seem normal for Fletcher's relationships with women. But if she was going to get another night with him she wasn't going to turn it down.

'I have to go,' Fletcher said, kissing her again.

'Yes, me too,' Fern said, and smiled when he kissed her again.

Finally he stepped back. 'OK, I really do have to go. I'll see you tomorrow night though, right?'

'Yes, looking forward to it.'

'I'll pick you up from your place around seven if you give me directions.'

'You can park in the car park outside Seahorses, take the path over the hill and my beach hut is the purple one right at the end, Turtle Cottage.'

'I'll be there. Oh by the way, just so you know, Theo is part of our pub quiz team. I hope that's not going to be awkward for you.'

'It's fine. If he has an issue with us being together, that's his problem.'

He kissed her again briefly and then walked away, but he kept looking over his shoulder at her as he made his way back to his car. She loaded Bones into hers, gave Fletcher a wave and then drove off up the hill.

She parked in the car park outside Seahorses and decided to get Shay and Carrie some pastries for breakfast as it was her first day working for them.

She opened the door to the café and smiled when she saw the local sea shanty group taking over the far corner. John was playing the accordion, Colin was playing the penny whistle, Marjorie was on the panpipes and a few others had tambourines and were singing and banging along to the beat. It sounded wonderful. Bones immediately went over to greet them all and those who knew him immediately gave him lots of fuss and attention.

Orla had just finished serving one of them when Fern approached the counter.

'Oh my god, you did it, didn't you?' Orla said as soon as she turned to greet Fern.

'How could you possibly tell?' Fern said.

'Because you walked in here as if you were floating and you look positively radiant. I've never seen you smile so much before in my life.'

'OK, OK, we did, last night under the stars, and it was the most incredible night of my life. I have never had anyone make love to me the way he did. And I don't even care that it will probably end in a week or two because I'm so happy right now and I deserve to be happy in a relationship for once. So many times I've dated a man and I always felt a little bit deflated – and not just with the ones that turned out to be complete twats, the normal, nice guys too. I always felt, is this it, is this the fairytale romance that I've always dreamed of. I'd started to think maybe it doesn't exist. But the last few days I've been with Fletcher I've been so gloriously happy. He is so lovely. He's kind, sweet, generous, romantic and the sex was…' she sighed happily. 'Magnificent. And he—' she trailed off when she saw the smile slip from Orla's face.

'Oh Fern, you've fallen in love with him, haven't you?'

'No, god no. I know what this is and it isn't that. My feelings are locked firmly away in my heart and my enjoyment of this thing with Fletcher is completely separate to that. It's a fling, a lovely, wonderful, incredible fling, but I am not in love with Fletcher Harrison. That would be ridiculous. Just because I think he is the most amazing man I've ever met in my life doesn't mean… Oh shit. I'm in love with him, aren't I?'

'It does seem that way.'

Fern rested her arms on the counter and let her head sink down on them. 'I'm an idiot,' she muttered into her arms.

'It's not your fault. Sadly our hearts have a mind of their own when it comes to love. We can't choose who we fall in love with or when. Besides, if you want to be angry at someone, then blame Fletcher. He made you fall in love with him by being so bloody lovely. If he'd been an arse, none of this would have happened.'

Fern laughed. 'You're right. It is his fault. What a dick.'

'Total dick.'

'Look, it's fine. Just because I'm in love with him, doesn't mean I'm *in* love with him. There's a difference. It's totally fine,' Fern said, ignoring the look of uncertainty on Orla's face. 'When it's over, it's over, it's not a big deal. It's like when you go on holiday and have an amazing time, of course you're going to be sad when you come home, but you don't not go on holiday just because you don't want to feel sad after. This is no different. I will enjoy it for what it is, of course I'll be sad when it's over, but then I'll pull my big girl pants on and move on, just like I've done with all the other men I've dated.'

Fern let out a heavy sigh, feeling like she was trying to convince herself more than Orla. 'Anyway, can I have a bag of pastries please?'

'How many do you want?'

'Better make it four, Shay will snaffle one in a matter of seconds and I want one for Carrie and me too. If Shay has two we stand more of a chance of eating ours. Get the custard ones for Shay, he loves those.'

'Are you excited about starting work up there today?' Orla said, bagging up the pastries and ringing them through the till.

'I am. This is a big job and it will take me quite a few weeks to finish it all but I love that every guest that stays at The Little Beach Hut Hotel will get to see my work. And it will give me loads of photos for my online portfolio.' She paid Orla. 'I better go, I need to have a shower. I've got sand in places that no one ever wants sand in.'

'That's what sex on the beach will do for you.'

Fern laughed, whistled for Bones, who was still having a load of fuss from the sea shanty group, and left.

'You're late,' Shay said, leaning up against the outside of the reception area.

Fern quickly checked her phone, as Bones bounded up to greet his uncle. 'You need to check your watch, as my phone says five to nine. You said to meet you here at nine.'

'I would have thought you'd come early if you wanted to make a good impression on your first day at your new job.' Shay stroked Bones's head.

'I don't need to make a good impression, you already love me. Plus I have these.' She held out the bag of pastries and Shay took it and looked inside.

'OK, you're forgiven.' He took her trolley from her and started walking off towards the new huts. Bones bounded along in front as if he knew the way. 'Right, follow me. We're not as far along as I'd like to be. I only have two huts that are ready to work your magic on, Otter and Narwhal. There will be quite a few more by the start of next week.'

'If the huts are already painted white inside like we agreed, it will take me approximately two days to finish each hut, some will take a lot less, some will take a bit more. So I should be finished with both of those huts by the time the other huts are ready next week.'

'Which one do you want to start first?' Shay said.

'Narwhals of course, who doesn't love a sea unicorn?'

Shay laughed and led her to a sky-blue hut. 'Can I see your designs?'

Fern pulled her big sketchbook out of her bag and flicked through the tabs to find the narwhal sketches. She showed him what she'd got. 'You can choose, realistic or whimsical.'

'Definitely whimsical, for the narwhal anyway.'

'That's what I thought, we can have a bit of fun with those. These are the sketches for the otters, I made them a bit more realistic.'

'These are perfect. I'm so glad we've got you doing this, the guests will love it and I can see all the Instagram posts now of people sharing pictures of the inside of the huts. I saw your mural in the tunnel. Fletcher's is good but yours definitely has the professional quality.'

'I think Fletcher's painting will appeal to a lot of people. It's quirky and charming.'

'Yeah, I can see that.' He paused, chewing his lip. 'Look, I'm sorry we interrupted you this morning.'

'It's no big deal. Bones had already stopped us from getting carried away, he likes to stare.'

Shay laughed. 'And I'm sorry about Theo, he's very protective over you, well we both are. But Fletcher's a good guy and it's nothing to do with us who you date. So I promise we'll be on our best behaviour tonight at dinner.'

'I hope so, I just want to play it down where Mum is concerned. You know what she's like.'

'Yeah of course. Right, I better get off. I'll check in with you later.'

Fern hooked a pastry out of the bag. 'Make sure Mum gets one of those.'

He laughed as if that was never going to happen.

Fletcher eyed the bookshelf he was making and sighed. It was supposed to look like a giant wave breaking. It had been ordered by one of his clients who loved surfing and it would take up the entire length of her lounge wall when it was finished. The shelves were curved with the flow of the waves but it had to have dividing vertical or diagonal sections inside so the books didn't just slide off the curves. It was relatively straightforward but for some reason he couldn't get his head round doing this today.

He smiled to himself. He knew exactly why his head wasn't in the right place today. All he could think about was Fern and the night before. Chatting to her, kissing her, making love to her under the stars. He knew what they shared was something special, something he'd never had with anyone before.

George put a cup of coffee down in front of him, distracting him from his thoughts. Fletcher loved George. He was eighty-five and a brilliant carpenter. As his first apprentice, Fletcher couldn't be more proud of how George had developed his skills. He was now a fantastic mentor teaching the apprentices with patience and an incredible attention to detail. He always wore a suit and would often have some pearls of wisdom to share.

'You're not really with us today, I see it in your eyes. Is it a woman?' George said.

Fletcher laughed. 'How can you possibly tell I'm thinking about a woman?'

'In my experience, there's only two things in this world that can make someone as happy as you look today: money and love. But money never lasts, the happiness it gives you is fleeting and empty, but love… well that's a different kind of happiness. Money doesn't give someone the glow that shines out of them like love does, it doesn't fill the heart and soul. Love is like the sun on a hot summer's day, this burning ball of light that is too bright to look at. It's standing on top of the cliffs in fifty-mile-an-hour winds, the force and power of the wind is so strong it can knock you off your feet, it makes you feel like you can't breathe, but as you stand there with your arms outstretched, feeling its strength as it roars past you, it makes you feel so alive. You, my friend, have that look that you're about to be knocked off your feet.'

Fletcher stared at him. 'Bloody hell George, you have a way with words.'

'But does it resonate with you? Does it feel like you've been burned by the sun and blown over by the wind at the same time?'

Fletcher thought about this for a moment, then looked at the shelf he was building. 'I think what I feel is what a surfer experiences when they catch the perfect giant wave. The excitement and anticipation of it coming, feeling that powerful swell build beneath your feet and that huge thrill of riding it expertly back to the beach.'

George stared at him in confusion. 'Your analogy is crap. Waves come and go, they ebb and flow, rise and fall. The sun is constant. It's always there.'

'Apart from at night,' Fletcher said. He loved winding George up.

'But it's still there for the other half of the world.'

'So that's not constant if we only have it for half the day. The wind isn't constant either. Sometimes the sea is as calm as a millpond, so I'm not sure that was a good analogy.'

'My analogy about the wind was about its power, not its constancy, as you well know. I see you Fletcher Harrison, you're being deliberately pedantic so you won't have to admit to yourself that you're in love with this girl. But you mark my words, a woman makes you smile that much, she is your sun, not some bloody wave.'

George strode away, muttering to himself.

Fletcher wasn't in love with Fern. He couldn't be. He'd only known her for a few days. He stood by his analogy. This felt different purely because he'd never caught the perfect wave before. He would enjoy the excitement and the thrill and when it came to an end he would look back with fond memories. So why did it feel like he wasn't riding that surfboard, he was falling off it and getting swept away with the tide?

CHAPTER SEVEN

Fern let herself into her mum's kitchen to see that Theo and Shay had already arrived and were trying to steal some of the chocolate chip muffins that her mum had made. Nothing ever changed. Her brothers always had massive appetites but rather unfairly always looked like they spent their lives down a gym, despite the amount of Carrie's cakes they ate, among other things.

'Hello my darling,' Carrie said, pulling Fern into a big hug and then giving Bones loads of fuss. 'Dinner's ready so why don't you all take a seat before there's no muffins left for dessert.'

Shay went and sat down, still chewing on the remains of a muffin, and Bones diverted his attention to him, but Theo came over and gave Fern a big bear hug. She smiled against him, she could never stay mad at him for long.

They went and sat down and Carrie dished up huge, heaped plates of meatball bolognese. The boys started tucking in greedily. Fern took a big bite, Carrie's meatballs were delicious.

'What's this I hear about you having sex on the beach?'
Carrie said.

Fern choked on her meatball and Theo slapped her on the
back. She quickly drank some water and then fixed her
brothers with her best stony glare.

'Don't look at us, we never told her,' Shay said.

'I've not said a word about it to anyone,' Theo said.
'Someone else must have seen you.'

'Wait, what?' Carrie said, suddenly looking confused. 'You
actually did have sex on the beach? When Marjorie said she
overheard you and Orla talking about you having sex on the
beach, I presumed you'd been talking about a cocktail. I had
to explain to her it was a drink and nothing more. Are you
telling me she actually got a bit of gossip right for once?' She
looked at Theo and Shay. 'And you two knew and you didn't
tell me.'

'It was definitely a cocktail,' Shay said.

'Don't give me that, I need to know all the details. I didn't
even know you were seeing someone. Who did you have sex
with? Wait, was it that lovely Fletcher Harrison you were
asking about the other day?'

Fern sighed. 'Yes it was.'

'Oh my god, I knew it, I knew you were interested in him.
Well, was it any good?'

'Mum, I really don't need to know those details, it was
bad enough finding them together,' Theo said, rubbing his
eyes as if trying to dispel that image.

'You saw them having sex?' Carrie said, aghast.

'No. No they didn't. We'd already… stopped by then.' This
conversation was going from bad to worse. She'd always had
a fairly open relationship with her mum but they didn't
really talk about sex too much. Well, Carrie was always more

than happy to talk about it, but Fern felt that some things should be kept private, so it was a bit of a balance to give Carrie enough titbits to stop her asking more questions without going into too much detail.

'So are you two dating?' Carrie asked, her own meal completely forgotten.

Fern thought about this for a moment. The night before had been a date, Fletcher had been very clear about that, and he was taking her to a pub quiz the following night, which she supposed was a date.

'Yes, I think we are,' Fern said and that gave her a delicious thrill. She was dating Fletcher Harrison.

'Oh look at that face, you're in love with him,' Carrie said, with hearts practically leaping from her eyes.

Christ, was Fern that obvious? Was she really such an open book that every person she spoke about Fletcher to would know she was in love with him?

'I'm not in love with him,' she insisted because there was no point in getting Carrie's hopes up that this was going to be something.

'Well your face certainly went gooey when you said you were dating.' Shay pointed at her with his fork before shovelling another meatball into his mouth.

'I like him, I think he's lovely, but I don't love him.' She tried to be firm, schooling her face not to show any signs of affection when she spoke about Fletcher.

'Please don't fall in love with him,' Theo said, seriously.

Shay backhanded his shoulder. 'Hey, leave her alone, it's not up to you who she dates.'

'I'm not saying she can't date him, she can sleep with him on every beach in England for all I care. Have some fun with him. I'm saying, don't fall in love with him.'

'I can fall in love with whoever I want,' Fern said.

'I knew you were in love with him,' Carrie said.

'I'm not but if I was that's my business, not anyone else's.'

'Look, Fletcher is a really good guy,' Theo said. 'There's no pretending to be something he's not. If he's being nice that's because he is a genuinely nice guy. But I've known him for many years and he has never had a girlfriend, ever. I've seen him flirting with women in a pub and I know he's probably gone home with that woman that night, but he never dates any of them. Most of the women never go beyond one night and if they do, it's only ever sex with him. He never wants more than that. He's not looking for a commitment or a happy ever after and I know that you are. I just worry that you're going to get your heart broken if you fall in love with him or expect anything more from him than just sex.'

Fern sighed, knowing Theo was right. She could tell herself it was fine and she knew what she was letting herself in for, that it would inevitably end, so she was prepared for it. But she knew the more time she spent with Fletcher the deeper in love she would fall and it would hurt when it came to an end. She'd never had her heart broken before. She'd been upset when relationships had come to an end, especially when the guy she'd been dating had let her down spectacularly, but she'd never been in love.

She had always guarded her heart so fiercely; growing up without love meant she had built walls around herself so she couldn't be hurt. When Carrie had fostered her and then adopted her, she told Fern she loved her every single day but it had taken nearly a year before she'd said it back. Handing over her heart meant it could be trampled on, crushed and rejected just like her birth mum had done. It had taken Fern a long time to trust Carrie and her brothers with her love. But with Fletcher it had happened so quickly, she hadn't even seen it coming, and now she'd laid herself wide open to getting hurt when it did reach an end.

'Maybe Fletcher just hasn't met the right woman,' Carrie said, optimistically.

'And I'm the right woman?'

'Of course you are. Any man would be a fool not to fall in love with you.'

Fern smiled at that lovely rose-tinted view. She looked at her brothers, who were watching her with concern.

She shrugged, trying to be blasé about it. 'It is what it is. I entered into this relationship with Fletcher knowing full well it would end. And yes I like him a lot and maybe I have feelings for him, but I'm having way too much fun to walk away from this now. If and when it ends, I'll deal with the fall-out then.'

'And we'll be here to help you pick up the pieces,' Shay said and Theo nodded.

Fern smiled. 'Thank you.'

Fern left Carrie's house and walked the short distance to Turtle Cottage. Although it was dark the paths to the different beach huts were very well lit, as were the beach huts themselves. The ten huts already in use were all in a row on the hilltops with fairy lights on the roofs of each one and around the decking, which was where the main entrances were. Each was quite a distance from the previous, affording the guests a little privacy. Turtle Cottage was the last one in the row and as she approached she could see the huge silhouette of Fletcher waiting on the decking. Waiting for her.

Her heart leapt and she quickened her step, Bones bounding ahead to greet his new best friend. She couldn't help smiling when she watched Fletcher greet him.

He stood up after stroking Bones and stepped off the decking to greet her, cupping her face and kissing her before she could even get a word out. She smiled against his lips.

'What are you doing here? We're not supposed to meet until tomorrow night.'

'I couldn't wait that long. I missed you too much.' He kissed her again then pulled back to look at her. 'God, you look like sunshine in that dress. You light up the darkness.'

She smiled at the lovely compliment. Her dress was bright yellow with gold sequins across the top. It was one of her favourites but not one of the men she had dated who had seen this dress had ever complimented it before.

She leaned up and kissed him again before he eventually pulled back.

'I better go, I have to be up early to drive to Plymouth to deliver a piece of furniture I've made.'

She frowned in confusion. 'You're going? But you just got here.'

'I just wanted to see you, kiss you and say goodnight.'

'You can stay if you like. Honestly, I'm too tired to do anything other than sleep but we can sleep together.'

Was that pushing the boundaries of their relationship when it was probably only going to be about sex? They had slept together the previous two nights on the beach but that had been slightly different. This was her home and he never stayed over at a woman's house.

'I'd love that,' Fletcher said.

She took his hand and moved up to the door, letting them all inside. Bones went straight to the kitchen to have a drink and then flopped down on the sofa, stretching himself out from end to end.

Fletcher stepped inside and shut the door, almost filling the lounge with his enormous presence.

'I'd show you round but what you see is what you get,' Fern said.

'I love the turtles. You have such a wonderful eye for detail.' He gestured to her mural.

'Thank you. The first ten huts, including this one, weren't painted with my designs. They were all in use every night so we'd have to close them off for a few days, so we agreed we'd do that once the new huts were up and running. But as I'm staying here I've had a chance to paint the turtles. I think they turned out really well.'

'I do too.' He stood staring at it for a few moments, taking it all in.

'Let's go to bed.'

He nodded and she led him upstairs, suddenly feeling nervous though she didn't know why. 'Bathroom's through there if you want to have a wash or anything. I have a spare toothbrush in the bathroom cabinet too.'

'Thanks.' Fletcher disappeared inside and closed the door.

Fern quickly changed into her pyjamas and then when Fletcher came out she went in and brushed her teeth and had a quick wash.

She stared at herself in the mirror. This didn't mean anything. Just because he was going to spend the night cuddling in bed with her when sex had been taken off the table, it didn't mean anything. So why did it feel like it did?

She stepped out the bathroom and her heart leapt to see Fletcher sitting up in her bed, waiting for her.

She got into bed, turned out the light and lay down. He settled down next to her, shifting onto his side to face her. He leaned over and kissed her. She smiled against his lips and he rolled on top of her as the kiss continued. She wondered if he would try to take it further but he was clearly more than happy just kissing her. She couldn't be happier too. There was no greater feeling in the world than being pinned to the bed by Fletcher Harrison.

CHAPTER EIGHT

Carrie was sitting out in her garden, sipping her cup of tea, watching the early morning sun sparkle off the turquoise sea of Apple Hill Bay. It really was a tremendous view from up here. She'd been thinking about Fern and Fletcher since she'd got up and what pearls of wisdom she could offer her daughter for the first time she was falling in love.

She looked over to see Antonio walking towards her. She waved at him and he let himself through the garden gate.

'What do you think about love, Antonio?' Carrie said, deciding to cut him off at the pass today before he could get out his latest complaint.

This clearly threw him. He hovered halfway through shutting the gate and she wondered if he would run away rather than talk about love with her.

But instead he came over and sat down next to her on the bench.

'Are you in love with someone?' he asked, his eyes still wide with surprise.

'If you say I'm too old for love, me and you are going to fall out. I'm forty-nine, I'm not decrepit.'

He put his hands up to stem the tide. 'I don't think you can ever be too old for love. And you have no control over it either. It just creeps up on you sometimes completely unexpectedly and suddenly they've taken up a place in your heart.'

She smiled. 'Good answer.'

He cleared his throat. 'Who are you in love with?'

'Oh, I wasn't actually talking about myself. Umm, a friend of mine actually,' Carrie lied, not wanting to openly talk about her daughter behind her back. 'She's seeing someone, a really lovely man who I think she's fallen in love with. But by all accounts he's not someone who ever has serious relationships so I don't think this is going to end well for her. There's a big part of me that wants to tell her to just relax and enjoy it, for however long it lasts, but she's been hurt before – not romantically, but by those who should have been there for her in the past and weren't. And I worry that if and when it comes to an end she'll get hurt.'

Antonio leaned back on the bench. 'Have you ever been in love?'

She smiled. 'Just once actually. What about you?'

He seemed to ponder that question. 'Probably twice.'

'Probably?'

'I'm in denial about the second one.'

'You can't deny love.'

'Don't I know it, no matter how inconvenient it is. But as you're now single I'm guessing your love story came to an end,' Antonio said.

'It did, it was very short-lived.'

'And do you regret it, that time when you were in love and everything seemed so much brighter and more exciting and wonderful? If you could do it all again, knowing it was still going to end exactly as it did, would you do it? Would you go through that heartache just for that fleeting moment of perfect joy?'

She grinned. 'In a heartbeat.'

He nodded. 'Love is a risk and sometimes it ends in pain but a life filled with safe choices is not a life worth living.'

She patted his leg. 'That's a good answer too. Cup of tea? And then you can talk to me about whatever it was you came to moan about this time.'

He patted her leg back. 'You know what, I think I'll save that for next time.'

He got up and gave her a wave as he walked out the gate.

Fern stepped back to admire the narwhal she'd finished painting. With its rainbow-coloured horn and big dreamy smile, the narwhal looked how she felt today: completely head over heels in love. She had spent what felt like hours kissing Fletcher the night before and it had been utter bliss. He kept stopping and looking at her with adoration before he kissed her again. And eventually when they did go to sleep, they'd cuddled up against each other, his arms wrapped around her, and he'd gone to sleep with a big smile on his face.

She was having a really hard time believing this was just sex for him but she was trying to stop herself from hoping for more.

He'd left early that morning to go to Plymouth and, when he'd woken her to say goodbye and that he'd pick her up at seven that night, his goodbye kiss had lasted over ten minutes and he'd had to drag himself away.

God he made her smile so much.

There was a knock on the door of the beach hut and she looked around to see Carrie standing in the doorway.

'I thought you might be hungry.' Carrie offered out a flask and a tin that was no doubt filled with her home-baked delights.

'I'm starving.'

Carrie came in and put the tin on the side, opening it and letting the smell of her delicious peach muffins waft out. Fern eagerly grabbed one as Carrie poured out two mugs of coffee.

Carrie moved to look at the wall where the narwhals were happily swimming around. 'This looks great. I love this fantasy style you've done.'

'I've had a lot of fun with this one.'

'Is that why you had the biggest smile on your face when I came in?'

Fern grinned. 'Maybe.'

Carrie laughed. 'You know, I was in love once.'

'With your husband, the dickhead.'

'Oh no, not him. I don't think I ever loved him. Which was stupid really because I married him.'

'Why did you marry him if you didn't love him?'

'Because I was twenty-three, all my friends had got married and were busy popping out children and I was deeply insecure about my appearance after a car accident left me with poliosis.' Carrie pointed to the silvery streak in her otherwise completely dark hair. Fern had always thought it was cool rather than ugly but she could see that as a young woman it might have impacted on Carrie's self-esteem. 'I used to wear headscarves to try to cover it, lord knows dye wouldn't do it. But so many boys would laugh at it and call me Lily Munster. Steve was nice, we got on well, and when he asked me to marry him I thought, well no one else will ever want me, so I said yes. Only to find out I couldn't have children a few years later and he ran for the hills.'

'Dickhead,' Fern said.

'Ah, I was better off without him as it happens. He went on to get married again and have three children and his new wife pretty much raised them by herself as he was such a useless dad. And being alone meant I could have you and your brothers and that was the best thing I ever did.'

'So who were you in love with?'

'A glorious man called Xavier. It was a year or so after Steve left me and we met while holidaying in Austria. The sex was incredible, he was insatiable, he couldn't keep his hands off me. He made me feel so desired, so beautiful. God, I fell in love with him so hard. But we both knew it was only for two weeks. He was going back to Ecuador, I was going back to the UK. There was never any talk of what would happen after the holiday was over. So we just spent the two weeks talking, eating, making love – a lot. It was utter heaven. On the last night, he told me he was very happily married with five children and that he would never see me again.'

'Oh my god, another dickhead.'

'I think in my heart I knew he was married. He never mentioned her until that night, never talked about his home life no matter how much I asked, he was always vague or changed the subject. But I was completely in love with him by then so I chose not to see the signs. I know that's a shitty thing to do but I had no idea when we first started seeing each other. It was really at the start of the second week that I started to have my suspicions but we only had a few days left by then. I knew when we said goodbye it would be forever so I decided to just make the most of the time we had left. I called him every name under the sun when he told me, but it was probably more out of guilt that I didn't stop it when I knew. I was also outraged on her behalf too, she was at home, looking after the kids, and her husband who she loved and trusted was away sleeping with another woman. He told me that he had never done this before and that he'd fallen in love with me too. It was probably a line that he trotted out to all the women he slept with, I don't know, I'm guessing I wasn't the first or last.'

'God, I'm sorry.'

'Oh no, honey, don't feel sorry for me. I didn't tell you about him as some kind of harbinger of doom warning about Fletcher. Xavier was the first and only time I fell in love and I know people say you can't possibly be in love after only two weeks when I clearly didn't even know the man but I was, unequivocally, and I fell in love with him after only one day. I don't regret my time with him, I regret that there was a wife involved, I do feel bad about that, but it was the best two weeks of my entire life. Everyone should experience that kind of love at least once in their life, to know the excitement and complete joy of that feeling. I know Theo would like to wrap you up in cotton wool and protect you from the world, but I want you to embrace this thing with Fletcher, to experience that beautiful, dazzling, breathtaking brilliance that is love. Don't be afraid of loving him deeply, with everything you have, bask in it, dance in it. Being in love is the most incredibly wonderful thing in the world and you should savour it, relish it with every fibre of your being, even if it is fleeting, even if it is destined to end in a few days or weeks.'

Fern smiled and hugged her mum. 'I bloody love you and your wonderful optimism. You make it sound so easy.'

'But it is easy, falling in love is the easiest thing in the world. Getting over it is the hardest. But we can't hide ourselves away from love because we're scared of the pain. That's no way to live.'

'I am scared by how much it will hurt when it comes to an end.'

'But you are one of the bravest, most resilient women I know. It will hurt but you will get over it and move on just like you've done before. But you will always be a little bit changed for the better because you've experienced love in all its heart-aching glory. That's a risk worth taking, isn't it?'

Fern smiled. Fletcher was bringing her so much joy right now, she had to embrace it, enjoy it for now and stop worrying about the future.

CHAPTER NINE

Fletcher knocked on the door of Fern's beach hut and heard Bones give a big deep bark inside. A few moments later Fern opened the door and he felt his heart leap as she stood smiling at him. Bones bounded out to greet him excitedly, shoving his extra-large head in Fletcher's hands before bouncing back inside and grabbing one of his many toys and shaking it around.

'Hey, come inside a sec, I'll just grab my jacket and put on my shoes,' Fern said.

She stepped back, holding open the door. He moved inside, took her face in his hands and kissed her. She shifted against him, wrapping an arm around his neck. God he could kiss her forever and never tire of it.

She pulled back slightly, tracing a finger down the inside of his collar, so it was a whisper against his skin. 'Well, we don't have to go the pub quiz, we could stay here instead.'

'Very very tempting, but my team would never forgive me if I didn't show.'

'Are you the brains of the team?' Fern said, stepping back and pulling on a pair of green sparkly Converse.

'I don't know about that, but I'm pretty much the only one that answers any question in the history round. How was your day painting?'

'I spent the day painting narwhals so it was a good day.'

He laughed. 'When does The Little Beach Hut Hotel officially open?'

'Just over five weeks. There's a big launch happening, Carrie's organised a funfair with traditional fairground rides, a helter-skelter, a big wheel, dodgems.'

'That sounds like fun.'

'We'll have to go together,' Fern said.

He suddenly noticed the dress she was wearing, a floaty black one with little dragons flying all over it.

'I love your dress.'

'Thank you, I wore it for you.' Fern shrugged on her jacket.

And that little gesture made another brick fall away from the walls around his heart. She had remembered his love of dragons in a throwaway comment he'd made when he'd been talking about his favourite books. He felt touched by that.

'Although I was going to wear my dinosaur dress. Dinosaurs, in my opinion, are far better than dragons.' She attached Bones's lead to his harness and stepped outside.

He moved outside and she locked the door behind them.

'I can't believe I'm hearing this,' Fletcher said, taking her hand as if it was the most natural thing in the world as they walked along the path towards his car. 'Dinosaurs are cool, granted, but how can they be better than a flying, fire-breathing dragon?'

'Because dinosaurs actually existed. There is scientific

proof they roamed the earth. As far as I'm aware there has never been any proof that flying, fire-breathing dragons existed.'

'Ah, but scientists and marine biologists are discovering new species all the time. We have oceans and seas that are so deep in parts that no one has ever seen the sea bed. Who knows what creatures are lurking down there?'

'Are you saying dragons are in our deepest oceans? Why do they have wings if they live underwater? Also, not much call for fire-breathing down there either, those flames would get put out pretty damned quick.'

He watched her as they walked, her eyes catching the light from the other beach huts. She made him so bloody happy. He loved that he could have this nonsense conversation about dragons with her. Everything about being with her was so easy. They just clicked in ways he'd never experienced before.

He unlocked the car and opened the back door for Bones. The dog jumped in without any hesitation, obviously excited for a new adventure. Fern climbed in and fastened the seatbelt through his harness before getting back out again.

'I think dragons are versatile,' Fletcher said. 'They know, above ground, the likes of St George would hunt them to extinction,' he added, closing the back door and opening the passenger side for Fern. She climbed in, tucking the dragon dress neatly around her. He walked round the other side and got in. 'So they live under the sea and only come out on land at night or in places where they're never likely to be seen. There are large parts of Canada that are completely uninhabited. I bet there's loads of dragons up there.'

She laughed and he loved the sound of it. 'I suppose it's possible that there are things or animals we've never seen.'

He started driving to the pub. 'I think you need to keep an open mind. Just because you can't see it, doesn't mean it isn't there. You read a lot of romance books, so you must believe in love, but that's not something tangible, something you can touch or see, but you believe in it.'

This conversation had suddenly taken an unexpected turn. What was he talking about love for?

'Oh I disagree with that, one hundred percent. Love is everywhere and you absolutely can see it. The love of a mother or father and their newborn baby, the love of a newly married couple, the love of a grandparent or a friend, even the love of a big slab of chocolate cake. You can see that love between them, it's visible. OK, the chocolate love might only be one-sided but even an unrequited love is something you can see.'

He glanced over at her as they stopped at some traffic lights. She closed her eyes, placing a hand over her chest.

'And you can feel it,' Fern went on. 'It's the butterflies of excitement when you see them. It's the accelerated beat of the heart. When they touch you that feeling inside is something way beyond lust and desire, it's something so powerful it takes your breath away. And when they look at you, you can see it in their eyes if they feel the same as you.'

He stared at her and he knew she was right. Love *was* a tangible thing. And it was highly likely he might be falling in love with her because he felt all those things she'd just described.

A horn blared behind him and he looked up and realised the lights had changed. He quickly drove off and then parked the car in the pub car park.

He got out and Fern was already out of the car and

climbing in the back to release Bones before he could get round there to open the door for her.

As they walked towards the pub, he got the distinct impression she was embarrassed for talking about love. He snagged her hand and pulled her back to him, wrapping her in his arms as he kissed her.

'I take back what I said about love. You are right, you can feel it and see it.' She looked up at him, her eyes wide and surprised he was saying these things. He was surprised himself. He cleared his throat. 'But I still stand by what I said. Dragons are better than dinosaurs.'

She laughed. 'You're such a nerd.'

They walked into the pub, ordered their drinks at the bar and then he led her over to his friends. They were all good blokes but he hoped they would be kind to her. He'd never brought a woman to quiz night before so he knew she would pique their interest. Theo was part of the pub quiz team and Fletcher wasn't sure if he was entirely happy about this new development between him and Fern.

Everyone fell silent as they arrived, apart from Ettie, Tom's wife, who let out an audible squeak.

'Everyone this is Fern, she'll be joining us tonight.' He gave her hand a squeeze. 'And this is Bones.' Bones rested his face on the table, which made everyone laugh. 'Fern this is Max, obviously you know Theo, and this is Tom and his wife Ettie.'

'Ettie is my best friend,' Fern said. 'I'd forgotten how small this town actually is.'

She smiled as Ettie got up and hugged her, whispering something in Fern's ear but Fern just laughed at whatever it was.

Tom gave her a hug next as Ettie greeted Bones.

'Good to see you again, Fern.'

'You too. Did you have a good honeymoon?'

Tom looked at Ettie and a big grin spread across his face. 'It was incredible.'

'Hey,' Theo said from the corner. 'You're turning up everywhere I am lately.'

'I'm just here to wind you up,' Fern said.

'Thought as much.' Theo diverted his attention to stroking Bones who had gone under the table to see him.

'Nice to meet you, Fern,' Max said from the other corner.

Fern smiled. 'And you. You're one of Fletcher's friends from school aren't you?'

'Yes, we go way back, but don't worry Fletch, your secrets are safe with me.' Max teased.

Although Max was only joking, Fletcher thought about that one big secret he hadn't quite found the courage to tell Fern yet and he shifted uncomfortably.

Just then they were interrupted by an announcement over the microphone and Fletcher knew that Dave, the landlord of the pub, was always a stickler for starting on time. 'Quiz teams, please take your seats, we're about to start round one. This week we'll be starting off with the history round.'

There were groans around the pub. Fletcher and Fern quickly sat down and Ettie grabbed the answer sheet and a pen. Fletcher felt Bones flop down against his leg, obviously happy to be part of the team.

'Question one,' Dave said. 'Who came to the throne when Queen Victoria died?'

'Christ,' muttered Tom. 'I really should know that.'

'Was it Albert?' Ettie said. 'That was her first child, wasn't it?'

'Victoria was her first child,' Theo said. 'But she wouldn't have been Queen as she had several brothers who would take that role ahead of her. Albert was her first son.'

'I don't remember there ever being a King Albert though,' Max said.

'There have been quite a few Alberts who became King,' Fletcher said. 'But they all took other names. Ettie is right, Albert did become King after Victoria but he used his middle name and became Edward the Seventh.'

Ettie quickly wrote that down and he glanced over at Fern, who was looking at him with a smile on her face. 'Such a nerd.'

'Question two,' Dave said. 'Which was considered to be the biggest dinosaur?'

Fletcher immediately looked at Fern, while Theo and Max were arguing about whether it was the T-rex or the Megalodon.

She laughed. 'I do know this actually, well according to the Natural History Museum, it was the Patagotitan. They think it was eight metres tall.'

Ettie wrote it down while Max and Theo were still arguing over who would win in a T-rex Megalodon fight.

'Dragons are bigger,' Fletcher said and Fern laughed.

'Question three,' Dave said. 'Which organ was left in the body and not placed in a canopic jar in Ancient Egyptian times? Was it the heart, the brain, the stomach or the lungs?'

'They used to throw away the brain because they didn't think it was important. I know that much,' Tom said. 'They'd shove a hook up the nose and yank the brain out through the nostrils and then throw it away.'

'Eww,' Ettie said.

'It was the heart,' Fern said, just as Fletcher was about to say the same. 'The heart stayed in the body because it had to be weighed against a feather in the afterlife. If the dead person had done awful things, the heart was heavy. Only if it was as light as a feather were they allowed into the afterlife.'

Fletcher stared at her in awe. 'You're a nerd too.'

She laughed and as he watched her he knew he could definitely fall in love with Fern Lucas.

Ettie followed Fern into the toilets and, before the door to the pub had closed behind them, Ettie was already squealing in excitement.

'Oh my god, what is going on between you and Fletcher? Last time I saw you, you'd just started painting the tunnel with him and now you show up to quiz night and you're holding hands and looking at each like you're completely head over heels in love.'

'We're not in love,' Fern said, although that wasn't strictly true. She knew she was in love with him, but she had no idea what he felt for her, though she guessed it wasn't love. 'We've had technically two dates, although nothing happened on the first date other than we cuddled under the stars, so I'm not sure if that really counts.'

'It definitely counts,' Ettie said, looking like she was about to burst with excitement. She suddenly gasped. 'He could be your One.'

Fern loved Ettie's optimism and excitement, it was a big part of what made her so endearing. She was also deter- mined to see Fern and Orla happily married too and was endlessly hopeful that every man who even looked their way could be their happily ever after. She genuinely believed everyone had their one person, their soul mate, and if and when they met each other it would be just like magic. She and Tom had connected in that way, he'd proposed after just four dates and Ettie had said yes. They'd got married three months later and were clearly still head over heels in love with each other.

'He is not my One,' Fern said, trying to temper Ettie's reaction, but she felt like that wasn't entirely true. 'He could be my One. I don't know if I'm his.'

Ettie squealed. 'Of course you are. That's how the One works. It's two soul mates coming together.'

'Ettie, I love your rose-tinted sparkly perfect view of the world, but we both know that in reality that doesn't happen.'

'It happened for me and Tom. He proposed after just one week. I knew without a shadow of a doubt that this was the man I was going to spend the rest of my life with.'

'You and Tom are perfect together, but you're the exception to the rule. Most people don't find their soul mate – if such a thing exists – or their life partner after dating them for one week.'

'Lots of people do. After Tom and I got engaged I did an article about it for the magazine I work for and I put a post out on social media asking for people's short engagement stories. I got loads of replies, people getting engaged after six weeks, four, two, even in one case after two dates. And when I questioned these people if they had any doubts, they all said they just knew he or she was the one. When you meet the One, everything will just click into place. Do you love him?'

Fern bit her lip and then nodded. 'I think so.'

'You think so?'

'I've never been in love, I know that much. And this feels so much more than anything I've ever felt before. My feel-

117

ings for him are so strong and powerful it fills me up.' She paused as she thought about it. 'Yes I'm in love with him.'

'And what would you do if he asked you to marry him right now?'

Fern laughed. 'He's not going to ask me to marry him. That would be ridiculous.'

'But what would you say if he did?'

'I'd tell him to ask me again in six months when we know each other well enough to make such a huge life-changing commitment.'

'Me and Tom didn't need six months.'

'You and Tom were lucky that you found something special in each other. But it would take a lot more for me to trust in that forever love. I never had that growing up, I was always moved on to the next family and the next. No one ever loved me until Carrie, Theo and Shay came along. The thought that someone like Fletcher or anyone could love me enough they would want to marry me and spend forever with me feels like an impossible dream. And I don't want to believe in that dream or hope for it, only to be disappointed. So right now, I'm enjoying being with him but I'm trying to keep a lid on all my feelings.'

Ettie nodded and put an arm around her shoulders. 'I get that, I really do. But you weren't too scared to let me love you.'

Fern smiled. 'You forced your way into my heart.'

'Well maybe you could be open to Fletcher loving you too.'

Fletcher watched Max disappear off to the bar. Tom was chatting to someone else across the room, leaving him and Theo alone together. Theo hadn't said much to him that night and Fletcher wanted to clear the air.

'Are you OK with me and Fern being together?'

'Would it make any difference if I wasn't?'

'Do you mean, would I stop seeing her? No, sorry, I wouldn't. I would do anything for a friend, but I can't do that.'

Theo folded up his receipt from the bar, making it into an intricate paper aeroplane. 'It's not that I don't think you're good enough for my sister. You're a good friend and a really decent bloke. I know you won't treat her badly like some of the other men she's dated, you're not going to cheat on her, steal money from her or hit her.'

'Christ no, I could never hurt her.'

Theo smiled sadly. 'But you will and that's the problem. You've never had a serious relationship in your life, well not as long as I've known you. This is going to end at some point and she will get hurt. She really likes you and, even though she puts on this brave front and says she's just having some fun or that she'll be fine when it ends, I don't think she will. I'm not sure how much you know about her past but she has a fragile heart and I worry about her.'

Fletcher nodded. 'I understand your concern but this relationship is different from anything I've experienced before. I really bloody like her and I have no intention of ending it anytime soon.'

'She wants forever though, the big fairytale love story, she's been searching for that in every relationship she's ever had. Are you really going to give her that?'

'I can't make you or her any promises about the future

but I've never felt this way before about anyone. She makes me want so much more. I think I could easily fall in love with your sister.'

Theo's eyes widened. 'Christ, I wasn't expecting you to say that.'

'I wasn't expecting to ever say those words either but she has changed everything.'

Theo had no words at all.

Fletcher checked that Bones was still snoring under the table and then stood up.

'I'm going to get a drink, do you want one?' he said.

Theo shook his head and Fletcher went to the bar, next to Max.

'Fern seems really nice,' Max said. 'You two suit each other.'

'She's incredible,' Fletcher said.

Max stared at him. 'This is something serious for you, isn't it?'

'I think it is.'

'Wow. I never thought I'd see the day.'

'Thanks very much.'

'I just meant you never let any woman get close. You've actively avoided any kind of relationship as far back as I can remember.'

'Fern is special. I guess I never found someone that I wanted to try with before.'

'Does she know about Lauren?'

Fletcher felt the horrible sinking feeling in his chest. 'Why does she need to know about Lauren?'

'Because, like it or not, she's a part of you and who you are today. I feel like you've always been afraid to have a relationship because of what happened with her, you've held yourself back, and if she somehow becomes a barrier for you and Fern, it would help if Fern knew what she was up against. And lastly, this is a very small town, people talk and one way or another she will find out eventually. It's far better coming from you.'

Fletcher felt sick at the thought of Fern finding out about Lauren, but he also knew Max had a point. If he had even the slightest chance of making this work with Fern he had to be honest about his past.

~

Fern stepped outside the pub and Fletcher took her hand as they walked towards the car. Bones was sniffing all the flower pots, wagging his tail frantically as he caught a scent of something exciting.

'I can't believe we won,' Fletcher said. 'You obviously brought us luck and wisdom. You'll have to come to every pub quiz night in future.'

'Now that feels like a big commitment, I'm not sure I'm ready for such a big step in our relationship.'

'Well how about another big step: would you like to spend the night with me on my boat?'

Fern stopped to look at him because that did actually feel like a big step. 'You never have a woman on your boat.'

'No.' He took her in his arms.

'You said the boat was too small to have someone there you didn't want.'

'But I do want you there, very much. And you're a very small woman, I'm sure we can find room for you.'

Fern laughed. 'But I come with a very big dog.'

'I have a super-kingsize bed. There's enough room for the

three of us. After I make love to you. I'm not sure I can do that with him watching us again.'

'He'll probably be quite happy on the sofa, or the floor if you don't want hair on the furniture.'

'A little hair is a small price to pay for a happy dog.'

Fern smiled, her heart filling with love for him. She leaned up and kissed him. 'Let's go back to yours.'

They got in the car, loading Bones into the back, and Fletcher drove off, over the hill and then down into the valley. The moon glinted off the river that headed out into the sea and, a few minutes later, Fletcher was parking his car in a small car park. They got out and walked along a well-lit towpath, keeping Bones on the lead in case he decided to take a swim in the river.

Fern hadn't been in this part of the town for many years and, when she had come, she'd never really paid attention to the number of canal boats that were moored here. She'd never realised these were people's homes. They were all beautifully painted with flowers or stars or other decorations. Many of them had flower pots filled with flowers on the roofs and the decking. People were sitting out on the decks, drinking glasses of wine or reading. Others were tucked up inside and as she passed different boats she could see people moving around beyond the portholes. She could hear the TV and music drifting out from most of them.

Fletcher suddenly caught her arm and nodded further along the path. She glanced round and her heart leapt when she saw a fox sniffing at one of the plants.

'Oh wow,' she said, softly.

'I'm pretty sure that's actually Copper,' Fletcher said.

'You name the local foxes?'

Fletcher grinned. 'I raised Copper as a cub last year. He'd

been abandoned, I think his mum had got hit by a car as I did see a dead fox on a road nearby. I hand-reared him and then released him back into the wild. I still see him round here sometimes and I give him the occasional titbit, especially in the winter.'

'What a lovely thing to do.'

'Oh, I think a lot of people would have done the same as me,' Fletcher said.

'I think you give a lot of people more credit than they deserve, I think most people wouldn't have anything to do with raising a wild animal.'

Copper disappeared over a wall and they carried on walking along the towpath.

'Well, I'm glad I did. I've seen him recently with a vixen who I've called Scarlet and they've made their den under a pile of rocks on the side of a dell just round the back of ReLoved. I did wonder if he chose there because he knows I'm up there or it's just a bit of a coincidence. I think Scarlet is pregnant. I haven't seen her for a while but I've seen Copper going backwards and forwards to the den bringing food so she might have given birth or be about to. If so we'll probably start seeing the cubs venturing outside in about four weeks' time.'

'That's so exciting. I can't wait to see them,' Fern said and then frowned. Would they even be together in four weeks' time? When everything was so perfect between them, it was very easy to start thinking about the future. Not in a marriage and babies kind of way, but planning things in advance like seeing the fox cubs together or going to the launch of The Little Beach Hut Hotel. She'd romanticised going on all the fair rides with him as a perfect date but they might not even be together tomorrow, let alone in four or five weeks' time.

She suddenly spotted a canal boat that was painted like one long purple dragon.

'No prizes for guessing which one is yours,' Fern laughed. 'It's a bit obvious.'

He stepped aboard and then held out a hand to help her over the edge of the boat.

'Will Bones need some help getting on—' Fletcher trailed off as Bones leapt over the small wall of the boat with ease. 'Apparently not.'

Fletcher's deck had a long cushioned seating area up one side and several pots of flowers and a barbeque round the other.

He let them inside and Bones took off with a big smile on his face as he explored his new surroundings.

Fern had been expecting something old-fashioned and poky but it was beautifully done inside so it was essentially one long room which gave it so much space. There was a large grey corner sofa in this part of the room, a big solid dining table that looked rough and rustic and misshaped with big knots of wood in it was a bit further along the room, and then there was a sizeable kitchen area. Up the very end, through an archway, was a huge bed that stretched from wall to wall. Everywhere was painted in tones of cream so it looked fresh and bright.

'Fletcher, this is beautiful.'

'Thank you. I'll just show you around. This is the kitchen, help yourself to any food and drink.' He grabbed a bowl from the cupboard, filled it with water and left it on the floor for Bones. He opened the door to another room at the side, which Fern could see was a large wetroom with a walk-in shower up one end and a toilet and sink up the other. 'There's a spare toothbrush in the cupboard under the sink.' He took her hand and walked through the archway into the bedroom.

'That bed really is huge,' Fern said.

'Do you want to try it out?'

Fern quickly toed off her shoes, shrugged off her jacket and crawled up the bed, plonking herself down in the middle, leaning up on her elbows as she waited for her big bear of a man to join her.

'Someone's keen,' Fletcher said, throwing his jacket off, kicking off his boots and crawling up the bed so he was over her. He settled himself down carefully on top of her and she wrapped her arms and legs around him as he kissed her.

After a while, when he was clearly not going to take it any further, she pulled back slightly.

'You know, for what we have in mind, it works better if we don't have any clothes on.'

'This works fine for what I want to do right now, we can get to that other stuff later.'

'The other stuff?'

'The kind of stuff that will keep my neighbours awake with your screams.'

She let out a little gasp. 'I don't scream.'

'Oh you do, I've heard you and it's wonderful. I've never been with a woman quite as vocal as you are.'

'I've never been with a man who makes me so vocal either. But you were quite noisy too.'

'That took me by surprise too. I think it was probably because it was the best sex I've ever had.'

She stared at him. 'Are you kidding me? All the women you've slept with, I was the best?'

'Oh undoubtedly. I've never made love to a woman like that before. It was incredible. It felt so... real. It made every other sexual experience fade in comparison.'

She stared at him. 'Are you serious?'

'I've never been more serious in my life. This is different for me. Everything about this is different.'

She leaned up and kissed him, feeling her heart fill for him. He ran his hands down her back over her bum and then, as he moved his hands back up her body, he started dragging her dress up too, pausing his kisses for only a second as he lifted it over her head and then threw it across the room. His mouth took hers again, his hands roaming across her body until she was humming with need for him.

He rolled back onto his knees and began undressing and she leaned up on her elbows to watch him, first taking his jeans off so she was able to enjoy the view of his massive thighs. He slowly started unbuttoning his shirt, teasing her with tantalising glimpses of that amazing chest.

When he finally peeled the shirt away she saw his impressive tattoo of a big scaly green dragon across the lower part of his chest and stomach.

She immediately moved up on her knees in front of him so she could get a closer look. When they'd made love on the beach it had been in the darkness, the only light being the candles in the lanterns, and she hadn't had much chance to look at his body properly. Now she could appreciate it in all its glory.

She traced her fingers across the dragon. 'I love this. You really are a dragon geek.'

'Oh I'm a complete nerd when it comes to dragons. I've always been obsessed by them, even when I was a kid.'

She studied the beautiful scales, the spikes, the wings, trailing her fingers over all of it. 'This is beautiful.'

He caught her hand as she traced the tail down towards his waistband. 'Do you have any tattoos?'

'I do, but you have to find it.'

'I love a challenge.'

He quickly removed her bra and then rolled her back, moving with her so he was pinning her to the bed. He kissed her deeply, igniting that fire deep inside her. He started trailing his mouth down her body across her chest.

'It's not here,' he murmured against her breast.

She swallowed and when she spoke her voice was high with need. 'Definitely not there.'

He moved his mouth down across her stomach, kissing her belly button. She arched off the bed, relishing in the feel of his mouth on her skin.

'Not here either.'

'Nope.'

He slid further down the bed, removing her knickers and then kissing the insides of her thighs. He moved his mouth slowly up, kissing her in the place that made her crazy.

'Fletcher, Christ,' Fern moaned.

'I'm just being thorough,' Fletcher said and then carried on kissing her.

Her orgasm ripped through her so fast and so hard it was as if it had come from nowhere.

'Definitely not there,' Fletcher said as she struggled to catch her breath. He kissed down to her ankles and then back up her legs again, driving her wild with need for him. He kissed all the way back up to her neck. 'Well, there's nothing here, I'm going to need to do a thorough investigation of the other side.'

She obliged him by rolling over and immediately he kissed the nape of her neck and then started kissing very slowly down her spine.

'Oh,' Fletcher said and she smiled into the pillow knowing he'd found it. 'That's Falkor, the luckdragon from *The NeverEnding Story*.'

'Yes it is.'

'Christ we really are soul mates. Maybe I should make love to you like this and then our dragons can play together.'

She bit her lip at the thought of him making love to her like this. 'That sounds like a great idea, they should definitely become acquainted.'

He carried on kissing down her spine and then knelt between her legs. She heard him dealing with the condom and she knelt up slightly, raising herself up on her elbows. He leaned back over her, kissing her spine as he wrapped an arm under her hips and slid deep inside her.

She gasped at the feel of him, clutching the duvet and arching back into him. He pulled her tight against him with one arm and leaned over her, bracing himself on the other arm as he held his hand over hers, entwining their fingers.

She was in absolute heaven, the feel of his strong body against her back, the scent of him surrounding her and every movement, every touch from him was as if they had been made to be together.

Suddenly he lifted her shoulders, rolling her back so they were both kneeling up on the bed together. She leaned into him, wrapping an arm round his neck, and he kissed her hard. She felt that sensation tighten in her stomach, spreading like wildfire through her. He moved his mouth to her neck and slid a hand between her legs.

She caught a glimpse of them in the mirror in the corner

of the room and watched him completely ravishing her, this desperate need to kiss her and touch her everywhere. Her eyes were wild, filled with lust and desire, and as his gaze locked with hers in the mirror, she could see how much he needed her. And then she was falling apart, crying out his name as that feeling exploded through her with such force and she felt him fall over the edge too.

They collapsed onto the bed gasping for breath and she snuggled into his chest.

She was never ever going to have enough of this man.

CHAPTER TEN

Fern packed up all her paints into her trolley, rolled up the plastic sheeting they'd put down to protect the floor and took one last look at the narwhals. The mural had turned out really well, with the magical-looking narwhals playing and swimming through the water.

She stepped outside. It was a glorious day, the sun painting the bright turquoise sea with ribbons of gold. She longed to go for a swim in it. Fletcher had gone off to Newquay this morning to deliver some furniture but he was going to be back this afternoon in time for the grand announcement of the winner of the mural painting competition. She wondered if he would like to go for a swim with her after that. A sunset swim could be beautifully romantic.

She wheeled her trolley over to one of the beach huts that Shay had commandeered as a site manager's office. Bones bounded after her sniffing every plant and clump of grass.

She walked in to find Shay on the phone, looking very stressed. He ended the call and moaned into his hands.

'What's up?' Fern said as Bones went round the other side of the desk to offer comfort to his uncle.

Shay stroked his big head. 'There's a leak in Otter Cottage. One of the builders was in there this morning, used the toilet and the flush handle came off in his hand. The toilet overflowed and wouldn't stop. We've turned the water off at the mains but I need a plumber to come out and fix it and trying to find one that can come out at short notice is a problem.'

'Is there anything I can do to help?'

'No, not today but, consequently, I won't need you to paint Otter today, there's water everywhere. You might as well take the rest of the day off but if you're free on Sunday you could make a start on Walrus or Hammerhead, both of them should be finished by tomorrow.'

'I can do that but are you sure there's nothing I can do to help?'

'No we're all good, well we will be. I might not make it down to the grand prize winner announcement this afternoon though.'

'Oh no worries, it isn't really a big deal. So many people have seen my murals and I've had quite a few phone calls already from people who want something on their walls so the exposure has worked. I'm not really fussed who wins now. Fletcher needs the money for ReLoved so I'd quite like it if he wins. They do such wonderful things up there, teaching people who don't get the opportunity. The money will go to good use.'

'It is a great place. Quite a few of the younger apprentices from there have worked on the beach huts here. Jobs are hard to come by in this part of the country so giving them a skill like welding or carpentry is something really useful to help them into work and something they can take to any city or town across the UK or the world. I have a lot of respect for what they do up there and for Fletcher for starting it all. Right, I better go and see if I can fix this bloody thing myself, at least temporarily. Leave your stuff here if you want.'

'OK.' She wheeled the trolley into the corner and then stepped outside while Shay locked the door. She waved him off.

'See you later,' he called and ran off up the hill.

She chewed her lip as she wondered what she could do with her day now it was suddenly free. She could take a book and read on the beach or go for that swim. Bones had already had his walk today and in this heat she didn't like to walk him again until it got cooler in the evening, at least not too far.

Suddenly she had an idea, why not go and see ReLoved for herself? Fletcher wouldn't be there so she wouldn't be disturbing him. It was only a short walk up the hill from here. She called for Bones as he was busy sniffing a patch of tulips and he lolloped ahead of her.

ReLoved was in a massive barn just on the other side of Carrie's land. Fern went through the gate and could see the huge double doors were open, letting in the sunshine. She could hear someone singing along to the radio, which made her smile.

She walked in, then hovered in the doorway and looked around. There were around six workstations in use, some taken up by mentors and apprentices, as she could see that there was teaching going on, while other work areas were occupied by individuals or pairs happily working away on some project. Some of the pieces were clearly going to be some kind of furniture, others more likely to be works of art.

'Fern? Hello, what are you doing here?'

She looked around to see George walking towards her.

'George, hello.' She gave the man a hug.

Bones bounded over to greet him as well and George gave him lots of fuss.

'Are you OK for him to come inside?' Fern said, holding onto her dog, who clearly desperately wanted to say hello to everyone else.

'Yes of course, I'm sure everyone will be delighted to make his acquaintance.'

She let him go and they watched Bones running round introducing himself to everyone.

'Are you here to do some woodwork?' George said, turning back to talk to her.

'Not really, I've just heard so much about this place, from you and others, and me and Fletcher are...' she paused. 'We've become really good friends over the last few days and I wanted to see where the magic happens.'

She wasn't sure how much Fletcher had told his colleagues about his relationship with her; he might want to keep it quiet so she didn't really want to announce to everyone that she was dating him. Saying they were friends seemed safer.

George studied her for a moment and then his eyes widened. 'You're his sun.'

'Sorry?'

'You're the girl he's been seeing, you're the blazing light in his life like the sun.'

Her heart leapt. 'He said that?'

'No, I said that.'

Fern was thoroughly confused.

'He said you were like a surfboard?' George said.

133

'What?' Fern said incredulously. How could she possibly take that as a good thing, was it that she was a fun ride? Christ, all of her illusions that Fletcher was feeling the same way she was were suddenly shattered.

'No hang on, not a surfboard, he said you were like catching a big wave on a surfboard.'

'Is that any better?'

'It was his analogy, not mine. The point is he's in love with you.'

Her heart soared back to life again. 'He said he loves me?'

'No, I did, why are you not getting this?'

Fern paused as she tried to take it in. 'You think he's in love with me?'

'Yes. Undoubtedly. I just don't think he knows it yet.'

'Because he sees me as a surfboard?'

'No,' George said in frustration. 'The thrilling feeling you get from surfing, from catching that perfect wave, or something like that, I didn't really understand it myself.'

Fern let out a heavy breath and decided to change the subject. Hearsay was not going to help in this conversation.

'George, why don't you show me around.'

George looked relieved the conversation was over. 'Of course, let me introduce you to everyone.' He moved over to one teenage boy who was making a beautiful animal hybrid sculpture out of what looked like bits of rubbish. It looked like it was part elephant, part snail. It was incredibly detailed. 'This is Leo, he is our resident artist. Some of his pieces have been sold to big corporate offices in London and one is on its way to Japan as we speak.'

'Hello Leo.'

'Alright.'

'This is amazing. Where did the inspiration for this come from?'

He shrugged. 'It's just something I've always done, doodles of animals crossed with other animals. When I came here, Fletcher asked me what I wanted to make. I didn't want to make any furniture so I showed him my sketches and he loved my hybrids. He worked with me to make the first one, showing me different techniques of how to join them together, and after that I started making them by myself.'

'That's fantastic. I love it. And I love that you're getting recognition internationally.'

'Thank you.'

George gestured for Fern to follow him to the next work-station, clearly he didn't want any dilly-dallying.

'This is Mo, one of our mentors, she's eighty-six today.'

'Happy Birthday,' Fern said.

'And this is Noah, one of our apprentices.'

'And who is this, George?' Mo said.

'This is Fern, she's Fletcher's sweetheart.'

Fern smirked at such an outdated lovely term.

'Oh, you're the one that has put a big smile on his face, are you?' Mo said.

'I'm not sure about that.'

'Well he's certainly had a spring in his step the last few days,' Mo said. 'I said to Pete that boy is getting jiggy with it.'

Fern snorted. 'What are you making here?'

'We're making a coffee table out of an old cot,' Noah said, hurriedly, obviously relieved to get away from the conversation about sex. 'The people who owned the cot wanted to keep it but make something out of it now they no longer need it as a cot. So we're using the wooden bars for the top of the table.'

'Oh this one has measurement marks on it, oh and that one,' Fern said, touching the lines the parents had clearly made to mark the length of the two babies at different ages. She smiled at the line that said, 'Felix six months', and on the other piece of wood was another mark that said, 'Isaac, nine months', among several other measurement marks.

'Yes, the parents wanted to keep that aspect on the coffee table. It's part of their memories.'

'I love that.'

'Let me introduce you to some of the others,' George said.

Fern turned to move on but Mo snagged her hand. 'That Fletcher is a good boy, he's done so much good here, you look after him.'

Fern smiled. 'I will.'

George gestured for her to come with him. 'The lad I'm going to introduce you to next, Oliver, he's completely blind. Many of the mentors didn't want to teach him in case he ended up chopping his finger off or hurting himself, which was ridiculous really. Blind people cut and prepare food for themselves and do all the things everyone does without causing themselves an injury. The mentors were also concerned about how they could show Oliver how to do something without actually showing him, if you get my drift. Anyway, Fletcher was insistent that we take him on as an apprentice as ReLoved is all about giving people the opportunity to do the stuff they would never get the opportunity to do. Oliver wasn't born blind but he had an illness when he was fifteen that caused him to lose his sight. Ever since then his mum has told him he can't do this because he's blind, he can't do that. He's here to prove her wrong. She has no idea he comes here, she thinks he goes to Blind Club, some fictional club Oliver told her about where they all sit around and talk and don't do anything risky at all. He's making her a dining room table and six chairs and he's filming it all so he can show her, he can do stuff on his own. He takes a bit longer to do everything than others might but he has a real talent for it. And so far no injuries either.'

Fern liked that Oliver was here because Fletcher had insisted he had as much right to be here as anyone else.

'Let's go and talk to him,' Fern said.

'Hello Oliver,' George said. 'This is Fern, Fletcher's girlfriend.'

So much for flying under the radar.

'Hi,' Oliver said.

'Hello.'

She looked at the table he was making; it was a big piece and looked fantastic. The legs were curved beautifully and the edges sanded to perfection. The top, however, was hollowed out so there was a deep rectangular area that looked like it was going to be filled with something. And that's when she saw all the buttons.

'This table looks amazing, but what are you doing with all the buttons?'

'My mum loves buttons. She's been collecting them all her life, buttons from every country, every place she's visited, but she keeps them all in a box and rarely gets them out. I asked her what she wants to do with them and she said one day she would get them all out and stick them on top of the old dining table which she hates, so she could look at the buttons every day. But that isn't practical, it doesn't make for a smooth surface to work or eat off, so I had the idea to make the top of this table recessed, glue on all her buttons and then cover it with an epoxy resin so they're secure. It makes the top smooth too. So I'm just sorting out the buttons. You can help me if you want. I can make a table and chairs by myself but I can't sort the buttons into separate colours.'

'I'll be happy to do that.'

She pulled up a stool. Bones came over to investigate and Oliver gave his head a stroke.

'I had the idea to have the big buttons in the middle then working out to the edge getting smaller and smaller, so I was just sorting them out into sizes. But I remember that from before I went blind, Mum always kept her buttons in little separate colour compartments so I wondered if I should do that on the table: have a blue section, red section, so there's a wave of each colour.'

'That's a great idea, I think it will look much more of a bold statement piece if you have the different colours in sections. I like the idea of starting off with the big ones in the middle, too. If we create a bit of a sun- or star-shaped pattern then we can have these wavy lines of different-coloured buttons coming from the middle to the edge.'

'I like the idea of that.'

'OK then, why don't I create a blue pile and then you can start positioning them on the table.'

'Sounds good.'

Fletcher stood in the doorway of ReLoved and watched Fern and Oliver laughing and chatting as they glued the buttons onto the top of his beloved table. He couldn't help smiling, his heart felt so full of her. Oliver had been very particular about not accepting help with his table because he wanted to say he'd done it all alone. Fletcher had demonstrated the techniques and with his assistance Oliver had practised those on other pieces of wood, but the table and chairs he'd completed all by himself, so Fletcher was surprised that Fern had been allowed to help with the buttons. But she was so easy-going and comfortable to talk to, he wasn't surprised Oliver had taken to her. Bones was lying fast asleep next to them, clearly making himself at home too.

It had been lovely to find her here but it also surprised him how much he wanted her here. He had always liked his own space. He'd never liked having a woman in his home, and he could never imagine a woman he was seeing turning up at his work, but she belonged here, just as she belonged in every aspect of his life. This morning, waking up with her in his arms in his bed, made him feel things he'd never felt before. He wanted her to wake up in his bed every morning and that stunned him. He was thirty years old and not once in his life had he ever wanted that. He'd actively avoided it. But this felt so right.

He wanted to kiss her right here although he knew he'd never hear the end of it from the mentors and apprentices teasing him. But right then he didn't care so he walked across the room towards her. Her face lit up at seeing him and then fell as he walked towards her like a man possessed.

She stood up. 'Fletcher, I—'

He cupped her face and kissed her, hard, and she let out a little gasp against his lips before she was kissing him back. He laughed against her lips when everyone suddenly cheered around him.

'What did I miss?' Oliver said.

'They're getting jiggy with it,' Mo said and Fern snorted against his lips.

∾

139

Fletcher hurried down the tunnel to Blackberry Beach, holding Fern's hand. After dropping Bones back at Fern's hut they were running a little late for the big announcement of the winner of the mural painting competition.

There were a number of people heading down there too. People had been voting for the last few days by putting tokens in the box next to the mural they liked the most.

Councillor Bishop was standing at the top of the steps that led onto the beach, greeting people as they passed.

'Fletcher, Fern, I'm so pleased you're here. I must say, these murals are fantastic. I would have such a hard time choosing a winner myself. I bet both of you get more commissions after this.'

'Oh no, I'll leave that to Fern, she's the professional,' Fletcher said.

'Well that's a shame, I like that cheeky charm in your paintings as much as I like the beautiful realistic images in Fern's. We'll be announcing the winner shortly so go on down.'

They went down to the beach and Fletcher was surprised by how many people had turned out to see who was the winner of a little local painting competition. There were lots of people from ReLoved there and several others he knew from around the town.

'Oh look, there's my mum with Shay and Theo,' Fern said. 'Are you up for meeting her? She's wonderful and I love her to bits but she's very over the top.'

'Of course. I'd love to.'

Fern led him over to Carrie, who he recognised from around the town.

'Fern my darling.' Carrie gave her a big hug. 'Your mural is beautiful. I've already voted.'

'Not that you're biased at all,' Fern laughed.

Carrie eyed Fletcher over Fern's shoulder and gasped. 'This must be the wonderful Fletcher that my daughter has fallen head over heels in love with.'

His heart leapt and he saw Fern tense in Carrie's arms.

'Way to play it cool, Mum,' Fern muttered.

'Oh, I'm only joking,' Carrie said, clearly backpedalling. 'I've just heard a lot about you over the last few days. Don't pay any attention to me.' She released Fern and opened her arms to give Fletcher a big hug. 'I'm Carrie.'

'Pleased to meet you,' Fletcher said, hugging her. He glanced at Fern, who was looking anywhere but at him. Was it true? Did she love him?

Carrie let him go and Theo patted him on the back. 'Carrie would like to see all three of us happily married, popping out a few children each so she is overrun with grandbabies she can adore. Consequently, the merest sniff of romance and Carrie has already bought the wedding hat.'

Carrie laughed. 'That's simply not true. OK, maybe a little.'

'I can shake your hand now,' Shay said to Fletcher. 'The last time we met I was too scared to in case your towel dropped and I ended up shaking something else. I'm Shay.'

'Good to meet you,' Fletcher said, his head still buzzing with what Carrie had said.

Just then Councillor Bishop switched on the microphone and it squeaked annoyingly, which got everyone's attention.

'Thank you all for coming to the first annual great mural painting competition,' the councillor said, as if it was a big event. 'I'm sure you've all had a chance to see the beautiful paintings done by our two finalists over the last few days and you've had a chance to vote. I'm sure you'll all agree they are both very talented. The votes have been counted and verified and the results are in.'

Someone handed her a gold envelope as if she was about to announce a winner at the Oscars.

Fern took Fletcher's hand and he looked down at her. 'I hope you win,' she said.

'You should win Fern, your paintings are amazing. You have an incredible talent.'

'You have a wonderful talent too. I voted for you.'

'You did? But I thought this was a fight to the death?'

'It turns out some things are more important to fight for.'

He frowned but then Councillor Bishop started talking again. 'This is incredibly close, the person in first place only has two more votes than second place, but the winner is...' she paused dramatically and everyone seemed to lean forward waiting to hear the name, 'Fletcher Harrison.'

Everyone cheered but Fletcher stood stunned. How the hell did that happen? But Fern was already giving him a big hug, while others were patting him on the back and urging him towards the stage where Councillor Bishop was waiting with a large, oversized plastic cheque for five thousand pounds.

He climbed the steps and looked out at the people cheering for him and no one was clapping louder and more enthusiastically than Fern. That touched him in ways that he hadn't expected. A win for her would have been important for her new business, but she still wanted him to win because she knew that the money could be used to help ReLoved. She was amazing and suddenly a realisation hit him like the force of a truck.

Councillor Bishop handed him the massive cheque, which was almost as big as him, and a photographer took his picture and then the councillor was handing him the microphone so he could make a speech. He hadn't expected to win, let alone stand up in front of all these people and speak.

He cleared his throat and the crowd quietened down. 'Thank you for voting. I had a lot of fun creating the painting so I'm pleased people will have fun looking at it too.' He found Fern in the crowd again. 'It was very easy to be inspired when I got to work with such an amazing talent as Fern Lucas every day. If you like what she did, she's started a business called The Big Picture painting murals in people's homes, shops and offices so please do check out her website if you're interested.'

Everyone clapped and Fern mouthed the words *thank you*.

'This money will go towards helping ReLoved and the work that we do up there. We'll be able to buy new welding gear and a lot more tools to help people create their masterpieces.'

There was another big cheer and Fletcher handed the microphone back to Councillor Bishop and walked down the steps with his huge cheque.

He found Fern in the crowd and she leaned up to kiss him but he stopped her. 'Fern, I need to say something.'

People were still cheering and clapping and patting him on the back. Maybe it wasn't the best time. Or maybe now was the perfect time, here where it all began.

'Before this thing between us goes any further I want you to know how much I... I appreciate you but—'

Fletcher echoed the words in his mind. *He appreciated her?* What was he doing? He was making a mess of this and it was important.

'You appreciate me?' Fern said.

People jostled around them, his friends from ReLoved were coming over to congratulate him.

'No, that's not what I'm saying. We've had fun over the last few days but—'

'Congratulations, Fletcher!' Abe, one of the men he'd taught at ReLoved, shook his hand.

'Thank you. I just need to—'

'Mr Harrison, can you come over and take some photos for the local paper?' A young woman was urging him to come with her to the tunnel.

'Yes, Fern should be in the photos too.'

'No, just the winner,' the woman said, rather unkindly Fletcher thought.

He turned back to Fern. 'I'll be right back, there's something I need to say to you.'

Fern smiled sadly as he was jostled away from her.

He spent a few minutes shaking various people's hands and having his picture taken and people started to leave but when Councillor Bishop was finally done with him he went back down to the beach to find Fern had gone.

Fern sat on her decking watching the sun go down as she nursed a glass of wine. Her heart ached. It was quite clear that Fletcher had been trying to break up with her this afternoon. After Carrie had unwittingly told him Fern loved him, he wanted to get rid of her quick before it went any further between them. *I appreciate you. We've had fun over the last few days but...* It was quite clear that *but* was going to be: *but I don't think we should see each other any more.* Or words to that effect.

When she saw Fletcher walking over the hills towards her, it was no surprise. She downed the rest of her glass and willed herself not to cry in front of him. She would be a grown-up about it because she'd known all along this day was coming. It was never going to be forever.

Fletcher stopped at the end of her decking. 'You left before we got a chance to talk?'

'Because I knew what was coming and I didn't want to hear it.'

'You didn't want to hear it?' This appeared to throw him, he rubbed his hand across the back of his neck and looked away over the sea. Why would he think she would welcome it? 'I thought… can I ask you, is what Carrie said true?'

Part of her wanted to leave this relationship with her head held high, for him to walk away knowing that it was just a bit of fun for her and of course she didn't love him; she didn't want him to pity her because she had fallen in love with a man who was scared of commitment. She didn't want him to know that she would cry herself to sleep tonight because the best thing that had ever happened to her was over. But there was a part of her that felt he deserved to know the truth, that he was loved, even if he didn't feel the same way.

She took a deep breath before she uttered the words she had never before said in her life. 'Yes, I'm in love with you.'

The smile stretched across his face, which she felt was a bit of a dick move since he was about to break up with her.

The smile fell. 'But then why would you not want to hear that I feel the same way?'

Her heart thundered in her chest. 'What? I thought you were breaking up with me.'

He smiled and stepped up onto the decking and took her

hand. 'Fern Lucas, I have fallen head over heels in love with you. I thought we were just having something fun over the last few days but somewhere between me chasing you down the beach in our water pistol fight and watching you laugh with the wind in your hair, watching a meteor shower with you, making love to you under the stars, realising you're a bit of a history nerd too and that you love dinosaurs almost as much as I love dragons, to seeing you today so bloody happy that I won, I realised that I've fallen completely and utterly in love with you.'

She gasped and the tears she had desperately tried to hold onto when he walked towards her little beach hut spilled over onto her cheeks.

'Hey, this is supposed to be happy news. I love you, you love me, this is a good thing, right?' He knelt down in front of her and gently wiped away her tears.

'I am happy,' Fern said. 'I just never thought anyone would ever say those words to me, especially not someone as wonderful as you.'

'I do love you Fern, so much. And if you invite me in, I'll show you just how much I love you.'

Fern laughed, wiping the last of the tears away. She leaned forward and kissed him and she could feel it in his kiss how much he loved her. She had tried so hard not to hope for the happy fairytale ending and now it looked like she might finally get one. She stood up and took his hand, leading him inside. Bones was already fast asleep, upside down on the sofa, so she shut the door softly and led Fletcher upstairs.

CHAPTER ELEVEN

FOUR WEEKS LATER

Fern threw her paintbrush back into its pot and stepped back to inspect her work. This hut was Puffin Cottage and she had really enjoyed capturing the beautiful colours of the birds' beaks, their unique clown-type eyes and their little black tuxedo jackets. She had painted the birds in flight, eating fish, bobbing on top of the waves, and their adorable little waddle walk. She had even captured the puffins kissing and cuddling up to each other in the bedroom, which the real-life birds seemed to do quite a bit. There was still quite a bit to do until it was finished, but she was really pleased with it.

'I'm going for lunch,' Fern said.

'You mean, you're going to see Fletcher,' Shay said, as he painted the banister.

She smiled, picking up the cool bag with her lovingly made sandwiches inside. 'Yes, I'm having lunch with Fletcher.'

'And do you not have anything in that bag for your favourite big brother?' Shay said.

'I'm not sure if you can hold that accolade, I'm pretty partial to Theo,' Fern teased.

'I'm mortally wounded. Go on, off you go, don't worry about me, starving to death.'

'Like you're not going to Seahorses for lunch to stare longingly at Orla.'

'That's an outrageous and scandalous thing to say. Orla does decent food. There's nothing more to my visits to her café than that.'

'Sure, you keep telling yourself that. I'll be back in an hour.'

Shay waved her off.

Fern stepped outside into the glorious sunshine and whistled for Bones, who was snoozing in the warm sun.

'Let's go and see Fletcher,' Fern said, and smiled when Bones wagged his tail ferociously and jumped to his feet. He took a long drink from his water bowl, probably longer than he needed to, and then lolloped off up the hill in search of the love of his life.

Bones had fallen completely head over heels in love with Fletcher, probably around the same time Fern had fallen under his spell. It had been four weeks since they'd got together and the three of them had been pretty much inseparable since then.

It was a beautiful spring day, the sun high in a cloudless blue sky, sparkling off the turquoise waters. Bluebells and tulips danced in the warm sea breeze. She walked past the brightly painted beach huts and smiled. What her mum, Carrie, had done with the place was nothing short of wonderful. The Little Beach Hut Hotel was due to open officially in just over a week and there was so much to do before then.

Fern neared the brow of the hill and saw the huge barn which was the home of ReLoved. She walked inside and looked around.

Joe and Rob, a lovely married couple, were bickering good-naturedly about the colour of a toy ride-on train they'd built. Leo was constructing something that looked like a dolphin with delicate iridescent dragonfly wings out of old bits of rubbish mostly found on the local beaches. Coral was doing something arty with an old vintage sewing machine, it looked like it was going to be the base to a small coffee table. Fern loved coming in here and seeing what was being made. It was something different almost every time she came. It was certainly an eclectic mix and she would often imagine, if she had a big house and of course lots of money to spend, she'd have all of these things in her home. Sadly her little beach hut wouldn't have enough room for a table lamp made from an old welly boot or a sculpture of a giant polar bear made from old ironing boards, as much as she loved them.

She glanced round to see Fletcher kneeling on top of a spiral staircase that he was building. She knew it had once been a glorious fifteen-foot, dark wood bookcase she had loved because of the tiny flowers carved into the wood. She had suggested that he used some of the leftover flowery wood as pieces of jewellery he could sell on his website. The staircase was now in graduating tones of blue and green and some of the flowers had been incorporated into the design. It also had a beautiful ornate banister that had once been a wrought-iron gate.

He must have seen movement out the corner of his eye because he suddenly looked over in her direction, a huge smile filling his face. He immediately climbed down and came to meet her. He cupped her face and kissed her and she couldn't help smiling against his lips.

Bones suddenly shoved his large head in between them, nuzzling up against Fletcher. They both laughed and Fletcher knelt down to stroke under Bones's chin. Bones slammed his huge body into Fletcher and then turned round so Fletcher could give him a bum scratch.

'Hey Bones, yes I love you too,' Fletcher said.

Bones bounded over to inspect Leo's dolphin and Leo gave him lots of fuss before he bounced over to take a long drink from the water bowl that Fletcher had left out for him, as if the short walk up the hill had given him a thirst he simply could not quench.

Fletcher turned back to face Fern.

'I brought sandwiches.' Fern held up her cool bag.

Fletcher grinned. 'How did I get so lucky to find you?'

'You must have done something amazing in your former life,' Fern said.

Fletcher laughed. 'You know what I love about you, your complete modesty. You don't go shouting your virtues from the rooftops.'

She leaned up to kiss him again. 'I don't need to when you do such a good job of it. Listen, if you don't have time to stop for lunch that's fine, just make sure you have something to eat while you work.'

'I always have time for you. I have something to show you,' Fletcher said, taking her hand and leading her out the barn and over to a large dell in the side of the hillside. Bones bounded after them.

Fern suddenly realised where they were heading. 'Is it Copper's cubs?'

Fletcher's huge grin was all the answer she needed.

They'd been keeping a close eye on the den over the last week, hoping to get a glimpse of the cubs. Copper had diligently been bringing food every day and they'd heard little yapping noises coming from inside so they knew it was imminent.

They approached the rim of the hollow and Fletcher sat down on the edge, Bones flopped down next to him, his huge head in Fletcher's lap, looking up at him with complete adoration. Fern sat on his other side and unpacked the sandwiches, taking out a few slivers of chicken for Bones too.

'I saw them first thing this morning,' Fletcher said, quietly. 'I reckon they're about four or five weeks old.'

'How many are there?' Fern said, excitedly.

'I only saw three, possibly two males and a female, though I'm not sure. At this age they are kind of the same size. They were pouncing on each other and chasing butterflies. I saw Copper too and he brought them back inside but I've seen the one who I thought was a female cub a few times. She's brave and curious. I saw the largest cub a few minutes ago, too. They've obviously been cooped up inside for the last few weeks and now they're ready to come outside and have adventures.'

Fern watched the entrance to the den in anticipation. It was funny to think that four weeks ago she'd been wondering whether she and Fletcher would still be together to see the fox cubs come out their den and now she knew without any shadow of a doubt that she would be with Fletcher forever. They just clicked together perfectly. The last four weeks had been complete heaven. Impossibly, she loved him even more now than when they first started seeing each other. He was so affectionate and she loved that; he was always touching or stroking her if they were watching TV together or if they were talking. Even something as simple as him stroking her fingers while they lay in bed together made her smile so much, as if he always needed that physical contact with her. Sometimes they took a shower together and, if she'd had a bad day, he would just hold her in his arms under the spray of the water and it helped all the frustrations ebb away. He was such a wonderful man.

Fern handed Fletcher his sandwich. 'I guess we should be quiet, or they won't come out.'

'They'll smell us anyway. Besides, Copper knows me, he knows the cubs are safe.'

Fern took a bite of her sandwich and they sat in companiable silence for a few moments, enjoying the sunshine and the views of the sea beyond.

'Is Leo ready for tomorrow?' Fern asked.

Fletcher paused, his sandwich halfway to his mouth. 'I am sorry that I'll be missing most of your birthday tomorrow for this exhibition. I—'

Fern put her hand on his thigh to stop him talking. 'You have nothing to apologise for. You're taking me for a lovely meal tomorrow night. And I couldn't be prouder of you and the work you've done with these kids and the other people that work at the barn. ReLoved is a wonderful initiative you've started, you're teaching skills that aren't available in the average school or college, you're helping them get jobs in the community and you're changing their lives. Look at Leo, he was always getting into trouble and spent a lot of time on the streets and now, with a little bit of old rubbish and your brilliant guidance, he has created incredible works of art that people are paying small fortunes for. You did that. And him obviously, but he would never have been able to do it without you. I'm excited for him to show his work off tomorrow in Plymouth and of course you must be there to support him.'

Fletcher smiled at her and then leaned forward to kiss her on the temple. 'I love you Fern Lucas. I think you're pretty bloody brilliant too.'

She smiled and blushed. 'Eat your sandwich.'

Fletcher put the rubbish and flasks back into Fern's bag and leaned back on his elbows as he took in the view: the sea, the beaches, the amazing woman next to him and her big, crazy dog. It felt like life was perfect right now.

Just then Leo appeared at their side and Fletcher sat up to talk to him.

'Sorry to interrupt, but I'm off now.'

'Do you have everything you need for the exhibition tomorrow?' Fletcher said.

'Yes, it's all set up ready for the opening, I just came back here to grab a few bits, but I couldn't resist working on the dolphin for a few hours before I went back up to Plymouth tonight.'

'I love the dolphin,' Fern said.

'Thank you, it still needs a lot doing to it, but as an artist yourself, you know that you could tweak and tweak and tweak it and you're still never perfectly happy with it.'

'So true. And I'm sorry I can't make it to the opening tomorrow. My friends booked afternoon tea at Merryport

Castle for my birthday months ago. But I'm hoping to come up and see it next weekend.'

'Well it'll be there for two weeks.'

'I'm so excited for you, the world finally gets to see the genius that is Leo Donnelly.'

'Thanks, I'm a bit nervous but it's a wonderful opportunity.' Leo turned to Fletcher. 'I'll see you tomorrow?'

'I'll be there, front of the line,' Fletcher said.

Leo grinned and waved as he walked away.

Fletcher stroked Bones's big, beautiful head. 'I better get back.'

Bones let out a moan of disapproval.

'Yes, me too,' Fern said, getting up and stretching. 'Hopefully Copper's family will make a showing another day.'

Fletcher stood up and looked down to the pile of rocks and saw a little brown face, poking its nose out from the hole underneath, sniffing the air. 'They must have heard us getting ready to leave.'

Fern looked down and gasped. 'Oh my god, it looks like a baby bear.'

He smiled, she was right. The cub had yet to grow into its nose, which would give it that distinctive fox-face shape, and its ears were small not pointy like Copper and Scarlet's. It wasn't even a deep red, fiery colour yet like its parents, much more of a dark brown. It was joined by another fluffy face. The first one ventured out, followed shortly after by two more.

Fletcher quickly grabbed Bones in case he decided to bound over and play with what he would see as puppies.

Copper was next out. He sniffed the air and stared straight at Fletcher and Fern, before he sat down and started licking his paws, keeping an eye on the cubs as they jumped on each other and rolled around on the ground, making weird yapping noises.

Suddenly they were joined by a fourth cub which was far smaller than the others and looked a lot more timid too, standing next to Copper instead of playing with its siblings.

'There's four,' Fern whispered.

Fletcher looked over at her and couldn't help smiling when he saw her enchanted face. She was staring at the cubs like they were a treasure chest filled with gold. He couldn't take his eyes off her as she watched them play and jump. She was the most incredible woman he'd ever met.

'Copper is a great dad, isn't he?' Fern said.

Fletcher tore his eyes from Fern's face to see that Copper was now lying down with the smallest cub climbing over him like he was a giant climbing frame and one of the others playing with his tail. Copper was lying there patiently letting them do it.

'Yeah he is,' Fletcher said, softly.

'You raised him well,' Fern said, leaning into him. He wrapped an arm around her, kissing her head. 'I think you'd make a wonderful dad too.'

The thought of that made his heart ache. That felt like a future he definitely didn't deserve but one he wanted so much.

She looked up at him and he cupped her face and kissed her. He looked down at the cubs again, clearing his throat. 'They need names.'

She paused as she clearly registered the subject change. 'Yes, how about, Ruby and Cherry for the two girls?' she gestured to the two cubs playing with Copper. 'Presuming they are girls as they are smaller than the other two. And the boys can be called Chestnut and Ginger.'

'Great names.'

They watched the cubs playing a bit longer before Fletcher pulled away. 'I really better go. Come to mine tonight, the weather is lovely, we can have a barbeque on the deck.'

She nodded, leaning up to kiss him on the cheek. 'Sounds good.'

He walked away and then looked back to see her standing on the edge of the dell, the spring breeze blowing her hair as she continued to watch the cubs. She would make a wonderful mum too.

He dragged himself away and went back inside ReLoved.

Fern walked into Seahorses on her way back to get Shay a cake. Although ordinarily he would be in there for lunch, flirting with Orla, she knew he would probably work through lunch in order to try to finish the hut they were painting and forget what time it was until his stomach protested. Bones quickly went off to the kitchen door to beg some scraps from one of his many fans, Marty the chef.

Fern smiled when she saw Orla chatting away to Ettie. Orla pointed out that Fern was there and Ettie turned and excitedly gestured for her to come over.

'What's up?' Fern said as she joined Ettie at the counter.

'I have some news,' Ettie said, looking fit to burst.

Fern smiled at her friend, fondly. Everything was exciting and wonderful in her world.

'Are you sure we should tell her?' Orla said.

'Well now you have to tell me,' Fern said.

'Fletcher is going to propose,' Ettie blurted out.

Fern's heart leapt.

Orla cringed. 'I'm sure Fletcher would rather have kept it as a surprise.'

Ettie waved it away like it wasn't important. 'Fern should know.'

'Are you sure?' Fern said. Four weeks felt like such a short time to get engaged. She certainly hadn't been expecting that. She knew Ettie and Tom had got engaged after a week and it had worked out perfectly for them but most people didn't get engaged until they'd been together for a year or two. But she suddenly knew that if he did ask she would say yes. She knew they were meant to be together forever.

'I'm a hundred percent sure.'

'You're not a *hundred percent* sure,' Orla said.

Fern looked at Ettie. Yes, this was a mistake. Ever since Ettie had got married she had been desperately trying to find happy endings for her friends. This was what this was, seeing the fairytale even if it wasn't real.

'I saw Fletcher looking at diamond engagement rings this morning in The Velvet Box,' Ettie said. 'I saw him point out a few rings, he was obviously trying to decide which one to get. I think he then noticed me looking so I ran off but I kept an eye on the door from a distance and I saw him come out carrying a bag with what looked like a small square box inside.'

Fern's heart soared with hope.

'Oh my god,' she said softly, those dreams she'd had as a child of a fairytale marriage blooming suddenly to life.

'What's going on?' Anna, Orla's new assistant, came over.

Fern sighed. If gossiping was an Olympic sport, Anna would surely win gold.

'Fletcher is going to propose,' Ettie said, barely able to contain her excitement.

'Really?' Anna wrinkled her nose. 'Are you going to say yes?'

'What's that face for?' Orla said, defensively. 'Fletcher is a wonderful man and he adores Fern.'

'I just never pictured Fern with someone like Fletcher Harrison.'

'What's happened?' Mira asked as she came over and joined them. She was Anna's next-door neighbour, she'd moved to Apple Hill Bay a few years before and she and Anna had been inseparable ever since. She could win platinum in the Gossiping Olympics, if such a prize existed.

'Fletcher is going to propose,' Ettie said.

'Oh shame, he's hot,' Mira said.

Fern rolled her eyes. Mira had no filter, she just said whatever was in her head without realising how inappropriate it was.

'Are you really going to say yes?' Anna said again.

'If he asks, I would,' Fern said.

'I always pictured you with someone like Shay not Fletcher,' Anna said.

'Ewww,' Mira said. 'He's her brother.'

'Well not really,' Anna said before Fern could get a word in. 'Carrie adopted all three of them when they were in their teens. They're not related at all.'

'Christ Anna, you're so indiscreet,' Orla said. 'Fern might not want her life history broadcast across the town.'

'Everyone knows, it's not like it's a big secret,' Anna said, completely unabashed. 'I'm just bringing Mira up to speed.'

'I never knew you were adopted,' Mira said, aghast, as if it was the most horrifying thing in the world when for Fern it had been the most wonderful.

'I have the best mum in the world with Carrie, so I wouldn't feel sorry for me. And Shay is my brother, even if it's not by blood. I've never looked at him or Theo in any other way.'

Anna shrugged. 'I didn't mean that you should get together with Shay, I said, someone *like* Shay. Fletcher is too... nice, I've never heard him raise his voice to anyone, he lives on a canal boat like some eighty-year-old, and I've even seen him wear slippers when I've walked past on the towpath. No real man would wear slippers?'

'They're not slippers, they're rubber shoes,' Fern said, defensively. 'The outside of the boat gets quite slippery sometimes so he needs shoes with a good grip when he moves around the outside. And so what if they were slippers, I'd take a man with a hundred slippers over raised voices anytime.'

'And he does all that work for charity,' Anna said, her nose wrinkling in distaste. 'All those deadbeats he hangs around with.'

Fern let out a gasp of shock.

'Yes, what a terrible person Fletcher is,' Orla said, sarcastically. 'What could Fern possibly see in him?'

'The people he works with have not had the opportunities in life that other people have or they've had some really bad luck and ended up living on the streets. Christ, I nearly ended up on the streets myself a few times in my life. I think the work he does with them, teaching them new skills to restore and renovate old furniture, is wonderful. We all need a helping hand sometimes and Fletcher is passionate about helping them.'

Anna sniffed, clearly not convinced that charity was a good thing.

'I'd still do him,' Mira said. 'He's sex on legs.'

Fern exchanged looks of outrage with Orla. Why would she say that with Fern standing right there?

'But would you marry him?' Anna said.

'I don't know, depends how good he was in bed,' Mira said.

'But Fern *is* getting married to Fletcher,' Ettie said, clearly getting frustrated that her big news was getting lost. 'Did you miss the part where I said he was going to propose and she said she'd say yes?'

There was a big gasp behind her. 'You and Fletcher are getting married?'

Fern turned round to see Carrie standing in the doorway, her eyes alight with happiness.

'Yes, he's going to propose,' Ettie said, clearly delighted to be imparting this news to everyone and anyone. 'I saw him buy an engagement ring.'

'We don't know that for sure,' Orla tried.

But Carrie was clearly not having any of it either as she all but charged across the café and pulled Fern into a big hug. 'I'm so happy for you. You and Fletcher were meant to be together. Oh, this is amazing news. We need to go shopping for a dress. Tomorrow is your day off, isn't it? We can go down to Something Sparkling tomorrow and have a look at the wedding dresses. We need flowers, we need a venue, where are you thinking of holding it? We need somewhere big to fit everyone in. Will you have a band or a DJ? We need a photographer and maybe a videographer. We need—'

'We need to wait for Fletcher to actually propose before we get carried away,' Orla said. 'And we need to let Fletcher and Fern decide what kind of ceremony they want rather than pushing them into something they don't want.'

'Of course, of course.' Carrie batted her comments away and turned back to Fern. 'When do you think he might propose?'

'I don't know whether he will. This feels very soon. It's been four weeks.'

'Tom asked me after only one,' Ettie said.

'I know, I just didn't see it coming at all.'

Fern suddenly thought back to a few nights before. 'Oh my god. We talked about weddings the other night. We'd been watching this film and the couple got married on a beach and I said I'd love to get married on the beach. And he asked me if I'd want to get married on Blackberry Beach or somewhere more exotic like in the film. I told him I'd love to get married on Blackberry Beach where it all began for us and then he... well, he seemed really happy with that.'

Fern smiled as she remembered how Fletcher had made love to her right there on the sofa, telling her how much he loved her and how happy she made him.

'See, I told you he's going to propose,' Ettie said, excitedly.

'Will you say yes if he asks?' Carrie said.

'Yes, I would. I know it's sooner than any of us expected but we're going to be together forever, I'm a hundred percent sure of that.' Fern thought for a moment. 'He's taking me to the Tulip Garden tomorrow night for my birthday, maybe he'll ask me then.'

The thought that in a little over twenty-four hours she could be sitting at her favourite restaurant, newly engaged, filled her with nothing but joy and excitement. She was finally going to get the wedding she'd always dreamed of.

No, she couldn't get carried away. What if Ettie was wrong?

'I think Orla is right, we need to wait for Fletcher to propose first,' Fern said. She saw that Ettie was about to protest. 'I'm sure your information is right. But he could have been buying a ring for his grandmother for all we know, or maybe he doesn't intend to propose just yet and is planning some big surprise. Let's just put a pin in any celebrations or plans for a little while.'

She watched Carrie's face fall. 'I suppose you're right. And we don't want to ruin his big surprise, we won't say a word.'

Fern looked at Anna and Mira; half the town would know by this afternoon thanks to these two. She glanced around the café, which was almost entirely filled with locals. Almost all of them were looking over in her direction, having heard Ettie's exciting news themselves. She was sure the few people in town who Anna and Mira hadn't told would hear it from the rest of Orla's customers. Poor Fletcher; if he was planning a big surprise, it was well and truly ruined now.

'Orla, can I get a slice of that caramel chocolate brownie for Shay, I best be getting back.'

Orla dished up the cake into a takeaway box and handed it over. Fern paid, whistled for Bones and then waved goodbye to everyone, but before she had even closed the café door behind her, she heard the place erupt into excited chatter.

She walked back to the beach hut she and Shay were painting, with Bones bounding eagerly by her side. The emerald sea sparkled today in the endless sunshine creating a picture postcard with the brightly painted beach huts.

When she was younger, Fern had spent a lot of time imagining what her dream wedding would look like. There'd been a big flouncy dress, a seven-tier pink and white cake, the ceremony and reception would take place in a big castle and, of course, she would arrive in a horse-drawn carriage. But she hadn't given any thought to what her real wedding to Fletcher would look like because they'd only been together for a few weeks.

She quite liked the idea of getting married on the beach, despite it having been a throwaway comment the other night. Blackberry Beach had played such an important part in their relationship. She could imagine the candles and the flowers in the tiny cove, Fletcher waiting for her at the end of the aisle. They could have a barbeque after with some music so people could dance under the stars. She didn't need the seven-tier cake or the meringue-style dress.

She smiled to herself. But maybe she could still arrive in a horse-drawn carriage.

She walked back into the hut and Bones flopped down outside in his favourite sunny spot.

'Wow, what happened to you, did you win the lottery?' Shay asked as he looked down from his spot on the stepladder as he painted the ceiling.

'Well, I kind of have. I think Fletcher is going to propose. Ettie says she saw him buying an engagement ring.'

His eyes widened and he quickly climbed down the ladder. 'Fern, that's amazing. But are you sure? It's so soon.'

'I know it is. And no, I'm not sure, but Ettie was pretty adamant about what she saw.'

'Well, I'm over the moon for you, I know you two will be

very happy together,' Shay said, stepping forward to give her a big hug.

'Are you not going to ask if I'm going to say yes?'

'I think the huge smile answered that question for me. And I get to give you away, right?'

'Yes of course,' Fern said. 'You and Theo can both give me away.'

'Damn it.'

CHAPTER TWELVE

Carrie was taking some coconut and chocolate muffins out of the oven when she saw Antonio coming over the hills towards her house. She'd just made herself a tea so she quickly made him one too, remembering to add a sugar.

She flung open the door. 'My lovely Antonio, there is nothing you can say to me today that can burst my bubble, so do your worst.'

'Fireworks,' Antonio said, holding the leaflet advertising the launch in the air.

'How can you possibly have a problem with fireworks? Everyone loves fireworks.'

'Too noisy, do you know how much it will echo around the bay? The poor animals will—'

'These are silent ones, no wildlife or pets will be disturbed by these fireworks.'

His face fell; he'd clearly not read that part of the leaflet. Now he had nothing to complain about and he didn't like it.

'Come on, have a cup of tea and a cake before your long walk back around the bay,' Carrie said, handing him the mug.

'What's got you in such a good mood today?' Antonio said, clearly miffed. He sat down and helped himself to a muffin, unwrapping it carefully as it was still hot.

'My daughter is getting married.'

'Oh, congratulations. How old is your daughter?'

'She's twenty-nine.'

He studied her for a moment. 'And you have two others, how old are they?'

'Shay is thirty-two, Theo is thirty-three.'

'You must have been a child yourself when you had them.'

'I'll take that as a compliment about my youthful beauty. They're adopted. I adopted Theo first when I was twenty-nine. He was thirteen. Then I adopted Shay a year later, followed by Fern after that when she was fourteen.'

'Adopting older children can't have been easy.'

'Neither are babies and dirty nappies and sleepless nights. You just have teenage angst and doors slamming instead.'

Antonio took a sip of his tea and for once he didn't wince, which was a little disappointing. 'What made you decide to adopt older kids?'

Carrie picked up her mug and held it in her hands. 'It was a long road. I couldn't have children for medical reasons and my husband left me because of it.'

'Well, he sounds delightful,' Antonio said, dryly.

'Oh, the man was an idiot. He remarried and popped out a few babies very quickly. I saw his new wife in a café with her three-year-old, one-year-old and pregnant with her third and the poor woman was exhausted. She was moaning to her friend that he never helped her, never lifted a finger with the night feeds or nappy changes, never helped in any way, and I felt relieved we never had a chance to have that life.'

She took a sip of her tea. 'I started fostering because I

always wanted a family and I was so surprised how many older kids had been in the foster system for years and I knew I wanted to do something to help. Local authorities tend to move towards permanent foster homes for older children rather than putting them up for adoption but there were many kids searching for a permanent foster home and you have to find the right match. When Theo came to me he was such a subdued withdrawn kid, like life had beaten any joy or happiness out of him. He was always moving on to the next foster home and the next, and I knew he needed some permanence. He stayed with me for six months before I applied to adopt him. It's supposed to be a year but there are ways round it. The first time I really saw him smile was when I asked him if I could adopt him. He was so used to moving around, he was always waiting to be transferred to the next foster family. In the months after, while we waited for the adoption to go through, he just blossomed, he opened up into a lovely, playful, mischievous boy. I knew I wanted to do the same for other children too.'

'Wow, that's a wonderful thing to do.'

Carrie smiled. 'I never regretted it. And now they're all grown up and doing well. Theo is a CEO of a very successful business that he built up from scratch, Shay is managing the whole development of The Little Beach Hut Hotel and Fern has her own small business painting large murals – those ones in the tunnel to Blackberry Beach, she did those. Although I suppose you would complain about them too.'

He frowned. 'Why would I complain, they're very good.'

'Because you complain about everything.'

'I do not.'

She couldn't believe he had the audacity to deny it or to smirk when he said that.

'Of course you do, you complained about The Little Beach Hut Hotel being built, you complained about the bright colours of the huts, the construction noise, the dust that apparently travels all the way across the bay, you complained about the lights on the pathways keeping you awake, you've complained that the grass is too long and the grass is too short, and those are only a handful of complaints on a very long list.'

To her surprise, he burst out laughing. And what was more surprising was how much she loved to hear it. He smiled very occasionally but this was a full rich loud laugh.

'The grass is too short,' Antonio chuckled. 'Even for me that was pretty tenuous. I'll have to do better at coming up with more plausible complaints.'

She stared at him in confusion. 'We don't need more complaints, dare I say it, but we probably need a lot less of them.'

Antonio finished his drink and stood up to go. 'But then you'd miss this.'

She felt her mouth fall open. 'Do you come by here every day, just to wind me up?'

'That's an outrageous thing to say. I'll see you tomorrow.'

Carrie quickly found her voice. 'Not tomorrow, it's Fern's birthday, I won't be here.'

'The day after then, and I'll make sure it's a good one.'

He walked out the door, giving her a wave.

She watched him go and felt her heart leap. Was there really more to Antonio's visits than she'd thought?

~

Fern slipped her favourite red dress over her head. It was a charity shop purchase and had cost her two pounds fifty. It was a lovely cotton dress with tiny sequins across the chest and thin spaghetti straps, she felt so pretty in it. When she spent most of her days in dungarees as she painted, it was nice to wear something a bit more feminine. She gave her eyes a flick of sparkly rose-gold eyeshadow and swept her favourite candyfloss lip balm across her lips. She pulled her hair up into a knot and threw her feet into her gold sandals.

Despite the fact that she and Fletcher had been dating for a few weeks now, she always felt the flutter of excitement at seeing him as if they were going out on a first date.

She went downstairs and poured herself a glass of apple juice, smiling at Bones lying upside down fast asleep on the sofa. She walked past him and went and stood out on the decking, looking out over the spectacular view.

She loved her little beach hut and living here had meant that she'd been able to save a small amount towards a deposit on a house. Maybe that house would be one she'd be sharing with Fletcher at some point in the future, although with the possibility of a proposal on the horizon it could be sooner than she'd thought.

She knew it was silly to get carried away with the proposal idea when it was so soon into their relationship. But if he did propose it would be the delicious cherry on top of their perfect relationship. Maybe she could put the feelers out tonight, find out what he thought about their future. Then she could either put this idea to bed or allow herself to get excited about it.

She finished her drink and whistled for Bones. Suddenly she was looking forward to seeing Fletcher even more.

~

Fern curled her feet up under her and watched the sun-kissed clouds drift across the pale pink sky. Dragonflies skated over the water, their iridescent bodies shimmering in the setting sun. Lots of people were sitting out on the decks of their boats too, enjoying the warm spring evening. Bones was snoozing at her feet after enjoying a few bits of sausage.

She loved being here on Fletcher's boat, it was peaceful and quiet and she enjoyed the camaraderie between the other boat owners. She and Fletcher split their time between here and her little beach hut but, if she had to choose, she preferred it here. She could imagine living here together.

Fletcher came out and handed her a glass of wine, looking happy and relaxed in baggy shorts and a loose shirt. He was just about to sit down when Mrs Gillespie from the neighbouring boat shouted over.

'Fletcher. Fletcher dear, can you come over and change my gas bottle for me?'

'Sure, no problem,' Fletcher said, slipping on his boat shoes which Anna despised so much before climbing onto the towpath and back onto Mrs Gillespie's boat.

He disappeared inside.

'Sorry Fern, I won't keep him a moment,' Mrs Gillespie said. 'Those pipes are too fiddly for me to do with these old fingers.'

'No problem,' Fern said.

'You look radiant tonight in that red dress, my dear,' Mrs Gillespie said.

'Thank you.'

'You're absolutely glowing,' Mrs Gillespie said, thoughtfully, as Fletcher stepped back out onto her deck. 'Isn't she, Fletcher?'

'She looks beautiful,' Fletcher said. 'She always does.'

Fern smiled at the compliment.

'But there's something different about her tonight.' Mrs Gillespie pulled at his sleeve so he had to bend down and she whispered in his ear.

Fletcher smiled and shook his head. 'Not yet?'

'Well get a move on, dear.'

'Hopefully soon,' Fletcher said.

Fern frowned in confusion. Was Mrs Gillespie asking whether he had proposed to her yet? Had he confided in his neighbour about his big surprise?

He waved goodbye to Mrs Gillespie and climbed back aboard his own boat and Fern couldn't help smiling at the rubber shoes as he toed them off.

'You know, Anna doesn't like those shoes. She says no real man would wear slippers.'

Fletcher burst out laughing. 'I think my masculinity is safe, they're not technically slippers. Although what's wrong with slippers?'

'I have no idea. I think her problem is more with you than your shoes.'

Fletcher took a sip from his bottle of beer and closed down the lid of the barbeque. 'Is that right?'

She smiled. He was so laid-back. 'Does that not bother you?'

He shrugged. 'I don't really care what anyone thinks about me, except you. And Anna has been shirty with me ever since I turned her down when she asked me out.'

Fern's eyes widened. 'She asked you out?'

'Yes.'

'But she's really pretty, why would you turn her down?'

He turned back to look at her in surprise. 'Because looks don't mean anything to me. I'm more concerned with the person on the inside and Anna's insides are not pretty. Also she asked me out the day after I told you I loved you for the first time, and Anna knew we were together. Her words were something like, "Why settle for dry white wine when you can have sparkling champagne?"'

Fern felt her eyebrows shoot up. 'The cheeky cow, what did you tell her?'

'That I'd tried champagne and I didn't care for it. I was more of a lager man myself.'

She laughed. 'So what does that make me?'

He pondered that for a moment. 'I've never been good at analogies but maybe a shandy.' He looked over at her, sizing her up. 'A half-pint of shandy.'

She laughed again. 'I don't know whether to be flattered or insulted by that.'

'Fern Lucas, from the moment I met you, I was completely head over in heels in love with you. There has never been anyone else for me since then and there never will be. You are the most wonderful woman in the world and no one else will ever compare to you, even if they are champagne or whisky or a pint of the finest ale. It will always be you.'

She smiled and stood up, sliding her arms around his neck and reaching up on her tiptoes to kiss him. 'I love you Fletcher Harrison.'

He kissed her and then pulled back slightly to look at her. 'I have something to ask you actually.'

Her heart leapt, the *yes* already on her lips.

He frowned slightly. 'Although maybe we can talk about

it tomorrow night, like I'd planned. Right now, I'd like to dance with you.'

Was he really going to ask her to marry him tomorrow, was that what he meant?

He led her inside. She was never much of a dancer until she'd met Fletcher, but he loved to dance with her and she loved it too. Although mostly she loved the way he held her like she was the world's most important treasure.

Bones followed them inside and made for the bedroom at the end of the boat.

Fletcher swiped his phone a few times and put it down as music started drifting out of it. She laughed as she realised he was playing 'Lady in Red' by Chris de Burgh.

'Too cheesy?' Fletcher came back to her, putting his hands round her waist.

She slipped her hands round his neck. 'Just the right level of cheese.'

As Chris de Burgh started singing, Fletcher joined in with the lyrics, staring at her as he sang about how gorgeous she was and how much he loved her. Fern swallowed the lump in her throat. They started moving slowly round the room but before Fletcher had finished the second verse, she leaned up and kissed him. His hands slid up her back as he kissed her too. He placed soft kisses on her cheek, his gentle hands caressing the skin on her back.

He kissed her shoulder, lingering lovingly, but it was that kiss that changed the atmosphere between them. Her heart leapt and his hands tightened at her waist. He swept her hair off her shoulder and slowly slid her strap off, following it with his mouth.

She eased her hands under his t-shirt, feeling his rock-hard stomach before sliding them round his back, trailing her fingers up and over his muscular shoulders. Although the t-shirt was just getting in the way so she tugged at the hem and pulled it up over his head. She stepped forward, leaning up to place a kiss over his heart. She looked up at him and he cupped her face and kissed her hard. She moved her hands to his jeans as he pushed her dress off her shoulders so it slithered to the floor. He quickly removed her bra, as she pushed his shorts down over his massive thighs. He knelt down and helped her out of her knickers and placed a kiss on her inner thigh. Her breath caught in her throat as he trailed his mouth upwards but then he stood back up before he'd got anywhere near her most sensitive area. She let out a groan of frustration and he chuckled as he kissed her again.

She loved the anticipation, the build-up to being with him, almost as much as the main event. Almost.

He kissed her again, letting his hands explore her body, making her gasp every time his hands grazed across her breasts. She loved it when he drove her wild with need and he knew that. He bent his head to kiss her shoulders then her neck before dipping his head lower and kissing across her breast.

'Oh god Fletcher.'

He kissed her on the mouth, shuffling her back against the wall. He hooked her leg around his hip and slipped his hand between her legs, making her cry out. He knew exactly where to touch her to make her weak and tingles started to explode through her body until suddenly her orgasm ripped through her hard, leaving her gasping for breath.

He continued kissing her as she came down from her high, stroking her arms, her back, clearly in no rush, but she was desperate for more now.

'Fletcher please,' she whispered against his lips.

'What do you need?' His touch was featherlight, sending her crazy for him.

'You.'

He lifted her and as she wrapped her legs and arms around him he moved deep inside her, kissing her hard.

She let out a sigh of relief as he started rocking against her. 'It's always you,' she muttered, mindless with pleasure. 'You are always what I need.'

He slowed then stopped, pulling back slightly to look at her, his breath heavy against her lips. She stroked his face, wondering why he'd stop now.

'I want forever with you Fern Lucas, I want to grow old and grey with you. Will you...' he trailed off.

Her breath caught in her throat. Was he really going to propose now? During sex wasn't the most romantic proposal but she'd still say yes.

'Do you want forever with me too?'

She saw the vulnerability in his eyes and she knew he was scared of asking her. She wanted him to have no doubt whatsoever of her feelings for him.

'Fletcher Harrison, I love you and I want to wake up with you every morning and go to bed with you every night. You are my missing piece and I want forever with you too.'

He broke into a huge grin and kissed her again, moving against her with an almost desperate need. She clung onto him, tears pricking her eyes, and she couldn't help the huge smile spreading on her face as she continued to kiss him.

She was going to be with this man for the rest of her life.

And it was that thought of forever that sent her roaring over the edge.

~

As Fern lay in Fletcher's bed she thought that there was no greater feeling in the world than being wrapped in his arms as he stroked her head. The moon was streaming through the windows and she could hear the water gently lapping against the boat. Bones was stretched out on their feet. Right then her heart couldn't be more full with happiness.

She looked up at him, stroking her fingers across his chest. 'In your vision of our future, do you see children?'

Fletcher's face lit up and he let out a groan of need. 'Christ Fern, the thought of you pregnant with my child is the biggest turn-on. Let's make a baby now.'

She shrieked with laughter as he rolled on top of her. Bones sighed at the intrusion and got off the bed, wandering off to the lounge.

'I'm on the pill, as you well know, but I can stop taking it after...' she trailed off. She had been going to say after the wedding but she didn't want him to know that she knew about the proposal. And she still didn't know if he was going to propose, though everything in her heart was saying he was. 'After the big opening,' she quickly amended.

He started playing with her fingers, stroking around her knuckles, her palm and up and down her fingers. 'Yes, the next few weeks are going to be busy but there is nothing that I want more than for us to have a whole football team of children. Umm... I've started saving for a deposit on a house with a large garden for Bones and all of our children to enjoy.'

She stared at him in surprise. 'You want to move out of here? But you love it here.'

'I do but I love you more. A boat is no place to raise a baby and I want that future with you more than anything.'

She suddenly realised he was stroking her wedding ring

finger, swiping his finger round and round it as if drawing a wedding ring on her finger.

That was the future he wanted with her: marriage, babies, a big house.

Fern swallowed a big lump of emotion in her throat and smiled. 'You've put a lot of thought into this.'

'Of course I have. You and our family are the most important thing in the world to me.'

'I've been saving so I could afford my own place again but at the back of my mind I hoped it would be a place we could move into together. I want that future with you too.'

They stared at each other, big inane grins on their faces, as they thought about that big, beautiful, happy future. She stroked his face and kissed him, excitement bubbling in her chest at the thought of them having a baby together. 'How did I get so lucky to find someone as wonderful as you?'

He frowned slightly. 'I'm the lucky one.'

She smiled and kissed him. 'You know, I think we should practise making a baby now, we need to get this right.'

He grinned. 'I think so too.' He kissed her softly. 'You are going to make such an amazing mum.'

'Are you kidding, our baby will have the best dad in the world.'

He frowned slightly but kissed her again before trailing his mouth down her chest and across her stomach as he shifted down the bed. He kissed below her belly button and then moved his head lower.

'I'm pretty sure that's not how you make a baby,' Fern said, stroking his head lovingly.

'It's well known that multiple orgasms can increase the chances of the woman getting pregnant,' Fletcher said.

She laughed. 'Is that so?'

But the laughter changed to a gasp when he kissed her at the very top of her legs, adoring her, making her orgasm rip through her as if it had been bubbling beneath the surface. He shifted back up her, kissing her body as he made his way up to her mouth.

'I love you,' Fletcher said, moving deep inside her.

'I love you too,' Fern said, knowing that what they had was forever.

CHAPTER THIRTEEN

Fletcher pulled his t-shirt over his head as he watched Fern sleeping with a smile on her lips. God, he loved this woman so much.

She stirred and stretched and when she saw him watching her, a huge smile spread across her face.

He climbed up the bed and kissed her. 'Happy Birthday, beautiful.'

'Thank you.'

'I'm sorry that I can't spend it with you.'

She shook her head. 'You don't need to worry, the exhibition is important. Leo has worked so hard on it and you can't let him down.'

He frowned. 'You're important too.'

'I'm fine. I'm meeting Carrie, Shay and Theo for breakfast and then Carrie is taking me shopping and then later I'm having afternoon tea with the girls and you're taking me to my favourite restaurant tonight. Sounds like the perfect day.'

'Are you sure you don't mind?' he asked.

'Not at all.'

He kissed her again and settled himself carefully on top of her as the kiss continued.

She pulled back slightly, holding his face. 'What time do you need to go?'

He checked his watch and groaned. 'About five minutes ago.'

She laughed. 'Go, we can pick this up tonight.'

'And we'll do your presents at the restaurant.'

Her face lit up. 'I look forward to it.'

He gave her another kiss and shifted off the bed. 'I'll see you at the restaurant.'

She waved and cuddled back into bed. He was so tempted to climb back into bed with her. He shook his head, grabbed his stuff and hurried out.

Fern walked into Seahorses just as Orla was unloading breakfast onto the table where her brothers and Carrie were sitting. It looked like they'd ordered enough to feed a small army. Pancakes, waffles, croissants, toast, bacon, avocado, sausages, fruit, cereals, yoghurt, it looked like her brothers had ordered every single breakfast item on the menu. Bones shot over to the table, nose in the air as he smelled all the wonderful, delicious treats. Shay was going to look after him today while she went shopping with Carrie.

'Christ, are you guys hungry?' Fern said, as Theo stood up to give her a hug.

'Happy Birthday, Fern. We didn't know what you wanted so we just ordered one of everything.'

'That seems a bit wasteful,' Fern said and then shook her head; her brothers would no doubt polish off every single thing on the table. By the looks of their wet hair, they'd both been surfing already this morning and were probably ravenous. They always were.

'I think we'll manage,' Shay said, getting up to give her a hug too.

'And I hear congratulations are in order,' Theo said as he sat back down.

'Am I not going to get the big lecture about it being too soon?'

Theo shook his head. 'I honestly can't see that I'll ever get married, as I don't think anyone would put up with my shit. But if I ever found someone who loved me and who I loved like you two love each other, I'd be popping the question too. I'd be holding onto that woman and never letting go. I know I had my reservations at the start but you two were meant to be together, I know that. He makes you happy so I have no problem at all about you two getting married. But surprisingly I didn't even hear it from my own family first, half the town must have told me before Mum phoned me last night.'

'Oh shush,' Carrie said. 'I tried to call you yesterday afternoon as soon as I heard, but you never answer that damn phone. I'm not sure what the point is of having a mobile phone when the thing is always on silent.'

'It's on silent because it never stops beeping with Facebook, Twitter and Instagram notifications. The hazards of owning a successful business, I keep getting tagged in people's comments about Pet Protagonist. It's wonderful to hear how much people are loving it but I need to prioritise my time more wisely.'

'Then just remove the apps from your phone,' Shay said.

'But what if I miss something important?' Theo said.

Shay rolled his eyes.

'But the point is, why didn't *you* phone and tell me Fletcher is going to propose?' Theo asked Fern.

'Because it hasn't happened yet,' Fern said, giving Carrie a hug. 'But I think it's definitely going to happen tonight.'

'Really?' Carrie said, her eyes lighting up as she sat back down.

'We had a chat last night and he told me he wants forever with me, we talked about trying for a baby and how he wants lots of children. And he's started saving for a house for us because he wants to have a garden for our children. He also said he has a question he wants to ask me tonight. I can't tell you how happy I am. We're going to be a proper family: me, Fletcher, Bones and our children.'

'Oh my dear, I'm so happy for you,' Carrie said, taking Fern's hand.

'Thank you. It just feels so wonderful that we're on the same page.'

'So we're going to be uncles,' Shay said. 'Wow, that's a lot of responsibility.'

'It might be time that you grew up then,' Theo said.

'Never,' Shay laughed.

'I'm so excited for you,' Carrie said as she walked through town with Fern. Carrie thought she might actually be more excited for this wedding than Fern was right now. Fern had wanted to wait to go dress shopping until Fletcher had actually popped the question but Carrie didn't see the point in delaying. Fletcher was head over heels in love with her and, after what he and Fern had talked about the night before, it was so obvious he was going to do it tonight. After Fern's childhood had been so lacking, Carrie wanted Fern to have the perfect wedding. She was more than happy to push the boat out to give her an amazing day and that was going to start with the perfect dress.

'I'm excited too but, if we're going to go to the dress shop, we're going just to look, not to buy anything,' Fern said, firmly.

'Of course,' Carrie said. 'Have you given much thought about what type of wedding you would like? Would you want a traditional church wedding or something a bit more glamorous like a hotel?'

'I think that kind of thing is something I should discuss with Fletcher.'

'Of course,' Carrie nodded. 'But if you could choose what would you like to do?'

Fern grinned. 'I would like to create the perfect wedding that me and Fletcher would both like.'

Carrie laughed. 'But you must have an idea in your head.'

'Honestly, I hadn't given it much thought until yesterday. When I was a kid, I always dreamed of arriving at my wedding in a horse-drawn carriage, I think I would still love that. Beyond that, I'm not sure what I want from the big day. As long as Fletcher is there, sliding the ring on my finger, I'd be happy with anything.'

'We can definitely do a horse and carriage,' Carrie said.

'*We* don't have to do anything, I'm not expecting you to pay for all this.'

'But I can pay for some of it.'

Just then Carrie spotted Antonio coming out of one of the shops and her heart leapt. She'd been thinking about him a lot since his visit the day before and what he'd said before he'd left.

'Oh look, your moany neighbour is over there,' Fern said.

'Oh yeah,' Carrie said, trying her best to sound disinterested.

Almost as if Antonio knew she was there, he suddenly turned his head to look at her and his smile warmed her insides.

Instead of carrying on with his day, he waited for them to get closer.

'Good morning Carrie,' Antonio said, politely.

'Good morning Antonio. Thought of any more pointless complaints?'

His mouth twitched into a smile. 'I'm working on it.'

'You're infuriating.'

His smile grew. 'I try.'

They stared at each other before Antonio dragged his eyes away to look at Fern. 'Hello Fern, Happy Birthday.'

'Oh thank you,' Fern said, in surprise, looking between the two of them in confusion.

'And I hear congratulations are in order.'

'Well, probably, he hasn't actually popped the question yet, but I think he will tonight. It's supposed to be a surprise, but of course half the town knows.'

Antonio smiled. 'Well you better work on your shocked happy face.'

Fern laughed. 'I will.'

This was too weird, watching Antonio be warm and chatty. Carrie had always thought he was a bit antisocial, kept himself to himself apart from bothering her with his complaints. But he was being nice.

'Well, we must go,' she said.

Antonio returned his attention to her. 'Of course. I'll see you tomorrow.'

'If you insist,' Carrie said.

'Oh I do.'

'Well, I look forward to it then,' Carrie said, dryly.

She walked off with Fern.

'What's happening tomorrow?'

'He's coming round to complain again.'

'He's booked in an appointment for it?'

'I'm not quite sure what's going on actually,' Carrie said, feeling thoroughly confused about the whole thing.

'If I didn't know any better, I'd say Grumpy McMoany-face has a thing for you.'

'That's ridiculous,' Carrie said, but she was starting to think the same thing.

She turned back to look at Antonio to find he was watching them go and it made goosebumps erupt across her skin. Suddenly she was looking forward to tomorrow even more.

Fletcher watched Leo schmoozing with the people who'd come to his art exhibition and couldn't help but feel an enormous sense of pride. Leo had come to him as a sixteen-year-old kid, angry at the world. His parents had a volatile divorce when Leo was fourteen. He had ended up getting into trouble at school and had been suspended several times so he'd been out on the streets causing trouble there too. Giving him the opportunity to turn that anger and passion into something constructive had changed his life. Leo had never been that academic at school, art being the only subject he felt he was good at, but sculpture was not really something he'd ever had the opportunity to do. He was always doodling

185

animal hybrids with highly detailed and accurate drawings and Fletcher had encouraged him to make them into sculptures. He'd showed him some techniques, taught him to weld, and it turned out that Leo had an incredible talent for it and it was something he clearly loved. Leo ended up coming to ReLoved every day, even at weekends. When he'd sold a couple of sculptures to some offices, he'd set up a website selling the rest and his career had suddenly taken off. The sculptures had got bigger, as had the price tags, but that hadn't stopped the sales. He'd even been featured on local BBC news. A few weeks before, Leo had put a deposit down on a lovely seafront flat. He was only eighteen and the future looked very bright indeed.

Leo excused himself from the group he was chatting to and came over to talk to Fletcher.

'What do you think?' Leo gestured to all the sculptures around the room, there was a lot of interest from the people who had come.

'I think I'm in the presence of greatness.'

Leo grinned. 'Mate, all of this is down to you.'

Fletcher shook his head. 'Absolutely not. You can't make milkshake out of vinegar. I could have taught a hundred people the same thing that I taught you and none of them would have produced something as amazing as this. I may have given you the tools, but you created all this with your incredible skill and imagination. I didn't give you that.'

Fletcher took a sip of his orange juice.

'But you did give me the opportunity. No one wanted to give me the time of day because I was such a little shit and I don't blame them. You didn't judge me on my past, you took the time to see past my angst and your patience teaching me was unending. None of this would have happened if it wasn't for you. ReLoved is such a wonderful place for kids like me. I'm gutted for you that it's coming to an end.'

Fletcher choked on his drink. 'What do you mean, it's coming to an end?'

Leo frowned in confusion. 'My mum's a secretary for the town council. She said she wrote to you a few days ago to say the funding for ReLoved was coming to an end.'

Fletcher cursed under his breath. One of the downsides of living on a boat was that no post was delivered. He would collect it from the nearby marina office once or twice a week. He didn't get that much so he didn't think to collect it that often.

'I haven't seen the letter. Shit, I had no idea.'

'Oh mate, I'm sorry. I thought you knew.'

'Christ, the other mentors, they depend on that money.'

Fletcher depended on it too. Although a lot of his income came from the sale of the items he made, his teaching and mentoring salary from the community trust covered almost half of his monthly income. But some of the others, George especially, had managed to get off the streets using the salary he got from the community trust. Fletcher felt sick that he was going to have to explain to them all that they were no longer going to get paid. There was no way he could afford the rent on the barn on his own either, so the mentoring would have to come to an end too and he'd end up back in the little shed where it had all started. He had seen the huge impact ReLoved had had on the community over the last few years. The kids, like Leo, who struggled academically or were getting into trouble had gone on to have jobs in carpentry and metal fabrication. The lonely retirees or widows had found a place to learn new skills and make new friends. Three of his mentors had come from living on the streets. It was an important part of the community.

'There has to be something we can do,' Leo said. 'So many people will miss it if it closes. It has helped so many people.'

'I'm not sure what we can do. I suppose the town council doesn't have a bottomless pit of money.'

'Well, spending it on frivolous things doesn't help. The local park just had some new signs put up saying, "Welcome to Apple Hill Park". Sure the shiny green signs look smart, I suppose, but how does that benefit anyone in the community? There are eight of them too, one on each entrance. They're, like, two foot big. That cost the council nearly ten thousand pounds. Why are they spending that kind of money on stupid signs? If they wanted to spend money on the parks, they could have put out more benches, more flowers and trees, better play equipment for the children, and if they had spare money lying around then they could have put it towards ReLoved.'

Fletcher smiled, despite the circumstances. 'If your art career doesn't work out, maybe you should go work on the town council.'

Leo let out a grunt of disgust. 'Politicians are all corrupt. I certainly wouldn't want to be a part of that world.'

'But you could make a difference, be the change.'

Leo weighed it up. 'I would make a brilliant prime minister.'

Fletcher smirked at the confidence of youth. 'But until that happens, I'm not sure there is anything we can do to help ReLoved.'

'We can't give up, let me talk to my mum, maybe she can get us a meeting with Councillor Bishop. Talk to her about how important ReLoved is. Maybe we can invite her down so she can see it for herself.'

Fletcher nodded despite knowing how fruitless it was to ask for anything from the powers that be. 'We can give it a go. Now, don't worry about any of that for now. This is your night, all these people are here for you, go and enjoy yourself.'

Leo looked around. 'OK, but we'll come up with a plan, Fletcher. I'm not letting this go.'

'I wouldn't expect you to.'

Leo clapped a hand on Fletcher's shoulder and moved away.

Fletcher's heart sank as a string of swearwords ran through his head. He had to save ReLoved but he had no idea how.

CHAPTER FOURTEEN

Carrie all but bundled Fern into the wedding dress shop. Fern wasn't sure that buying a wedding dress before Fletcher proposed was a great idea but perhaps it wouldn't hurt to have a look.

Mrs Allbright came hurrying out from behind the counter, looking delighted. 'I've heard the good news Fern, you and Fletcher are going to make a lovely couple.'

Fern suppressed the urge to say that they already were. Although getting married was a dream come true, it wouldn't change anything between them.

'Thank you.'

'Now what kind of dress are you looking for?' Mrs Allbright said. 'Let's start with the top: strapless, one strap, two straps, spaghetti straps, thick straps, bardot, capped sleeves, three-quarter-length sleeves or big billowing ones?'

'I think something with sleeves maybe,' Carrie said, fingering a beautiful beaded gown with little t-shirt sleeves.

'Oh, we have lots like that.' Mrs Allbright started pulling

dresses out and hanging them on a rail. 'What kind of length are you looking for, do you want a train?'

'Oooh a train would be lovely,' Carrie said.

'Actually Mrs Allbright, do you remember that dress I tried on when Ettie was buying her wedding dress?'

Fern and Orla had come here a few months before to help Ettie find her dream wedding dress and Ettie had tried on so many and they were here for so long that Orla and Fern had started trying on some themselves as a laugh. Mrs Allbright had been more than accommodating. And there had been one dress that Fern had completely fallen in love with.

Mrs Allbright gasped as she clearly remembered. 'The one with the flowers.'

'Yes, that's the one, do you still have it?'

'I do, this one is beautiful, it's made by a wonderful designer called Meadow Brookfield.' Mrs Allbright bustled off to the back of the shop and flicked through a few dresses before pulling it out.

Fern felt goosebumps erupt across her body as Mrs Allbright brought it towards her. When she'd put it on a few months before, Fern had known it was the perfect dress although at that point she hadn't even met Fletcher.

Mrs Allbright took off the plastic wrapping and offered it out. 'Would you like to try it on?'

It was a strapless simple dress in raw silk so it had that beautiful sheen to it but flowers of every colour were hand-embroidered around the bust, trailing down towards the hips. It was stunning. Some of the flowers had tiny beads or sequins sewed into them, making the material twinkle as the dress moved.

'Yes please,' Fern said, reaching out to trace her fingers across one of the flowers.

'Oh Fern, this is beautiful,' Carrie said. 'And such a perfect dress to celebrate your marriage to Fletcher.'

Mrs Allbright gestured for her to go into the extra-large changing room and hung the dress on the hook inside. 'Let us know if you need any help getting into it or being zipped up.'

Fern stepped inside and pulled the dress on, carefully zipping it up from behind. It fitted perfectly and looked so beautiful as it shimmered in the light. She stared at her reflection, imagining Fletcher's expression when he saw it. She watched a huge smile fill her face as she thought about her wedding to the man she loved. She could see it all: the flowers, the bridesmaids, and Fletcher's face when she walked towards him wearing that dress.

This all felt so surreal. She'd never thought this day would come. She had spent so many years of her life in and out of foster care when her birth mum couldn't or didn't want to look after her and then when she had been taken from her mum permanently she had spent the next six or so years being passed from foster carer to foster carer like she was a broken toy that no one wanted. She had grown up believing that no one would ever love her or want her forever. And although Carrie had shown her that she was loved by adopting her, Fern had never really thought that she was lovable. Until Fletcher came into her life. And now he wanted forever with her and he wanted to stand up in front of everyone and declare how much he loved her. There was something so wonderful about getting married, that commitment to each other for the rest of their lives.

She stepped out into the shop area where Carrie and Mrs Allbright were waiting for her. They both gasped when they saw her.

'Oh my darling, you look incredible,' Carrie said, reaching inside her bag for a tissue.

Mrs Allbright fussed around her, fluffing out the dress and inspecting it from every angle before turning Fern to face a giant mirror. It really was the perfect dress. It was like it had been made for her.

'I don't even think it would need any adjustments,' Mrs Allbright said. 'It fits perfectly.'

'It feels like magic,' Fern breathed.

'We'll take it,' Carrie said, her voice choked.

'Wait, we can't,' Fern said.

'The price is very reasonable,' Mrs Allbright said. 'Meadow Brookfield wants her designs to be affordable to everyone.'

Mrs Allbright showed Carrie the price tag.

'Even better,' Carrie said.

'We can't because Fletcher hasn't actually proposed yet,' Fern said.

'Oh, that boy is crazy in love with you,' Carrie said. 'Of course he's going to propose.'

After the conversation with him the night before, Fern felt sure she was right.

'We have had quite a bit of interest in this dress,' Mrs Allbright said, clearly sensing the sale was teetering on a knife edge. 'There was a young lady in here last week trying it on, she said she'd come back this afternoon and try it on again.'

'That does it, we're buying the dress now,' Carrie said.

Fern looked at herself in the mirror again. The truth was she couldn't bear to take this dress off and put it back on the rail for someone else to buy. This was the perfect dress for her perfect wedding. But she shook her head.

'No, we're not. I can't buy a dress when he hasn't even proposed. I know we're on the same page about our future and that he's going to propose and probably tonight but I'm not going to jinx it by buying a dress. I'm sorry, Mrs Allbright, but if he does propose tonight, I'll be straight back here tomorrow to buy it. And if it's gone, then it wasn't meant to be.'

'Well, I'll try and put this other woman off, but I can't make any promises,' Mrs Allbright said, shaking her head regretfully as if the dress had already been sold.

'That's OK,' Fern said, trying not to wince at the thought of someone else walking off with her dress.

She went back into the changing room, carefully took it off and zipped it back into its case. She threw her clothes back on and stepped outside.

Carrie was standing near the till with the biggest grin on her face.

'I bought it for you.'

'Mum!'

'Oh shush. Why are you holding back from getting this dress? You know he's going to propose. You deserve this,' Carrie said. 'You've waited your whole life for this.'

'It doesn't seem right, I feel like we're jumping the gun.'

'We can return it, can't we Mrs Allbright, if he doesn't propose tonight, we can bring it back tomorrow?'

'As long as it's not been worn, absolutely.'

Fern couldn't help the smile from spreading across her face. The perfect dress was hers.

'Thank you but let me pay half.'

'No, let me do this for you.'

'No, no way,' Fern said. 'I have some money in my savings.'

'No, this is on me. What's the point of having money if you can't do something good with it?'

'I think building a whole holiday resort and employing all the people of the town to build and run it is definitely something good.'

'But I haven't done anything for you.'

Fern smiled and shook her head. 'You gave me a loving home and a family, that's more than enough.'

'Fern Lucas. I am your mother. You'll do as you're told, young lady. You're going to let me pay for this wedding, do you hear me?'

Fern smiled and hugged her. 'I love you so much. But you're not paying for the wedding.' Carrie made to protest but Fern reached forward and gently held her lips closed. 'I've never been good at doing what I'm told, you should know that by now.'

Carrie grunted her disapproval. 'Fine, you'll let me get the dress and we'll discuss the rest of the wedding later.'

Fern rolled her eyes.

'Are there any adjustments you'd like on the dress?' Mrs Allbright said.

'No, it's perfect exactly how it is.'

'Very well, do you want to take it now?' Mrs Allbright said.

'Can you deliver it this afternoon?' Carrie said.

'No problem at all.'

Fern took one last look at her perfect dress before they walked out.

'Thank you for that,' she said to Carrie. 'You didn't have to do that.'

'Of course I did, you're my daughter and I couldn't let anyone else get their filthy little hands on it.'

'You know that was just a sales tactic, don't you, there probably isn't anyone else. And even if there was, I'm sure we could have contacted this Meadow Brookfield and asked her to design me a new one.'

'It wouldn't have been the same.'

'Well thank you. I can't wait to see Fletcher's face when he sees it as I walk down the aisle.'

'Right, you're having afternoon tea at Merryport Castle, aren't you?' Carrie asked as they walked outside.

'Yeah but not until later.'

'Well we could go up there and have a cup of tea,' Carrie said, trying to act as if a cup of tea was the only thing on her mind.

Fern looked at her through narrowed eyes. 'What are you playing at?'

'There is a wedding at the castle today, we could go up and have a look.'

'Gatecrash someone's wedding?'

'No, it's not on until this afternoon, but the reception and ceremony rooms will already be set up.'

'No, absolutely not. This is me putting my foot down. We are not looking at venues until I have a ring on my finger. Once he has proposed we can do all of that stuff together, with Fletcher obviously so he can actually have some say about his own wedding, but I'm not booking a venue and the flowers and the photographer until he actually asks me the question.'

'Don't you just want to have a look? It will give you an idea of what the place looks like when it's dressed for a wedding, and whether it's something you want. And if you don't like the castle as a location, at least the decorations and flowers might give you an idea for your own wedding.'

'I don't even know if I want to get married in the castle, I'm not sure Fletcher would either.'

Carrie looked like she was going to try to persuade her some more.

'Come on, you can help me choose a dress for tonight, something that will definitely persuade Fletcher to pop the question.'

'Oooh, I know just the dress,' Carrie said.

Fern smiled. 'Of course you do.'

Merryport Castle towered over the tiny town of Apple Hill. There was certainly nothing medieval or even particularly historical about the place but it was a hotel that looked like a castle and had been part of the town's history for about a hundred years. It was a ridiculously extravagant place designed by one of the richest bachelors of the Victorian period, Pierre Merryport. Sphinxes stood sentry either side of the driveway, which seemed entirely pretentious. The garden, with its elaborate fountains, waterfalls, neatly mani-cured trees and hedges, and flowers from all over the world, was always a bit of a tourist attraction. It even had its own maze. Inside there were Renaissance-style paintings on the ceilings, an impressive marble staircase with bronze balus-ters and enough gold and gilt to rival the crown jewels.

Fern had worked here when she was sixteen, waitressing at the big events or parties, and she had always dreamed that one day she would be the one holding an extravagant party here, the one being served champagne and course meals. She'd never longed for the life of the rich and glamorous, she was happy living in her tiny beach hut or moving in with

Fletcher on his canal boat, she didn't need the big houses, the swimming pools, the private jets, but she couldn't deny that her younger self had imagined that her wedding would be held in a place like this. In reality, a wedding on Blackberry Beach was much more up her street now but she couldn't fail to be impressed by the place.

As soon as she stepped into the reception area she was stunned by the huge floral centrepiece that was obviously part of the wedding as it was the same beautiful blues and purples of the flowers that lined the red carpet outside. Tiny fairy lights were interspersed with the flowers, making it look magical. The famous marble staircase had garlands of blue and purple flowers woven around the banister too.

The reception area was busy with staff clearly getting ready for the upcoming wedding but just off the reception was the banquet room where the wedding guests would be sitting down to a five-course meal. No one was in there and, after a surreptitious look around, Fern walked inside.

It was exactly how she remembered it from her waitressing days where many hours were spent ensuring the room looked absolutely perfect for their guests. Every table was covered in pristine white tablecloths, with large arrangements of purple and blue flowers and fairy lights twisted through them. The tables were laid with all the cutlery you could possibly need to eat four or five courses of the finest foods. Crystal wine glasses sparkled in the light, as did the sequins scattered on all the tables. Over in the corner a huge wedding cake sat on a table. It had seven tiers covered in a pearlescent icing and flowers trailing down the sides. It would have matched her wedding dress exactly. On the top was a bride and groom and a black dog. This would be the perfect wedding cake for her own wedding.

Getting married here would be ridiculous and silly and over-the-top. Fern looked around at the magic of the room trying to stop her imagination from getting carried away with dreams of dancing her first dance here as husband and wife under the canopy of fairy lights, of walking down the aisle in her perfect wedding dress and seeing Fletcher standing at the end waiting for her, of the fine food and wine to celebrate their big day.

'Can I help you?' a woman asked behind her, rather sternly, Fern thought.

'Oh I'm sorry, I'm here for an afternoon tea.'

'That's not in here, that's in the orangery.'

'Oh I know, sorry. It's just that… my boyfriend is going to propose tonight and I was just looking at…' she gestured round at the opulent magnificence.

The woman clearly softened. 'Why don't I get you a wedding brochure so you can look at the different packages we offer? If you and your fiancé feel like Merryport Castle is the right place for you, you can come back and we can give you a proper tour and talk through the different options.'

'Oh yes, that would be lovely,' Fern said, following her back out to the reception.

The woman grabbed a brochure which was all cream and gold, matching the elegance of the place perfectly. 'Give us a call next week if you want to discuss anything, the events manager will be happy to answer any questions.'

'Thank you.'

'The orangery is through there.'

Fern traced her finger over the gold wedding bands on the outside of the brochure and walked off to the orangery.

∾

Orla and Ettie arrived just as Fern had finished reading the wedding brochure from cover to cover. She stood up to greet her friends.

'Happy Birthday, lovely,' Orla said, giving her a hug.

'Thank you and thank you for taking this afternoon off for this.'

'Oh I wouldn't miss it.'

Fern moved to greet Ettie, who looked like she was bursting with excitement. 'Happy Birthday.'

'Are you OK, you look like you're going to explode?' Fern asked as they hugged.

'I'm fine,' Ettie squeaked. 'Well, I have some news but let's do your presents first.'

Fern exchanged glances with Orla as she sat down. 'Do you know this news?'

'No, but she's been bubbling with excitement ever since she picked me up.'

'Come on, Ettie, out with it. I'm not going to be able to concentrate on these yummy cakes when you're vibrating like a washing machine on a spin cycle.'

'I'm pregnant,' Ettie blurted out and then clapped her hand over her mouth. 'And me and Tom agreed we wouldn't tell anyone until I'm at three months, but I had to tell you two.'

'Oh my god Ettie, that's wonderful news,' Fern said, standing back up to give her friend another hug. 'I'm so happy for you.'

'Oh Ettie, this is incredible, you're going to be a mum!' Orla said, joining the group hug.

'I know, I can't believe it. We've been trying since we went on our honeymoon and now I'm pregnant. I'm so excited, I can't even begin to tell you.'

'Well I would suggest we celebrate with champagne but I guess alcohol is off limits for the next few months,' Orla said.

'Yes, there's a long list of things I can't have, but fortunately we can celebrate with some delicious scones with cream and jam,' Ettie said.

'I think you mean jam and cream,' Orla said as they all sat back down.

Ettie grinned. 'I'm from Devon, we do it the right way there.'

'The Irish way is butter then jam then cream, or cream then jam, but always butter first. Fortunately for me and my newly adopted home, I don't like butter, so I do it the Cornish way: jam then cream,' Orla said.

'The way I see it, a scone has two halves, you can do one of each and see which is the best,' Fern said.

'I already know which is best,' Orla said.

'Me too, and it's cream first,' Ettie said.

The waitress came over then. 'Hello, can I get you all a drink while you're waiting for your afternoon tea? We have wine or champagne if you're celebrating something.'

'No thanks, just an orange juice for me please,' Ettie said. 'But you two can order champagne, it is your birthday after all.'

'No, I'm fine, I'll just have a tea please,' Fern said.

'Me too,' Orla said.

The waitress moved away.

'Anyway, enough about me, are you excited about tonight?' Ettie said, waggling her eyebrows. Her eyes suddenly fell on the wedding brochure and she gasped. 'Are you thinking of holding the wedding reception here?'

'No I don't think so, I think I'd prefer something simpler like getting married on a beach and I'm pretty sure Fletcher would too. I was just looking at the reception room that was decorated for a wedding this afternoon. It's so beautiful.'

'Can you imagine getting married here, imagine the photos,' Ettie said dreamily.

'We still don't know for sure that Fletcher is going to propose,' Orla said. 'Let's not get too carried away.'

'It's a bit late for that, Carrie's bought me a dress,' Fern said, almost bursting with her own excitement now.

They both stared at her for a moment then Ettie squealed. Orla just stared at her with her mouth hanging open.

'Wait, did you buy *the* dress?' Ettie said. 'The one you tried on when I was trying on mine?'

Fern nodded. 'It was still there.'

'Oh my god, that dress was made for you. It was perfect, wasn't it Orla?' Ettie nudged her, clearly hoping that Orla would join in with the excitement.

'I just…' Orla started. 'You looked beautiful in that dress but…'

'I know, I know,' Fern said. 'But me and Fletcher had a big chat last night about our future and we talked about getting a house and having children together and I just know that he's on the same page as me. And he said he had a question for me. Of course I went to the dress shop today just to look, but the dress was still there and it looked so beautiful when I tried it on. I wasn't going to buy it today but Mrs Allbright said someone else was interested, which I know was just a ploy to get me to buy it. Anyway, Carrie bought it for me and I'm so excited for Fletcher to see it.'

Orla paused. 'I want to get excited for you, I really do. And if Fletcher does propose I will be over the moon for you. You two are perfect for each other. He is a wonderful man and I can't wait to be your bridesmaid and watch you sail off into the sunset with the man of your dreams, I can't wait to hold your baby or babies and watch them grow up. I want to be there for all of that but we still don't know for sure that he is going to propose and I don't want you to be disappointed if he doesn't.'

'Are you forgetting the part where I saw him buy an engagement ring?' Ettie said.

'You saw him buy something, not necessarily an engagement ring, and we don't know it was for Fern, it could be for his sister or his mum or great-aunt.'

Fern tried to stamp down on her disappointment that Orla wasn't sharing in her excitement but, in her heart, she knew her friend was right. She was letting herself get carried away and Fletcher hadn't even popped the question.

'Look, it's no big deal,' Fern tried to reassure Orla. 'If he doesn't propose then I take the dress back.'

'But won't you be disappointed?' Orla said.

'Of course I will but it won't change anything between us. Just like when I bid to be the artist on a big mural project and I don't get it, it's disappointing but I pull on my big girl pants and move on. I know you're trying to protect me but I'll be OK.'

Just then the waitress returned with their drinks. After she had left Orla raised her mug in a toast. 'Here's to a long and happy future with Fletcher, in whatever form that takes.'

'Hear, hear!' Ettie said, raising her mug.

'Cheers to that,' Fern said.

Fletcher drove past Merryport Castle on his way to meet Fern at the Tulip Garden. Now the news had sunk in a bit, he was determined he had to do something to save ReLoved. He really felt like he was doing something good with his life helping the people who came to the barn. When he'd been eighteen, he'd been a stupid, self-absorbed arsehole. And yes he'd been a kid but people had got hurt. Working at ReLoved felt like he was giving something back, being part of the community instead of always looking out for number one like he had when he was younger. Losing ReLoved would make such a difference to so many people. He would schedule a meeting with Councillor Bishop and see if anything could be done. Or maybe he could get together a petition, although he doubted whether the people of Apple Hill Bay would totally understand or appreciate the impact it had on the people who went there. Would offering to give up his salary make a difference? His salary from ReLoved might just cover the rent and bills, although it certainly wouldn't cover the salaries of the other mentors.

He really needed to have this discussion with Fern. They had a future planned, a house with a big garden, children. Giving up half his monthly income would impact on that. He didn't want her to have to carry them financially or feel he was letting her down, or that ReLoved was more of a priority than her and their family as that simply wasn't the case. But then if ReLoved closed, he would lose that salary anyway, although he would have more time to make his own furniture so could probably make up some of the shortfall.

He sighed. He would talk to her tomorrow and most likely she would have some amazing plan to fix it. Tonight was for celebrating.

CHAPTER FIFTEEN

The Tulip Garden was Fern's favourite restaurant and she loved that Fletcher had chosen it for her birthday celebration and for their big proposal. It was just over the headland from The Little Beach Hut Hotel and had an incredible view over the sea and the pretty harbour below them. It was such a beautiful place, it was a large room, with vines climbing the walls inside entwined with tiny fairy lights. But tonight Fern couldn't concentrate on any of that. Her heart was hammering against her chest as she walked into the restaurant hand in hand with Fletcher. He'd been waiting for her outside, carrying a giftbag with some presents neatly wrapped inside and she was so excited that one of them was going to be an engagement ring she was practically trembling.

Fletcher gave his name to the hostess who took them to a reserved table in the corner right by the sea view window. The setting sun looked dramatic as it sank into the waves, casting cranberry and blueberry ribbons across the water. It was beautiful.

They both slid into the booth and it was then that Fern noticed Carrie, Shay and Theo all sitting at a table on the opposite side of the room trying not to look at them or at least trying not to make it obvious they were looking.

She suppressed a smile that of course Carrie would want to be here for the proposal, she couldn't help herself. And although Fletcher probably wanted a little privacy, it was sweet that her family wanted to be here for her special moment.

She glanced around and was surprised to see Ettie and Orla at another table, peeping over their menus at them. Anna and Mira were at another table and as Fern looked around she realised that the restaurant was filled with loads of people from the town who were all taking surreptitious looks over at their table.

'It's busy in here tonight,' Fletcher said, looking down at his menu.

Poor Fletcher, he had no idea that all these people were in on his big surprise and had come to witness the big proposal themselves.

Fletcher placed the giftbag on the table and her heart leapt. 'Have you had a good birthday?' he asked.

'It's been… fun,' Fern said, carefully, not wanting to reveal what it had included.

'Would you like your presents now?'

'Yes please,' she said, trying hard not to seem too desperate.

The waitress appeared at their table. 'Would you like some drinks while you decide what you want to eat?'

'Could we just have a few minutes,' Fletcher said.

'Of course,' the waitress said before moving away.

Fletcher nudged the bag across the table. This was it, the moment it felt like she had waited all her life for.

She opened the bag and peered inside. There were three presents inside and Fern carefully took them out and laid them on the table in front of her. There was a book-shaped package, a mug-shaped package and then the little square box.

'Which one should I open first?'

Fletcher smiled. 'Whichever one you want.'

She felt like she should give the other presents some love first because once she opened the present with the engagement ring inside the others would be all but forgotten about.

She opened the book-shaped package and let out a little gasp of delight when she saw it was the latest book from her favourite author and her smile grew when she realised it was a signed copy.

'This is wonderful, thank you so much.'

She opened the mug-shaped present and smiled to see a mug with a photo he had taken of her and Bones snuggled up together on the sofa.

'This is lovely, thank you. What a brilliant photo.'

'I have that as my screensaver on my phone, it's one of my favourite photos of the two of you.'

'That's really sweet. I didn't know you have that as your screensaver.'

'Well, you two are my family and now our family is going to get a little bit bigger.'

Her heart swelled with love for him. 'Thank you, that's really thoughtful. Maybe next year you'll be able to get me a mug with me, you, Bones and our baby on.'

He nodded and when he spoke his voice was rough. 'I would love to be able to do that.'

She reached across the table and took his hand. 'I love you so much.'

'I love you too and I can't wait to start that chapter of our life together.'

'Me too,' Fern said.

His eyes fell on the little box and she knew this was it.

She turned her attention to the box, her heart thundering against her chest. Her fingers shook as she unwrapped the paper and, sure enough, the little black box inside had a ribbon around the outside with *The Velvet Box* written on it.

She carefully opened the box and stared at a beautiful necklace. He'd incorporated a stunning blue moonstone with the tiny wooden flowers she loved so much from the old bookcase he'd been working on at ReLoved. It was a lovely necklace but she was confused about what she was seeing. There was no engagement ring. She almost wanted to tip out the little box to make sure the engagement ring wasn't underneath but suddenly the realisation hit her. He wasn't going to propose. She swallowed a lump of emotion that clogged in her throat, tears pricking her eyes. Oh god, she had got it all wrong. They all had. The restaurant was packed with people who were here to see her get proposed to and that wasn't going to happen.

'Are you OK, do you like it?' Fletcher said.

She nodded. 'Yes, it's beautiful.'

She didn't know what to say and do. She was so bitterly disappointed she didn't think she could sit here and smile her way through a three-course meal with Fletcher. She needed to get her head round this. Was it possible that he had planned a proposal for another time or was there no proposal coming at all? When they'd spoke about their future the night before, the house with the big garden, having children together, she'd assumed all that came with marriage because when she envisaged that kind of fairytale ending for them, she'd always imagined that marriage was a part of that. But what if it wasn't for Fletcher?

'Congratulations!' Carrie cheered, suddenly appearing at their table.

'Carrie, hello, how lovely to see you,' Fletcher said, with some confusion.

Fern looked on in horror as Carrie popped open a champagne bottle and poured it into two flutes and the room erupted into applause and cheers. Her brothers, Ettie, Orla and several other people from the town started coming over to offer their congratulations as well. They must have seen her nod to say she liked the necklace and assumed she'd said yes to his proposal.

She couldn't find the words to explain and suddenly she didn't want to.

Fletcher looked thoroughly confused. He glanced over at her to see if she knew why the whole restaurant wanted to congratulate them and she felt the tears spill over onto her cheeks. She saw the realisation pass over his face. She quickly snapped shut the jewellery box and stood up.

'I have to go,' Fern muttered, shoving the box in her handbag and running out.

'Fern, wait,' Fletcher called.

She ran as fast as she could over the headland and back to her little beach hut and threw herself through the door. Bones came bounding out to greet her and she knelt down and cried into his soft black fur. Why had she let herself get carried away with this stupid fantasy?

'Fern.'

Fletcher was standing behind her in the open doorway. Bones extracted himself from her embrace and bounced over to Fletcher, excitedly wagging his tail. Fletcher absently stroked his head.

Fern stood up, wiping the tears away but they were just replaced with more. Fletcher immediately moved towards her, wrapping her in a big hug.

'You were expecting me to propose tonight?'

Fern closed her eyes as she leaned against him. She nodded, unable to speak. Her chest hurt from the disappointment.

'I'm sorry. I love you so much, I hate that I've hurt you but why would you think I was going to propose?'

'Ettie saw you in The Velvet Box and she was adamant that you were buying an engagement ring. And then you said you had a question for me tonight.'

He shook his head. 'I wasn't expecting to have that chat about our future last night, I wanted to talk about all that with you tonight, I was going to ask you to move in with me. I'm sorry to disappoint you.'

'No, it's fine, it's so soon for us. Everyone was getting all excited for me and I got carried away with the dream.'

She felt him tense under her arms and he pulled back from her. 'Your dream is to get married?'

'I've always dreamed of getting married one day. When I was a kid I had it all planned out, the dress, the cake, the horse and carriage. I know it's only been four weeks for us but after we spoke about getting a house and having children I thought you wanted that too.'

'I want that future with you, but Fern, I can't marry you.'

She felt the impact of those words like a punch in the stomach. Her hopes and dreams of getting married to Fletcher withered and died.

'Not ever?'

'No.'

'But the other night we talked about getting married on Blackberry Beach.'

'That was... that wasn't what you think. I love you but we can never get married.'

She stared at him, all her words stuck in her throat. She was never going to get married. Not ever. How was she going to get past that? Could they have a future together if marriage wasn't a part of it? She loved him so much but marriage had always been such a big part of her fairytale dream.

'Is that... a wedding dress?' Fletcher pointed to the dress that was hanging over the banister.

It was in a protective bag and they could only really see the back from where they were standing but there was no escaping what it was. When Carrie had brought it over after Fern had got back from her afternoon tea she'd considered hiding it away so as not to spoil the surprise for Fletcher but there had been a huge part of her that wanted to show him, maybe just a tantalising peep. At the time, when she had been so confident about the proposal, she'd thought Fletcher might find it funny that she'd already bought a dress. Now, though, he was looking at it in horror.

She nodded, biting her lip to stem the tears. 'I ended up trying on dresses with Ettie a few months ago when she got married, just for a laugh, and there was this one dress that was so beautiful, so perfect for me. Carrie insisted I went dress shopping with her today as she was almost as excited as I was about the proposal and the dress was still there. When I tried it on, all I could see was your face when you saw me wearing it as I walked down the aisle.'

She swallowed down the pain because that was never going to happen now.

He took a step towards her. 'Fern...'

'It doesn't matter, it was just a silly dream and I allowed myself to get swept away with the tide of excitement.'

She was dismissing the dream she'd had all her life, pretending it didn't mean anything to her, and that didn't feel good.

He shook his head as he moved away from her. 'Except it clearly did matter or you wouldn't have pinned all your hopes on me proposing tonight and got so upset when I didn't. And you certainly wouldn't have bought a dress if it didn't mean that much to you.'

'I just got caught up with all the excitement. All my dreams were coming true and—'

'I've taken that away from you.'

She didn't know what to say. She had to get her head around that, if she stayed with Fletcher, she would never ever get married. That dream would never come true.

He stared at her and then walked across the room again, pushing his hands through his hair.

He turned back to face her and he looked absolutely broken. 'You deserve to be with someone who will help you realise your dreams, not ruin them.'

Her heart leapt in fear because living her life without getting married wasn't great but living it without Fletcher was unthinkable. 'No wait, it was just a silly dream. People dream about winning the lottery too, doesn't mean their life is ruined when they don't win.'

He shook his head. 'Fern, I can't be the man you want me to be.'

Panic started rising in her. 'I don't want you to be any man apart from the man I love with all my heart.'

'You want me to be your husband and I can't give you that. I love you and I only want you to be happy.'

'You make me happy.'

'Not happy enough though. Meeting you was the best thing that ever happened to me but I can't stay with you knowing that I'm never going to make your dreams come true.'

Fresh tears filled her eyes. 'You're... you're breaking up with me?'

'Because I love you and can't bear to hurt you,' Fletcher said as if it was the most obvious answer in the world when it was actually the most ridiculous. They were supposed to be together forever.

Anger filled her. 'You're being absurd. Last night we talked about how we wanted forever, children, a house with a big garden. None of that has changed. We love each other, why would you throw that away?'

'But you thought all of that would come with marriage, that was your dream. You should never compromise on your dreams, Fern.'

She stared at him. How was this happening? Last night she had been so happy and now it was all over.

He moved towards her, took her face in his hands and kissed her. She clung onto him, tears coursing down her cheeks as she kissed him.

'I love you, Fern, I always will,' Fletcher said. Then he turned and walked away, closing the door softly behind him.

Bones bounded up to the door, wagging his tail in confusion that Fletcher had gone without him.

Fern sank onto the sofa, sobbing into her hands, and Bones immediately moved to her side, trying to lick her face through her fingers. Ordinarily, this would cheer her up, but nothing would ever ease this pain in her heart.

CHAPTER SIXTEEN

There was a knocking on her door the next morning. Fern hadn't even made it to her bed the night before, spending the night crying on the sofa. She'd barely slept a wink all night but must have fallen asleep an hour or so after the sun had started to rise.

Bones, who would normally bark and go rushing for the door, was obviously empathising with how she felt, because he couldn't be bothered to get up either.

She opened the door and saw Carrie, Shay and Theo standing there.

Theo immediately folded her into his arms, holding her tight. 'Are you OK?'

She shook her head, fresh tears filling her eyes.

'Oh honey, I'm so sorry you didn't get the proposal you wanted,' Carrie said.

'And I'm so sorry we cheered at your non-proposal,' Shay said. 'We saw you nod after opening the box and we just assumed you were nodding to say yes.'

'It's OK,' Fern said, her throat raw.

She pulled away from Theo and moved back into her house so they could come in. The little beach hut was so tiny that there wasn't really room for two big men, Carrie and Bones but they all squashed onto the sofa.

'I don't even care about the proposal, not really. Fletcher broke up with me.'

There was a collective gasp. It was clear no one had been expecting that. Even Fern had never seen that coming.

'Over a silly misunderstanding?' Carrie said, her voice choked.

Fern sat down on the armchair.

'He told me last night that he can't ever marry me. He said I should be with someone who makes my dreams come true, not ruins them. He said he can't be the man I want him to be. He thinks he's doing the right thing so I can find the perfect man who *will* marry me.'

Fern could hear how empty her voice sounded. She reached down and stroked the fur on the back of Bones's neck, but he barely stirred.

'I can't believe he broke up with you,' Theo said. 'The man is crazy in love with you.'

'That's why he did it, apparently,' Fern said.

'He'd rather not be with you than just suck it up and marry you?' Theo said.

'Jesus Theo, I don't want him to suck it up, or marry me just to make me happy, he has to want it too and for whatever reason he doesn't. I'm OK with not getting married, I really am, but he can't see that, he thinks he's ruining my life. He saw the wedding dress and thinks that it's really important to me.'

'But it is important to you. Are you really OK about not getting married?' Carrie said.

'Honestly, I'm crushed that I'm never going to get that, but when I pictured my perfect dream life it was me and Fletcher together forever with Bones and our children. Marriage is just the cherry on the top of that. I need him more than I need a ring.'

They were all silent for a moment.

'There's something more to this that we're not seeing,' Shay said.

'What do you mean?' Fern said.

'He said, I *can't* ever get married. *Can't*. That's an odd choice of word, isn't it? I know some people don't believe in marriage or see it as important and some people are really anti-marriage but "can't" suggests an actual reason bigger than just not wanting to.'

Fern thought back to the night before. Fletcher had said *I can't marry you*, and *we can never get married*. It was an odd way to say it. She hadn't noticed it before because she was in the middle of having her heart broken but it felt like there was something physically stopping him from doing that. Maybe Shay was right. Was there something else going on?

'Did he say why he didn't want to get married?' Carrie asked.

Fern shook her head. 'We didn't discuss it last night. I know his parents never got married until Fletcher was around eight. They were very much in love, as far as his eight-year-old memory recalls, and after the wedding they hated each other and were always screaming and shouting at each other so I guess that could be the reason why he is a bit anti-marriage. But that seems a bit far-fetched to blame marriage on their inevitable break-up. They were probably having problems way before they tied the knot. And their issues are theirs, I can't see how that would impact on Fletcher to such an extent.'

'Maybe this is something you two should talk about,' Carrie said. 'If there is a reason why he doesn't want to get married, a real reason that's holding him back, maybe you can help him with it.'

Fern shook her head. 'We didn't split up because he didn't want to get married, we split up because he thinks that means more to me than he does.'

'Well, you have two choices,' Carrie said. 'You either convince him that he is more important than marriage or you help him see that marriage is not this big scary thing he clearly thinks it is so he can be the man that makes your dreams come true. He broke up with you because he feels he can't offer you that. If you can help him see that marriage is not something to be afraid of maybe you can get past all this.'

Fern wasn't convinced that trying to persuade Fletcher to get married was the answer, she never wanted him to do something he would later regret just to keep her happy. But in a way Carrie was right, she had to do something, because not being with Fletcher was simply not an option.

Fern was sitting on the floor of the decking, her bare feet on the wet grass, having forced down a few mouthfuls of toast. She was just about to go back inside and get ready for work when Orla and Ettie arrived. She could see they were worried about her. She couldn't decide whether to be angry at Ettie or not. On the one hand, none of this would have happened if Ettie hadn't convinced her Fletcher was defi-nitely going to propose. However, Fern had let her excitement get completely out of hand and Fletcher had then overreacted so she wasn't sure any one person was to blame for this.

'Hey,' Fern said, softly.

'I'm so so sorry,' Ettie said, tears filling her eyes.

Fern patted the space next to her and Ettie and Orla sat either side of her, taking her hand.

'I don't understand,' Ettie said. 'I know I saw him looking at engagement rings.'

'You must have been mistaken,' Fern said. 'He never wants to get married. Ever. In fact, he feels so strongly about it, we broke up.'

Ettie let out a little gasp. 'Oh no, I'm so sorry. This is all my fault. You two were supposed to be together forever and I ruined that.'

'You didn't. I'm not mad at you.' Fern squeezed her friend's hand. 'OK, I wouldn't have got excited about the proposal if you hadn't told me you'd seen him buy an engagement ring. But we'd started talking about having children the night before last. I think if we'd got to the point of trying for a baby I probably would have brought up marriage myself because in my mind the two would go together. Of course we don't need to get married to have children, but I probably would have asked about it so we would have been sat here anyway.'

'He broke up with you because you wanted to get married?' Orla said, incredulously.

Fern shook her head. 'He thinks the dream is to get married, he doesn't want to stand in the way of my dreams.'

'But you've always talked about getting married, would you really be OK never getting that?' Ettie said.

Fern sighed. How was she ever going to convince

Fletcher that marriage wasn't important to her when her friends and family were so convinced it was? Even the week before, if someone had asked her, she would have said that it was but suddenly it wasn't so important any more.

'I've always dreamed of the big love story and I know marriage was part of that too but it wasn't the most important part, not even close. Fletcher is my love story, he is my beginning, middle and end. And a relationship is about compromise, give and take. I give up the dream of not getting married and I get to spend the rest of my life with the man I love with everything I have. I could never ever be disappointed with that.'

'I can't believe he broke up with you. He loves you. You're Fletcher and Fern, Fern and Fletcher, you're two halves of a whole,' Orla said.

'He wants me to be happy, he doesn't realise he's the thing that makes me happy.'

They were silent for a while.

'What are you going to do?' Ettie said.

Fern stared at the sea twinkling beneath her. 'I don't know, I'm so angry at him right now. I thought what we had was forever and now it feels like our relationship is fragile and easily broken and that scares me. I know he wants to do the right thing for me but he should never have walked away from us.'

'This is a blip for the two of you,' Orla said. 'You never fight, you've never even fallen out before. This is just your first one. You mark my words, a few weeks from now, you'll be looking back at this time and laughing about it.'

Fern looked at her. 'Do you really think so?'

'I do. Because I don't think Fletcher can walk away from you that easily.'

Fletcher threw down his piece of sandpaper in frustration. He had been sanding so hard and for so long that the sandpaper now had holes in it. The necklace he was making was looking good though, although perhaps a bit distressed now with all the sanding.

He felt broken, that was the only way to describe it, as if a part of him had been wrenched out of him and now he was bleeding and raw. He had never felt sadness like it. He felt sad for himself that his future with Fern was over but he felt heartbroken for Fern that her dreams of getting married were in ruins. To see her sobbing on the floor when he'd caught up with her at her house after she'd left the restaurant had been gutting. He'd destroyed her and the guilt clawed away at him. And then when he'd ended things between them, he'd broken her heart all over again. He'd been awake all night, wondering if he'd done the right thing, but it would be completely selfish of him to go back to her now. She wanted marriage and he couldn't give her that.

To top off his entirely crappy day, he'd had to tell the mentors that ReLoved was coming to an end and that had not been an easy conversation to have.

He looked up at movement in the doorway and was surprised to see Ettie standing there. Although he didn't know Ettie that well, the times he had met up with her and Tom she'd always been this bubbly happy, woman with a permanent smile on her face. Today she looked pissed off.

'Can I have a word,' she snapped.

He moved to the door and gestured for her to take a seat at the picnic bench outside. They sat down opposite each other.

'What the hell is going on?' Ettie said.

This was so out of character for her, he almost wanted to laugh, but she was clearly here about Fern and there was nothing to laugh at in that regard.

'I appreciate that you are concerned for Fern but this is between me and her so—'

'Don't give me that. You and I both know that you were looking at engagement rings the day before her birthday.'

His heart sank. 'You're mistaken, I was there simply to buy the moonstone so I could incorporate it into the necklace I made for her.'

'That's insulting, Fletcher, and I thought better of you than that. Do you think my eyes are painted on? Do you think I'm just some dumb blonde who can't see past the end of my nose? I was standing outside the window when you asked the assistant to get several engagement rings out of the cabinet. I saw you holding one in your hand. The assistant even modelled one for you on her finger. So don't lie to me.'

Fletcher swore under his breath. He was really hoping that all Ettie saw was him going in and coming out of the jewellery shop.

'So either you had this big surprise proposal planned for some time after her birthday and I ruined that or you were buying the engagement ring for someone else.'

'There was no big proposal planned, I never got that far, and there is no one else. How could there be, Fern is my entire world.'

'And yet you've destroyed her by breaking up with her.'

'I did that for her, she deserves someone who wouldn't think twice about marrying her and making her dreams come true. I can't do that for her, I thought I could but I can't.'

'So you were looking at engagement rings for her and then you changed your mind?'

'It was stupid. I was kidding myself when I thought I could propose to her. I could never get married. The thought of it terrifies me.'

'Jesus Fletcher, if you ever get back together with Fern, never ever tell her that the thought of marrying her terrifies you.'

'It's not marrying Fern that makes me feel like that. I want forever with her, it's marriage that scares me. Apparently it's a thing, gamophobia, a fear of marriage brought about by a traumatic experience.' Labelling it didn't do anything to make him feel better about it. He felt like a coward.

'Have you had a traumatic experience?'

An image of Lauren flashed through his mind and he rubbed his eyes, trying to dispel it. 'Yeah, you could say that.'

Her face softened a little. 'Do you want to talk about it?'

He shook his head. As much as he liked Ettie he couldn't unload his emotional baggage on her.

'Does Fern know?'

'No, I never told her. I probably should have so she would never have had that expectation of me. It's too late now though.'

'It's not too late to talk to her, explain why marriage can never be on the cards for you.'

'But it boils down to the same thing, I can't give her what she wants.'

'She wants you, you idiot. She wants a lifetime with you. And she would forego all other dreams to have that.'

'She shouldn't have to abandon her dreams for me.'

Ettie thought about this for a moment. 'Tom hates cats. Always has. And I love them. I always wanted a cat when I was living with Fern but the landlord had a no pets rule. When I moved in with Tom I was desperate to get a kitten. So Tom got me one. You could say Tom gave up his dream of never having a cat. You should see the two of them together, he carries this little thing around on his shoulder, it cuddles up on his lap, he picks it up and takes it to bed with us. He adores it. And that's what you do when you're in love, your dreams change and adapt and then you make new dreams together.'

Ettie made it sound so simple, when the truth was far more complex.

She stood up to leave.

'Ettie, are you going to tell Fern you were right about the engagement rings?'

'No, I think I've done enough damage by telling her in the first place. None of this would have happened if I hadn't opened my big mouth. I was just so damned excited for you both that I couldn't keep it in. You two were meant to be together so you need to find a way to make that happen. Whatever it takes.'

He sighed as she walked away. He had no idea how he could do that.

Carrie was sitting at the kitchen table, staring at the sandwich she had made for herself and not eaten, when there was a knock on the door.

She looked up to see Antonio standing there. She didn't know whether to be happy or annoyed by his arrival now. She waved him in.

He opened the door and stepped inside. 'Why is there not

a vegetarian option for the food trucks that are coming to the launch? There's burgers, sausages, kebabs, hog roast, bacon sandwiches—'

'Can we not do this today,' Carrie said, holding up a hand to stem the tide.

His face creased in concern. 'What's happened, are you OK?'

'I just feel... a bit sad.'

That felt like an understatement.

'Well, I'll put the kettle on and you can tell me all about it,' Antonio said, busying himself with making two cups of tea.

Carrie sighed. 'You'll think I'm such an idiot.'

'I could never think that about you,' Antonio said, seriously, and that made her smile.

'Well we all thought Fletcher was going to propose last night at Fern's birthday meal. Her friend Ettie said she saw him buying an engagement ring and then Fern had a conversation with him the night before about their future and he'd talked about having children and getting a house and he intimated that he was going to propose, well at least Fern thought he did. I was so excited for her and, after her childhood was so crap, I wanted her wedding to be special for her and pull out all the stops for her, so... I pushed her into going wedding dress shopping. We found the perfect one and I bought it for her.'

Antonio put two mugs down on the table and sat down next to her. 'I take it he didn't propose.'

Carrie shook her head, pushing a plate of biscuits she'd made that morning towards him. 'It gets worse. He broke up with her because he didn't feel he could make her dreams come true. He thinks marriage is more important to her than he is and he wants her to find someone who can tick that box for her. I just feel like I made the whole situation so much worse. I was getting more excited about it than she was and she got caught up in my frenzy. If I hadn't insisted that I buy her a dress then she could have passed it off as a silly misunderstanding. But she can hardly say that marriage isn't important to her when she has a wedding dress hanging in her lounge. I just worry I've ruined everything for her.'

'I wouldn't take the weight of this on your shoulders. When something this big divides two people in a relationship, it rears its head eventually. My ex-wife wanted to live in London, I wanted to live here. We spent a few years living in London, then we moved here and she hated it. She wanted to move back, I didn't. In the end that was the thing that broke us. Don't get me wrong, things were not great between us, hadn't been for a long time, but that was the straw that broke the camel's back. If marriage really is that important to Fern, she would always be disappointed not to have that. Maybe Fletcher is right and she needs to find someone who will give her that.'

Carrie shook her head. 'They are perfect for each other.'

'I don't know them so I don't want to speak out of turn but isn't being in a relationship about wanting the same things? I don't mean, what shall we have for dinner or where shall we go on holiday or what colour shall we paint the spare room, but the big stuff: children, where you want to live, marriage. I think that kind of thing is important to agree on.'

'It depends on how important those things are to you. Fern would love to get married, but being with Fletcher is more important to her. I think if your ex-wife was the single most important person in the world to you and you were the same for her, it wouldn't matter where you lived as long as you were together. And I'm not judging; as you said, there were other factors between the two of you and I'm certainly not an expert when it comes to marriage. For Fern, her priority is a future with Fletcher. For Fletcher, his priority is Fern's happiness, even if that means she'll be happier without him. She has to convince him that he is the thing that makes her happy more than anything else and I just don't know how she's going to do that.'

Antonio took a long sip of his tea as he thought. 'Do you think you should talk to him, tell him how much you were involved yesterday? The little I know of you, you're a force to be reckoned with and Fletcher would know that too. It'll take the flak off Fern a little if he knew how much of that came from you.'

'If I knew it would help I would do it in a heartbeat but I don't know if me interfering would make things worse.'

Antonio helped himself to a biscuit, he took a bite and nodded his approval. 'These are good.'

'Thank you.'

'I could talk to him.'

'What?'

'He owns ReLoved, doesn't he?'

Carrie nodded.

'So do people just turn up and ask to work on something?'

'Yes, I think so initially, just to see if it's something they would like to do. Some people just turn up once a week and put a few hours in, others turn up every day.'

'I know my way around a bit of woodwork and carpentry to make something rudimentary, I could go along and get some tuition from Fletcher, bond over a block of wood and a wood plane and we can chat. I can tell him how much you pushed Fern into this, put all the blame on you, in the nicest possible way.'

'I take full responsibility for it, so I'm happy for you to make me look like the bad guy in that regard.'

'I don't know if it will work or if anything I say will hold any sway but it's worth a go, right?'

'If you do this and it works, I'll make every food truck vegetarian at the launch.'

Antonio helped himself to another biscuit and stood up. 'That's a shame, I was really looking forward to the hog roast.'

She frowned in confusion. 'Wait, you're not a vegetarian?'

'Oh hell no, I love meat.'

'Why are you complaining about the food trucks then?'

'It was better than complaining about the length of the grass.'

With that he walked out, giving her a wave.

She smiled. The man was completely infuriating.

CHAPTER SEVENTEEN

Fern finished painting a patch of wildflowers and stepped back to look at them. Flowers were nice and easy to do and didn't require a lot of thought or skill, especially these, which were kind of childlike flowers among the long grass. This felt like something safe to work on today when her heart was physically hurting and her eyes kept filling with tears.

She grabbed her cool bag and pulled out two packets of sandwiches she had made out of habit this morning before remembering.

'Here,' she said to Shay, tossing him one.

He caught the packet. 'Ordinarily, I would be over the moon to be honoured with one of your sandwiches. But maybe you should go and give this to Fletcher so you can talk to him.'

Shay tossed it back but she immediately threw it back to him. 'I'm too pissed off to talk to him. We had a future planned, children, a house with a big garden, and he threw all that away.'

'By the sounds of it, he did that for you so you could have the future he thinks you want.'

'I don't want a selfless boyfriend, I want someone selfish who would hold onto me no matter what.'

Shay laughed. 'You definitely picked the wrong man if you want someone selfish. There isn't a selfish bone in Fletcher's body. He's probably feeling as lousy as you are right now that he can't be the man you want.'

'He is the man I want.'

'Maybe you should go and tell him that.'

'I tried that last night.'

'To be fair to him, I'm not sure I would believe that getting married wasn't a priority when you'd bought a wedding dress.'

Fern sighed in frustration because Shay was right. She might as well have turned up wearing the wedding dress with Ettie and Orla wearing bridesmaid dresses. What had she been thinking?

'I'm going to share my lunch with Bones, at least he doesn't judge me.'

She walked outside and sat down on the grass next to Bones, who didn't even stir. He looked as thoroughly depressed as she felt. She pulled out a few chicken slivers and offered one out to him. He lifted his head with great effort, sniffed the chicken and then put his head down. He never turned down chicken or any food for that matter. Could he really be missing Fletcher this much already? Or was he just empathising with how she felt? She was so angry at Fletcher but she had to admit she was angrier with herself. Why had she let herself get so caught up with a silly unimportant childhood dream when her adult dreams had been on the verge of coming true? Sure, a wedding would be lovely but forever with the only man she'd ever loved was far more important. Shay was right: after what she'd done, how could she convince Fletcher that getting married meant nothing to her? But she had to do something, it hurt so much and now it seemed Bones was hurting too.

~

Fletcher made his way along the towpath back to his boat and saw his friend, Max, waiting for him, holding a box of beers under one arm.

Fletcher sighed. He was not in the mood for socialising tonight.

'Hey,' Fletcher said.

'I heard what happened at the Tulip Garden last night, and that you two broke up. I came by to see if you were OK.'

'To be blunt, no I'm not.' Fletcher climbed aboard and Max didn't wait for an invite before he followed him.

Max offered him a can of beer but he shook his head. He wanted to keep a clear mind, not drown himself in a fog of grief.

'What the hell happened?'

Fletcher shook his head as he tried to unravel the absolute shitshow that had been the last few days.

'We were watching this film a few nights ago and the couple in it were getting married on the beach. Fern said how much she would love to get married on a beach, on Blackberry Beach more specifically, and I just knew I wanted that too. I know we've only been together a month but I suddenly knew I wanted forever with her and I wanted to get married to her where we'd met. I was in the jewellery shop the day before her birthday, I had planned on getting her a blue moonstone for a necklace I was making for her. But I spotted the engagement rings and the next thing I was asking to see a few of them. And that's when it hit me.'

'Lauren,' Max said, grimly.

Fletcher nodded. 'All I could see was Lauren attached to all those machines, those wires, those tubes keeping her alive, her chest rising and falling because the machines were breathing for her. Every time I feel like I can move on with my life, my brain reminds me of the most horrific thing I've ever seen. And I did that to her.'

'You can't blame yourself.'

'Of course I can.'

'How can you possibly think it was your fault?'

'How can you possibly deny that it wasn't?'

Max let out an exasperated groan and walked away from him to the other side of the deck. 'You were eighteen.'

'It doesn't make me any less responsible for her.'

Max shook his head. 'So what happened in the jewellers?'

'I told the assistant to put them back and I just bought the moonstone as planned. Unfortunately, Ettie saw me looking at rings and told Fern I was going to propose. Of course that didn't happen.'

He explained about the wedding dress and how obviously important marriage was to her and that he'd broken up with her because he could never give her that.

'Does she know about Lauren?'

Fletcher shook his head. 'I was an absolute arsehole back then, I didn't want Fern to know about that.'

'You were not an arsehole, you were a normal eighteen-year-old kid. And you behaved far more admirably than most kids your age. In fact, if it had been me I think I would have behaved far worse. Besides, you're a completely different person now. You have to let go of this guilt, it's destroying your life.'

Fletcher sighed, pushing his hand through his hair. He had no idea how to do that.

'Fern and I had a chat the other night about our future, we talked about buying a house together and having a family. And I wanted that so much. I thought, as long as marriage isn't involved, I could do that.'

'But what difference does it make? Buying a house, having children together is still a huge commitment and a big responsibility. The only difference is that marriage comes with a piece of paper and a ring.'

'I know. I do know how ridiculous this sounds. How pathetic I'm being.'

Max came back to him, clapping a hand on his shoulder. 'I never said you were being pathetic. I know Lauren has been such a big stumbling block for you for years. I just wish I knew how I could help you get over it.'

'I do too.'

Max opened one of the cans of beer and took a long swig and, somewhere in the depths of despair, Fletcher found some humour in that. Fletcher's problem was enough to drive Max to drink.

'Would Fern be happy if you never got married?' Max said.

'She says she would, she says getting married was just a silly dream, but I don't want her to give up on her dreams.'

Max took another long swig and Fletcher smirked.

'You need to tell Fern.'

Fletcher felt the smile fall away.

'Whatever happens between the two of you, whether you can figure out a way past this obstacle to be together again or whether this is it for the two of you, she deserves to know the truth.'

Fletcher suddenly felt like opening a can of beer too.

Fletcher poked at his pasta, unable to eat more than a few mouthfuls. It was Fern's favourite recipe and all he could think about was how she wasn't here to share it with him, how she would never be here to share it with him again.

So he was a little surprised when he looked up from his meal to see her marching along the towpath towards him. She looked pissed off and he didn't blame her.

He quickly hurried to the side of the boat and helped her aboard.

'Hey,' Fletcher said, softly.

'Hello,' Fern snapped, putting her hands on her hips.

Yep, definitely pissed off.

'Are you OK?'

'Oh yes, absolutely peachy,' Fern said. 'I spent the night sobbing my heart out so yes I'm fine.'

His heart broke. 'Because I didn't propose.'

'Because you broke up with me, you idiot. I can't even begin to get my head around what happened last night. We're supposed to be together forever, we were going to have a family and you...' she swallowed. 'I'm so angry right now I can't even speak to you. And I'm angry at myself. But I didn't come about me, I came for Bones.'

Fletcher stared at her in confusion. 'Is he OK?'

'No, he's barely moved all day, he looks depressed and I can only assume it's because he's missing you. And while I can't even begin to understand why you broke up with me over this, it's worse for him, he has no idea why you've abandoned him. And I can't explain it to him either. You were as much part of his life as I am and you can't just cut him out of it, it's not fair. You need to take some responsibility for him too.'

He pushed his hand through his hair. She was right. This whole thing was a mess. He loved Bones almost as much as he loved Fern. The three of them had been together every single day and, although it had only been four weeks, it had become the norm so quickly.

'I could visit him. Take him out for walks.'

Fern nodded. 'He'd like that.'

They stood in silence for a moment. There was so much that he wanted to say.

'Should I perhaps come round now and see him?'

Fern thought about it. 'Come round after your dinner. I can give you an hour with him. I… don't have to be there if you don't want me there.'

Christ, he felt the knife twist in his heart. What had he done?

'I'd still like to be friends with you. I know I've hurt you, but I do think this is the best thing for you. I don't want this either, believe me, but I only want you to be happy.'

'I was happy, deliriously so. And now I'm miserable so you're doing a brilliant job of making me happy. And only I get to choose what's the best thing for me and, rightly or wrongly, I choose you.' She moved to the side of the boat and climbed over before he could move to help her. 'I'll see you in half an hour.'

With that she marched back down the towpath again.

$\sim$

Fern was sitting on the floor trying to persuade Bones to eat while he lay there refusing to move. This wasn't right. This was something a lot more than just missing Fletcher. He had been sleepy all day but she'd assumed he was sulking because he hadn't seen Fletcher. The thought that Bones might be ill simply hadn't occurred to her. He was always so full of life. He was never sick so this behaviour was really starting to worry her.

There was a knock on her door and she quickly got up to answer it.

Fletcher was standing there and all anger suddenly left her with her worry about Bones.

'Something isn't right, he's just not moving.'

Fletcher's face creased in concern and he moved past her into her house, kneeling immediately in front of her dog. And that's when she knew for sure Bones was very unwell because, as Fletcher stroked his head and talked softly to him, he didn't even wag his tail.

Fletcher must have thought the same because the next thing he was lifting Bones into his arms, no mean feat with fifty kilos of dog. 'We need to get him to the vets, he's completely unresponsive.'

Guilt flooded through her. 'He wasn't this bad today, just lying around and sleeping, but he was still eating and drinking. Well, he refused chicken at lunch but he had his breakfast this morning and a dental bone a few hours ago. But he was drinking loads. He just seems to have got like this in the last hour.'

'It's OK, I'm sure it's nothing, let's just go and get him checked out. I have my car with me.'

She grabbed her bag and keys and followed him up the path to the car park, watching as Fletcher very carefully loaded Bones into the back of the car, then she scrambled into the passenger seat.

'I should have taken him to the vets before now. He's been acting out of character all day, why didn't I realise he was ill?'

'Because Bones doesn't do ill and he was absolutely fine yesterday. Try not to worry, maybe he's just eaten something a bit dodgy.'

Fletcher drove off really quickly. He was usually such a careful driver, something she always teased him about, but tonight that care seemed to have gone out of the window. They were lucky – the vets where Bones was registered was a twenty-four-hour hospital but frustratingly it was in the next town, which was suddenly too far away for Fern's liking.

She glanced into the back seat where Bones was sleeping... or worse. He was still breathing though, she could see his chest rising and falling as if he was just in a deep sleep.

Fletcher made a call to the vets to let them know they were on their way and what the problem was.

She looked at Fletcher as he finished the call, his jaw clenched as he drove. He glanced over at her and her heart ached just looking at him. Was this really it? Were they really over or, as Orla said, was this just a blip that they would look back on and laugh at later? It was hard to believe when two people loved each other so much they couldn't find a way to make this work again.

They arrived at the vet hospital a lot sooner than she expected after Fletcher took some windy, narrow roads as shortcuts.

They quickly got out the car and Fletcher carefully lifted Bones from the back seat. The dog moaned in protest and struggled a little, he always hated being lifted. The fact that there was still fight in there was at least a good sign.

She followed him into the surgery and one of the vet nurses quickly ushered Fletcher into one of the rooms. But as soon as Fletcher had laid Bones down on the table, they were ushering them back into the waiting room again. 'We'll just run some tests and one of the vets will be out to speak to you shortly,' the vet nurse said.

Fern made to protest but Fletcher guided her to a seat. 'Let them do their job,' he said, softly.

She sat down and Fletcher took her hand. She stared at the way their hands were joined. There was so much she wanted to say but now didn't seem appropriate. So they sat in silence instead while her world was tilting off its axis. First she'd lost Fletcher, now she could lose Bones. How could her life go so spectacularly wrong and so quickly?

CHAPTER EIGHTEEN

Fern stepped outside the vet hospital with Fletcher, feeling numb.

'Oh my god Fletcher, diabetes, how are we going to cope with that?' Fern said, before realising there was no 'we' any more. 'I mean, how am *I* going to cope with that? I don't even like needles.'

'*We* will cope with it. As you said, I have to take responsibility for him as well. We'll face this together. And you'll get used to the needles, it will soon become second nature.'

Fletcher opened the passenger door for her and then got into the driver's side before driving off.

The vets were going to keep Bones in overnight to monitor him. It had been pretty much a blur of information since the vet had come out and told them Bones had diabetes. He wasn't even two years old. That felt like such a young age to be struck down with such a horrible disease. They had talked about food and calories and a whole bunch of other stuff which Fern had barely registered; all she could think of was that her poor boy had diabetes.

The vet had discussed giving Bones insulin twice a day and showed her how to administer the first injection. Her hands had shaken so much handling the syringe that she'd nearly dropped it twice. Bones had barely stirred.

The vet had said that it looked like it had been caught really early and everything else in his blood looked normal and healthy, which was at least something.

'Where are we going?' Fern said, realising Fletcher was driving away from her house and to the far side of Apple Hill Bay.

'We need to speak to someone with experience of a diabetic dog. The vets know the facts, but living with a diabetic dog day in, day out, is very different from what the science says. We need all the tips and advice we can get. One of my apprentices, Arthur, had a diabetic dog until recently when his dog passed away.'

'Did the dog die from diabetes?' Fern said, in horror.

'The dog was twenty-one years old, it was just his time. From what I can gather, Jasper was diabetic for around ten years before he died in his sleep. This isn't going to be a death sentence for Bones, despite what your mind is telling you, so stop coming up with the worst-case scenarios. There is no reason why Bones won't go on to have a very happy and healthy life, despite not being able to have titbits in future.'

Christ, she hadn't even thought of that. Poor Bones, he loved his titbits.

'Did I do something wrong? Did I do something to cause this?'

'No honey, it's an autoimmune disease, most likely genetic. I very much doubt it was something you did.'

They pulled into the drive of a very ramshackle cottage

overlooking the sea with a garden spilling over with flowers from watering cans, buckets, wellies, old tyres, wheelbarrows, even an old boat. It looked incredible.

The door opened and a man, probably in his seventies, stood on the doorstep dressed in a most impressive blue velvet waistcoat, embroidered with stars.

'Well, hello Fletcher, this is a lovely surprise,' the man said. 'And you've brought your girl with you. This must be Fern. I've heard so much about you. I'm Arthur.'

Fern smiled. 'Hello Arthur. I hope we're not disturbing you.'

'Not at all, I was just about to watch *Poirot* but it's been on before so it's not like I don't know what's going to happen.'

'Arthur, we need your help,' Fletcher said, clapping the man on the back. 'Our dog, Bones, has just been diagnosed with diabetes.'

The smile faded from Arthur's face, which did nothing to raise Fern's spirits.

'You best come in then.'

Arthur stepped back and Fern and Fletcher moved inside.

The house was painted in warm tones of yellow but the hall had tons of photos, mostly of a black and white collie with a big smile, clearly having the time of his life. There were photos of Arthur astride a motorbike with Jasper, the dog, wearing goggles sitting in a side car, a huge grin on his face. There were photos of Arthur and Jasper swimming in the sea together, hiking up mountains, playing on the beach. Fern couldn't help smiling at what a wonderful life Jasper had led.

'That's my Jasper,' Arthur said. 'When he was diagnosed with diabetes, I was so worried that his life would be short so I wanted to give him the best life possible in his remaining time, I wanted to photograph everything so I would have some fond memories to look back on. He lived for nearly eleven years after his diagnosis. All of those photos show a life with diabetes.'

Fern's smile grew.

'I know you're worried, love, and it is very overwhelming to start with but you'll soon find your way. And you can come and see me or call me anytime if you have questions. Come and sit down and I'll put the kettle on.'

He disappeared off down the hall towards the kitchen and they followed him. He gestured for them to sit down at the small dining room table.

'I was just sorting out some of his bits today actually, I was going to take them to the vets to see if anyone could make use of them, but I'd much rather they went to a good home.' He grabbed a large box off the side and brought it to the table. 'This is a FreeStyle Libre.' He held up a small yellow box. 'It's a blood glucose monitor that attaches to the dog for two weeks. You scan it with your phone to find out your dog's blood glucose levels. You're aiming for your dog to be within five and fifteen for the majority of the day but that will take several weeks to get there. The instructions of how to fit it are in the box. There's four in there, I bought a load before Jasper died.'

'The vet spoke about that, she said they might fit one for us before we pick him up,' Fern said.

'OK, good, I'll help you download the app on your phone in a minute and if he is wearing one when you pick him up, you can scan him straightaway as it takes an hour for the sensor to warm up once it's activated.' He held up another box. 'This right here is a bloody brilliant thing. It's called a BluCon and sits on top of the Libre, you can use a bit of double-sided Sellotape to attach it. It's a transmitter and will continually send the blood glucose level from the Libre to your phone so you don't have to scan the Libre with your phone every few minutes. It has alarms set on it so if Bones drops too low you are notified and can do something about it. It saved Jasper's life on more than one occasion, let me tell you. With these two bits of kit you can see his levels all day, every day. I love a gadget or a gizmo, so these were right up my street but they're very easy to use. You need to get yourself a diary and keep track of everything. What dose he is on every day, what food you are feeding, how much, how he seems in himself, what his levels were like. At some point down the line, you'll need to look back on it so you know what was working and what wasn't.'

He started sorting through the box and pulling things out one by one, explaining what they were, and Fern sat there trying to take it all in, wishing she could take notes.

The sun had well and truly set and Fletcher was starting to feel a little guilty about staying with Arthur so late but he seemed to be in his element talking with Fern about everything she needed to know about this disease. She had asked a ton of questions and Arthur had fetched her a notepad and pen so she could write stuff down. He could see she was feeling better about all of this already.

Just then Fern's mobile phone rang and she quickly scrabbled in her pocket to answer it.

'Hello?'

There seemed to be a lot of noise the other end of the phone, it sounded like a lot of barking.

'Really, he's OK?' Fern said. 'That's great, we'll be there in ten minutes.' She hung up the call. 'Bones is very much awake and making a lot of noise because we're not there. They said we can come and pick him up tonight.'

Fletcher stood up, grabbing his keys. 'Let's go and get him.'

Fern stood up too and turned to Arthur, who was already packing everything away back into the box. 'Thank you so much for all your help. How much do I owe you for all of this equipment?'

Arthur waved it away. 'Absolutely nothing. It's money I've already spent and I don't need it. But if you feel you must give something, then donate to Diabetes UK. It's a horrible disease and there's still so much we don't know about it. The research that can be done into treatments will eventually filter down to our dogs too.'

'I will, thank you.' She leaned forward and gave him a hug.

'And if you have any questions, Fletcher has my number. Call me anytime. Or pop in and see me, bring your little Bones with you.'

Fern snorted. 'Bones is a Bernese mountain dog, he's fifty kilos.'

Arthur's face lit up. 'Oh that's wonderful, I love big dogs.'

Fletcher hoisted the box under one arm and shook Arthur's hand. 'Thank you for this.'

'I'm glad I could help.'

They hurried outside and climbed in Fletcher's car.

'I can't believe he's OK, he was so unresponsive a few hours ago,' Fern said. 'They did say that with insulin treatment he would be back up on his feet in no time. I just didn't expect it to happen so quickly.'

'Bones is a fighter, as are you. I know you're going to be fine with all his treatment too and I'll be there to help you every step of the way.'

'Thank you, although when I said you had to take some responsibility for him, I didn't think it would involve helping me inject him twice a day.'

'We're a team,' Fletcher said and then realised he needed to quantify that. As much as it pained him, he still stood by his decision to end things last night. She deserved someone better than him. Someone who would make all her dreams come true. 'Just because we're not a couple any more, doesn't mean we can't work together, be friends, be there for each other.'

He saw her look out of the window and she was quiet for the longest time. As he drove towards the vets, he saw her surreptitiously wipe her eyes. God this was killing him. He wanted to pull over onto the side of the road, haul her onto his lap and kiss her until those tears were a distant memory. But if they got back together now she would always regret it, always be hoping and waiting for him to propose, always be slightly disappointed that he hadn't. She'd bought a wedding dress for crying out loud. This was hardly a passing fad for her. This was obviously something that was important to her and it was something he could never give her.

She cleared her throat and when she spoke her voice was rough. 'I want to put one of these FreeStyle Libre sensors on him tonight if the vet hasn't done it already. I know his blood glucose levels will be all over the place for the next few weeks until he settles down but I just want to get an idea of what the levels are doing, what causes his highs and lows so we... I can manage his treatment more successfully. I need to change his food right away, he has to be on a low-fat diet from here on in because his pancreas is ruined. Thankfully, Arthur had some leftover diabetic dog food so I think I'll start him on that tomorrow and go from there.'

Fletcher heard the change from *we* to *I* and winced.

'We're in this together, Fern. I will help you.'

She didn't say anything and he knew she was angry at him.

They arrived at the vets and hurried inside. Fletcher could hear Bones barking his head off from behind the reception area and he couldn't help but smile at how vocal he was. One of the vet nurses greeted them and called them into one of the surgical rooms.

'He's doing well, really well,' she said, closing the door. 'It normally takes a couple of doses of insulin before they rally round so we were quite surprised how quickly it affected him. But that's a good sign. His levels aren't that high right now and, while they might increase over the next few days, they shouldn't stay too high for long now we are treating it. We will probably increase his dose once a week until we find the right dose.'

They both nodded.

'I'll go and get him, I'm sure he'll be over the moon to see you both.' The nurse opened the back door to the room and the barking got a lot louder. Within a few moments, she was struggling to bring in a very excited, very strong Bones, who howled in delight at seeing them. He ran to Fern first, who crouched down and hugged him tight, before he wriggled free and threw himself at Fletcher for a brief stroke and then went back to Fern again so she could stroke his bum and then moved back to Fletcher for a chin scratch.

'OK, OK,' Fern laughed through her tears.

'We've attached a FreeStyle Libre on him for now so we

can keep an eye on him over the next few weeks and make sure his levels don't get too high or low,' the nurse said. 'This will take the pressure off you a little for the next few days until you get your head around everything. Do you have your phone ready with the app? If so you can scan him now to activate the sensor.'

Fern pulled her phone out of her pocket and with the nurse's direction scanned the sensor with it.

'That will start showing readings in an hour's time. It would be a good idea for you to learn how to home test too, which is testing Bones's levels by doing a blood prick test. As a bare minimum you should be testing before injecting to make sure his levels are above eleven so you know it's safe to inject the full dose. But you don't need to worry about home testing for the next few days because the Libre will do that for you. It's just an expensive way of doing it going forward as each Libre only lasts two weeks and then you have to buy a new one. Blood prick testing is a much cheaper way of doing it. We'll have him back in at the end of the week and we can look at his charts from the Libre and show you how to do the blood prick testing then.'

'OK,' Fern said.

'Right, I think you've got everything you need but you're bound to have questions over the next few days, so feel free to phone us and ask.'

'OK, thank you. Come on then Bones, let's get you home.'

Fletcher grabbed the dog's lead and they walked out into the reception area. He waited while Fern paid the eye-wateringly huge bill and then they were outside.

This time Bones bounded into the back seat by himself and pressed his face against the glass as he normally did. Fletcher strapped him into his car harness and climbed into the front next to Fern. He lowered the back window so Bones could stick his face out of the window and sniff the wind.

He started driving and they sat in silence. He hated this sudden awkwardness between them.

After about five minutes, Fern clearly realised where they were driving to.

'Why are we going to yours? I thought you'd drop me and Bones off at mine.'

'So I can help you with the injection tomorrow. And so I can be there for you and Bones throughout the night. I'm worried about him too.'

'I have to learn how to do it by myself. You won't always be there.'

'I will always be there for you.'

'No you won't. We're not together any more, remember. How would this work when you start dating other women? You'll leave them at the restaurant while you hurry round to mine to help inject Bones and then run back to them? Leave them in your bed in the morning after hot morning sex and, while she's still catching her breath, hotfoot it round to mine?'

Fletcher pulled a face. Dating other women hadn't even crossed his mind. The thought of making love to someone who wasn't Fern made his stomach turn.

'It's just not practical,' Fern said. 'I know I said you need to take some responsibility for him, and I do think you should visit him now and again, take him out for walks, but I can't expect you to upend your whole life for him. He's my dog. And I might as well start as we mean to go on and do this alone.'

Fletcher thought about this for a moment. 'I think it's a

good idea if we both learn how to do this. There will be times when you can't do it either and I'll need to look after him and handle the injections myself. And there's so much to get your head around for the next few days, there's no shame in getting help from a friend. Let me help you, at least until the end of the week.'

Fern sighed. 'Fine.'

Fletcher parked the car and they walked down the towpath towards his boat. Bones bounded aboard and, as soon as Fletcher opened the door, he made his way towards the bedroom. It was getting late now and Bones always liked to claim his spot right in the middle of the bed.

Fletcher and Fern stood awkwardly in the lounge. He had no idea what to say to her. She was so angry at him and he wondered if they ever could just be friends or if they really would go from lovers and best friends to hating each other.

'I think we better get to bed ourselves,' Fern said, quietly. 'If we're going to feed and inject him every twelve hours, we're going to have to get up relatively early to get ourselves into a routine.'

'OK. I'll, erm, take the sofa.'

She stared at him incredulously. 'I think we can be grown up enough to share a bed without tearing each other's clothes off.'

Fletcher wasn't sure he was grown up enough for that. Sex with Fern had always been incredible. There was something about making love to the person you loved more than anything. He could never get enough of that. And now he'd broken things off, he would never make love to her again, he'd never kiss her again, never dance with her again. The thought of that made him ache inside. But he had made this decision for her. He had to stand by it.

He swallowed. 'OK, if you're sure?'

She huffed out her annoyance and walked off towards the bedroom.

Fletcher grabbed the BluCon transmitter from the box and followed her through. 'If you give me your phone, I'll set up the BluCon on it too. That way we can be alerted in the night if Bones goes too low.'

She handed him her phone and he was quite glad they had this to focus on rather than talking about their relationship. At some point she was bound to ask him why he didn't want to get married and then he'd either have to lie or tell the truth, and neither one of those particularly appealed. If she found out why he never wanted to get married, she would probably never want anything to do with him again.

He spent a few minutes focussing on setting up the BluCon transmitter, deliberately not looking at her as she got undressed and changed then wandered off to the bathroom. He sat on the bed and attached the BluCon over the top of the Libre sensor and made sure it was communicating with Fern's phone.

She came back in and she was only wearing one of his t-shirts, just like she normally would. Her bare legs made his stomach twist with desire. He quickly averted his eyes as she got into bed. He was definitely not getting any sleep tonight.

'The BluCon is set up so if he drops below five the alarm will go off, but judging from what the vet, nurse and Arthur told us, he will probably be high the next few days or weeks rather than too low.'

'And there's nothing we can do about being too high?' Fern said.

'No, too high is not great, especially long-term, but being too low is the dangerous one. If he drops too low we can give him a biscuit or some kibble and if he drops really low we have to rub honey on his gums but I don't think we'll have that problem, not yet anyway.'

Fletcher pulled off his shorts, leaving his t-shirt and boxer shorts on. Ordinarily, he'd sleep with just his boxer shorts on or, on hot nights, absolutely nothing at all but there was already too much bare flesh in this room as it was without adding to it. He went off to the bathroom, cleaned his teeth, washed his face and then came back to bed. Fern was already lying on her side, curled round Bones, stroking his thick fur. He seemed no worse off for his ordeal.

Fletcher climbed into bed and curled himself around Bones too, just like he normally would. Except now he was looking right into Fern's face and that felt far too intimate for two people who were just supposed to be friends. He switched off the light and rolled over to face away from her.

They lay in silence for a moment.

'You know what, I think I might take the sofa,' Fern said. 'I can't lie here with you not being able to bear to even look at me.'

He rolled back to face her, snapping the light on. 'Do you think this is easy for me? It's killing me. I don't want this. Before yesterday, I was so happy and excited about our future, about getting a house together, having children, and now all that is gone because I can't give you the future you imagined when you agreed to all that.'

'I imagined you and me, growing old and grey together, raising our children in a house by the sea. The getting married part was the cherry on the top of that wonderful dream, but it was not *the* dream.'

He shook his head. 'I don't want you giving up your dreams for me.'

'You're not listening. *You* were always the dream. I don't need anything else.'

'You said you always dreamed of getting married when you were a child.'

'I dreamed of lots of things when I was a child. I remember when I was little I always wanted one of those Mr Frosty ice-drink makers – you put the ice in and it crushes it and you add juice to it to make a slushy ice drink. One of the kids at one of my many many foster homes had one and it was the coolest thing. I was never allowed to play with it or have any of the drinks from it because the kid was a little shit who didn't understand the concept of sharing. I always wanted one of my own so I could make iced drinks for all my friends – well, try to buy friends with my iced drinks as I didn't have a lot of friends growing up – and I always knew my life would just be a little bit better if I had one of those Mr Frosty drink makers in my life. I never got one. And you know what, I don't feel that I missed out because of it. I never look back on my life and think my life was worse because that dream never came true.'

He frowned. 'Are you really comparing the dream of getting married to the dream of having a plastic toy?'

'I'm just saying, sometimes we think that having something will make everything better when it doesn't. While losing something can make everything infinitely worse.'

'Are you telling me that if we stay together for the rest of our lives, you won't be disappointed if we never get married?'

Fern paused long enough for Fletcher to see the truth.

'Exactly,' Fletcher said. 'And I can't be the one to disappoint you.'

He reached up and snapped off the light, rolling away

from her again. 'And it's not that I can't bear to look at you, it's that I can't lie in bed with you, staring at you, without wanting to kiss you, touch you and make love to you.'

She was silent for a moment. 'You know what, I am disappointed. We had a plan for the future and one misunderstanding, one tiny disagreement, and you've turned tail and run. I'm disappointed that my beautiful future with you is now in tatters because you want to take some moral high ground.'

Fletcher sighed as he stared at the wall. 'You'll thank me one day when you get married to the man of your dreams.' The thought of that burned his insides.

'*You* were the man of my dreams, Fletcher. Now you're just an arse.'

He felt her turn around to face away from him.

He hated this. They had never once argued or had a cross word since they'd got together. He'd hoped they could be friends at least but now he didn't think they could even be that.

Fern woke in the middle of the night to a weird noise, which she immediately realised was coming from Bones. He'd moved to the very side of the bed with his face pressed against the small porthole window. She sat up, grabbing her phone to see that his blood glucose level was at sixteen, not ideal but not too high or too low. She crouched over him, stroking his head; he snuffled in his sleep and the weird noise stopped. She sighed with relief, it was obviously just a weird snore because his head was at a strange angle. Bones loved to sleep in the most awkward of positions, upside down, his head hanging off the sofa with his tongue lolling out of his mouth was his preferred position, but the more uncomfortable the better.

She stroked his thick mane, massaging his neck which he loved. She felt a hand on her own back.

'Is he OK?'

'Yeah he's fine, he was just snoring weirdly and I got scared something was wrong,' Fern said. She lay back down and cuddled into Fletcher's chest and he wrapped an arm around her before she suddenly remembered that they weren't together any more. But as he was holding her tight, he clearly wasn't that bothered by this inappropriate show of affection. Maybe at this time of day, in the darkness, it was neutral territory, no man's land. They could call a temporary truce and just be there for each other. They would worry about their angst and relationship problems in the light of day.

'Are you OK?' Fletcher said, his fingers running through her hair.

'Yeah. Just scared for him. I'm going to do everything in my power to get his levels stabilised and get him healthy but it feels like if I don't get it right his life is at stake. And this is not just a few weeks of care, it's the rest of his life. It feels like such a huge responsibility. I think I'm always going to be watching him like a hawk. I don't know how I'll ever have a decent night's sleep again.'

'You will. It will all become second nature soon enough. And if it doesn't then we can always take shifts.'

She smiled and closed her eyes. 'Because we're a team,' she said, sleepily.

'That's right. We are.'

CHAPTER NINETEEN

Fletcher woke as the sun peeped through the portholes. Fern was still wrapped in his arms, where she belonged. He glanced down and realised she was awake.

He stroked her head and she looked up at him.

'Hey,' she said, softly.

'Hi.'

'Sorry for this,' she gestured to her current position.

'There's no need to apologise. I hope we can be friends and as friends we can hug each other.'

She let out a sigh. 'Fletcher, I don't want to be friends with you.'

His heart sank. 'You don't?'

'I want *us* back, we were perfect together and I would rather never get married than not have you in my life. And if I can get past that, I don't know why you can't.'

Fletcher sighed. Could they really just sweep all this under the carpet as if it hadn't happened? Pretend that she hadn't got so excited about the possibility of marriage that she'd bought a dress?

'What is it about getting married that you are so against?' she asked. 'I don't want to push you into doing something you don't want to do, but if this is the sticking point between us, if you feel that marriage is so important to me and you can't give me that, maybe we can talk it through to address the problem.'

Fletcher felt himself tense and hoped she hadn't felt it too. He couldn't tell her the truth about that. Although if he really wanted a clean break from her, he supposed that was the way to do it.

'You know why. My parents loved each other completely until they got married, then they hated each other. I watched the change and it happened so quickly.'

That part was true. As a child he had blamed marriage for his parents' break-up and had grown up thinking he never wanted that for himself as it was clearly so damaging. With the wisdom of age, and having since talked to his parents as an adult, he knew now that wasn't the case. Their wedding was merely a feeble sticking plaster over a gaping wound.

'There's something else, isn't there?' Fern sat up to look at him, her face filled with worry. He should have known she would see right through him. 'There's a bigger reason that's holding you back. When we broke up you said, "I *can't* ever get married." What does *can't* mean?'

Fletcher felt physically sick at the thought of telling her the truth and her finding out about Lauren. He couldn't even begin to find the words to explain.

Her face fell. 'Are you married? Do you have a secret wife somewhere and when you said, I can't get married, did you mean legally you can't?'

He stared at her in shock. 'Fern... I... I'm not married.'

She let out a sigh of relief and he felt like such a shitbag for not being honest with her about this before.

'But there is something, isn't there? It's not just your parents' divorce that's made you feel this way, is it?'

He toyed with the words in his head but, no matter which way he spun it, he still came out of it looking like a completely self-absorbed bastard.

He shook his head. 'I just... have my reasons. Just as you have strong beliefs for marriage, I have strong beliefs against it.'

She sighed. 'Honestly, I was kind of hoping there was some big reason behind all this, rather than believe that you've simply broken up with me because you don't want to marry me.'

She got out of bed and called for Bones as she headed for the kitchen.

He watched her go, aching inside.

'So we're starting off at twenty units of insulin?' Fern said, holding the syringe in her hand and feeling the weight of its power. This was the thing that would save Bones's life, but if the dose was too much it could also kill him.

'Twenty is actually a bit of a conservative start. The vet said they normally start dogs on an insulin dose that's half of their body weight and then increase the dose from there. As Bones is fifty kilos, he probably should have been started at twenty-five units. He was given twenty units last night and he didn't drop below twelve throughout the night so we will probably have to increase his dose at the end of the week if we don't see an improvement in his levels. For now, I don't think we need to worry about giving him too much.'

Fern sighed, she hated this. Poor Bones would have no idea why they were going to be pricking him twice a day. He trusted her and now she was going to be hurting him. They were going to use a licky mat that Arthur had given them, filled with a small dollop of fat-free Greek yoghurt, which Bones loved, to try to distract him. All she had to do, once Bones was busy with his licky mat, was pinch the skin and stick the needle in. Simple. So why did she feel so sick at the thought of it?

She saw Fletcher glance at his watch.

'Sorry, am I keeping you?' she said, hoping it didn't come out quite as snippy as it sounded in her head.

'No, it's just the vet did say that we need to inject within an hour of feeding otherwise the food gets too far ahead of the insulin. I totally understand that you're nervous and, when I do it for the first time, I will be too, but it's been forty-five minutes so far since Bones had his breakfast, so we're kind of running out of time.'

Fern let out a heavy breath.

'You can do this, I know you can,' Fletcher said, gently.

'OK, OK, let's do this. Give him the licky mat,' Fern said.

Bones tucked straight into the yoghurt, licking it all up, and Fern quickly pinched the skin, fumbled with the injection for a moment to get the angle right and then it was in. She quickly pressed down the plunger and released the insulin a second later. Bones barely noticed.

She sat back and watched Bones get every last tiny drip of yoghurt and then look for more.

'You did that like a pro,' Fletcher said.

She smiled at him gratefully. 'A pro that needs plenty of

practice but I guess I'll get lots of that. I'm just so scared of hurting him.'

'He didn't seem remotely bothered so I think you did a good job.'

Fern stood up and stretched. She had to get used to it, she'd be doing it twice a day for the rest of Bones's life.

She noticed a letter from the Apple Hill Bay town council next to where she was standing and couldn't help pick out the title of the letter in clear bold capitals.

NOTICE OF COMMUNITY FUNDING TERMINATION

Her heart leapt and she quickly scanned over the rest of the letter.

'What the hell is this?' Fern said, holding the letter.

Fletcher looked up from stroking Bones's head. He winced when he saw the letter. 'They're cutting our funding. ReLoved has got three months left and that's it. Of course, we can carry on but the mentors won't get paid and they rely on that money and we won't be able to afford the rent on the barn either.'

'They can't do that,' Fern said, outraged. 'ReLoved is a hugely important part of Apple Hill Bay. It's helped so many people. The council saw its worth when they gave you this funding two years ago so why not now? It's gone from strength to strength since then. How can they not see how integral it is to the people of the town?'

'I don't know. The letter talks about how they want us to be self-sufficient but that's not the nature of our business. Yes, we produce pieces of furniture or art that we sell but that would never pay for the salaries of the mentors or the rent. The most important part of ReLoved is the teaching, the passing on of skills these people have never had the opportunity to learn before, it's giving them a purpose, it's giving them jobs or developing a passion; it was never about making money. I don't know how we can ever be self-sufficient enough to match the money we get from the council.'

'We have to do something. We can get a petition going. I see these online petitions on Facebook and the internet all the time, people trying to rally the troops.'

'I did think of that, I'm not sure if the townspeople actually know what we do up there.'

'I'll think you underestimate how much of an impact you've had on the town,' Fern said. 'And if they don't know, we have to show them. We need to make the council reprioritise what they spend their money on. Did you know they've asked local artists to submit designs for a full-size statue of Francis Drake and offered a hundred thousand pounds to the winning artist?'

'What? That's crazy money,' Fletcher said, standing up. 'And why the hell do we need a statue of Francis Drake?'

'Apparently he stayed in The Green Dragon when he was around eighteen, but no one can actually confirm that, especially as history books have him in Plymouth around that time. The only possible evidence they have is that an old guest ledger shows an F. Drake stayed there in 1559 and The Green Dragon have exalted this link ever since finding it.'

'I'm not entirely sure Francis Drake is someone to be exalted. From what I've read, he was nothing more than a pirate in his early life, stealing treasures from other ships and countries, and he was involved in the slave trade serving on his cousin's boat before that.'

Fern smirked. Of course Fletcher would know about the history of Francis Drake.

'Anyway, regardless of Francis Drake's good points or bad points, regardless of whether he stayed in the town or not, a hundred-thousand-pound statue of him is not going to help the town in any way, whereas ReLoved helps people from the town every single day.'

'You sound like Leo, he was the one who told me ReLoved was losing its funding. He was furious that the town council had put some new signs up at the park saying, "Welcome to Apple Hill Park", but then cut the funding for us.'

'Exactly, if they have that kind of money to waste, they have money to continue to support ReLoved. They've just commissioned me to do murals on the back of seven bus stops. Eight thousand pounds they've offered me. I'll go and see Councillor Bishop today and tell her she can keep the money.'

'Wait, no, you can't do that.'

'I can and I will. The town doesn't need pretty bus stops. But ReLoved is too important to lose.'

'But you need that money for…' he trailed off.

'The house with the big garden for our children to play in?' Fern snapped. 'Well that's not going to happen now, is it, so the money might as well be put to good use.'

Fletcher looked utterly broken as he pushed his hands through his hair.

'Look, I'll get other jobs. It's no big deal. I want to do this for you.'

'Why? You hate me and I don't blame you.'

'I could never hate you. I love you and I always will, but this is bigger than us.' She looked at her watch. 'I have to go to work and you need to go and be fabulous at ReLoved as always so we still have something to save.'

She grabbed her stuff and whistled for Bones but paused before she walked out the door. She moved back to Fletcher and leaned up to kiss him on the cheek. 'Thank you for helping with Bones.'

'Thank you for helping with this,' he gestured to the letter.

She smiled sadly. 'We make a good team, whether we're married or not. It's a shame you can't see that.'

He followed her out onto the deck. 'I'll be round later to help with his evening injection.'

She nodded. 'I won't lie and say I don't need you because I do, even if it is just for moral support. You can come for dinner if you like.'

He paused long enough for it to hurt. He clearly wanted a clean break and she kept dragging him back in.

'Seven OK? I can bring pizza,' Fletcher said.

'If you want to,' Fern said. 'You can just come round at half past to help with the injection.'

'I'll be there at seven.'

She nodded and he helped her to step over the side of the boat. She walked down the towpath and turned back to see that Fletcher was watching her go.

When Fern arrived at Puffin Hut, Carrie and Shay were already there admiring her mural, which gave her a small kick of pride.

'Hey,' Carrie said, turning to greet Fern. 'My friend Mary

said she saw you and Fletcher at the vets last night, is everything OK with Bones?'

The dog in question bounded through the door at hearing his name and went straight up to greet Carrie, wagging his tail as if he hadn't seen her in years. Carrie laughed and made a big fuss of her 'grandpup', as she called him.

'He has diabetes,' Fern said, hearing her voice crack as she said it.

'Oh no,' Carrie said.

'Oh shit,' Shay said.

'Yeah, exactly. I have to jab him twice a day with insulin, which is terrifying, and he has that sensor attached to him so I can see what level he's at throughout the day and monitor it so he doesn't go too low. We're having to change his diet so it's completely low-fat and he can't have any treats. But the vet and Fletcher's friend Arthur say there's no reason why he can't go on to lead a normal, healthy life.'

'Well that's good, I guess,' Carrie said.

'I know. I'm just sad for him, I can't explain why he can't have a little bit of my crumpets at breakfast any more, or why he won't be getting any treats or why I'm hurting him twice a day with the injection.'

'He still seems like his happy old self,' Shay said. 'He's with you and that's all that matters. I can't see his spirits getting dampened by this, or anything actually.'

Fern watched as Bones picked up his favourite lobster toy and tossed it in the air. 'Maybe you're right.'

'But Fletcher's been helping you with this?' Carrie said, a hint of hope in her voice.

'Yeah, he's been brilliant,' Fern said, then caught the little smile on Carrie's face. 'Don't look like that. I'm still angry at him and he's still taking the moral high ground thinking that breaking up with me is the best thing for me. And now he also has the added worry of ReLoved closing down.'

'What?' Carrie said.

Fern explained about the council cutting the funding for ReLoved.

'They can't do that,' Shay said. 'Fletcher and his mentors have helped so many people.'

'The council apparently want them to be self-sufficient but they can't pay the mentors or the rent out of selling a few bits of furniture here and there.'

'That's really annoyed me,' Carrie said. 'Councillor Bishop was the one that pushed me into having a funfair for the launch of The Little Beach Hut Hotel. I'm paying for half but the council are paying the other half. They've even paid for fireworks, which I thought was an unnecessary expense. Why do that if they don't have the money or if they have to steal money off community projects?'

'I don't know, but I'm going to go and see her at lunchtime, see if I can get her to change her mind,' Fern said.

'I'll go and see her this morning,' Carrie said, she gestured to the puffins. 'This looks good.'

'Thank you.'

'But you need to get a move on if you're going to finish Dolphin before the big opening on Saturday.'

Fern smiled. 'You're such a hard taskmaster. It will be finished.'

'Or you could let me paint my interpretation of a dolphin,' Shay said.

Fern snorted. Whenever they played Pictionary as a family, Shay's drawing always had them in fits of giggles and were never anything resembling the real thing.

'I think your talents lie elsewhere,' Carrie said, diplomatically.

~

Fletcher sighed as he sat on top of the staircase he was making, running his fingers across one of the tiny wooden flowers Fern loved so much. He couldn't focus on anything this morning. His head was full of Fern, how to save ReLoved and Bones and his diabetes.

'Hello.'

Fletcher looked up to see a man standing in the doorway. He forced on a smile and went over to greet him.

'Hello, I'm Fletcher, can I help you with anything?'

'I'm Antonio Garcia, I live in the blue house overlooking Apple Hill Bay. I've heard such good things about this place and I wondered if I'd be able to make something.'

'Of course, what did you want to make?'

'I thought maybe a wooden picture frame would be fairly easy but with objects or shapes round the face of the frame.'

'We can absolutely do that. Do you have much experience with this kind of thing?'

'Well, when I was a kid in secondary school we dabbled in a bit of woodwork but that was many many moons ago.'

Fletcher smiled. 'Well, let's see what you can remember and we can fill in the rest. Let's go grab some wood. As you may know, all the materials we use come from reclaimed furniture or scraps that have been thrown away. A lot of the bigger pieces of furniture can be painted and restored so when it's finished it's still a chest of drawers or a desk but with a new modern twist. But sometimes, if it can't be saved, we break it down and use the wood to make something else entirely. Here is some of the wood we have to use, there's some more out the back. What kind of size are you thinking for your picture frame?'

Antonio showed him with his hands.

'That's fine, I think these will be suitable.' Fletcher selected a few pieces of wood.

They moved back over to one of the workstations and Fletcher showed Antonio how to measure and cut the wood, and soon Antonio was working away.

'So I hear congratulations are in order,' Antonio said. 'I've become very good friends with Carrie over the last few months and your wedding is all Carrie's been talking about over the last few days. I think she was probably more excited about the wedding than Fern was. You know what Carrie's like, she gets so carried away and she's so over the top with her emotions,' he smiled, fondly. 'She kept telling me how she wanted this wedding to be perfect for Fern. I think Fern felt a bit railroaded, if I'm honest. I kept telling Carrie that she needed to let you and Fern choose the kind of wedding you two wanted, but Carrie is all about big extravagant gestures, you know that. She told me how she'd bought the dress for Fern despite Fern not wanting to.'

Fletcher stared at Antonio in surprise. 'I didn't know Carrie had bought it.'

'Oh yes. But don't worry, you just need to be firm with Carrie, tell her what kind of wedding you want, she'll soon come around. As long as Fern is happy, Carrie will be happy and Fern is happiest whenever she's with you – well, that's what Carrie says.'

Fletcher stared at the piece of wood Antonio was happily cutting up. He had to say he felt mildly better to know that the dress, in part, had come from Carrie. He knew what she was like and, as lovely as she was, she was very bullish about getting things done and getting her way. But Fern could be feisty and stubbornly determined too. If she didn't want to do something, she would have fought harder against it. She'd said that she'd let herself get caught up in the excitement of the wedding and, for as long as he lived, he would never forget finding her sobbing on the lounge floor. Regardless of the dress, she had been bitterly disappointed by the lack of the proposal.

'So when's the big day?' Antonio said.

'We're not getting married,' Fletcher said.

Antonio stared at him in horror. 'What? Carrie said you were going to propose, did we get it all wrong?'

'It was a misunderstanding.'

Antonio looked thoroughly confused. 'But... do you love her?'

'With everything I have... which is why I broke it off with her. She was so excited about these plans and she's always dreamed of getting married. I can't give her that. She deserves to find someone who will make her dreams come true.'

Antonio looked like Fletcher had spoken to him in Greek. 'But... I would think that for Fern the most exciting part of getting married is the happy ever after with the man she loves more than anything, not the actual wedding itself. That's why we get married, not for the big party or the gifts, but because we simply cannot imagine a future without that person.'

'I can't get married,' Fletcher said, his voice choked at saying that.

'Why not?'

'Because I'm scared I'll let her down.'

He was surprised how easily that answer came when the weight of that responsibility was like an anchor dragging him down.

Antonio stared at him. 'I'm not sure what happened in your past to make you think that, and it's none of my business, but if you talk to her and tell her your fears and she still wants a future with you, then don't you think you owe it to her to at least try? In ten years' time, if things don't work out between the two of you, for whatever reason, at least you can look back and say, I gave it my best shot, rather than I gave up before we even began.'

Fletcher started sanding down one of the pieces of wood Antonio was going to use. Could he really do that? Embrace the future they both wanted? The thought of it filled him with fear and joy in equal measure and he wasn't sure which one would win.

CHAPTER TWENTY

Carrie walked into Councillor Bishop's office and addressed June, her assistant.

'I need to see Michelle.'

'Umm, do you have an appointment?'

'No, but she'll see me,' Carrie said. 'Tell her it's Carrie.'

June phoned through to Michelle's office and, after a moment, June waved her in.

Carrie opened the door and strode in, closing the door. 'What the hell are you playing at, Bishop?'

Michelle rolled her eyes. 'What are you here complaining about this time, you miserable cow?'

'Well that isn't very professional, is it. Is that how you speak to all the townspeople?'

'No, just my best friend.'

Carrie laughed. 'You haven't changed, you had this attitude when we were at school.'

'You had the attitude, you just led me astray.'

Carrie sat down. 'You wanted to be led astray. I was providing a service.'

Michelle smiled. 'You certainly made my school years more entertaining. How's the plans for the launch going?'

'Good, but I have to say that when we sat here discussing it all, I didn't realise I'd be planning it all.'

Michelle laughed. 'Well, you're so good at it and I do have other work to do.'

'Yes, about that other work. I'm here about ReLoved. You can't shut it down.'

'We're not shutting it down, it's just the funding that's coming to an end.'

'But that will cause it to shut down. They can't afford the rent on that huge barn without the funding and the mentors won't get paid either. ReLoved is a wonderful initiative and, dare I say it, it's probably the best thing you've done for the town since you've been elected.'

Michelle frowned. 'I'm not sure if I should take that as a compliment or a criticism.'

'Well, if I'm honest, and I'm always honest with you, it's probably a bit of both. When you started here, you were all about making a difference, a real difference, the kind of projects that changed people's lives for the better. Now it feels like you're more focussed on the appearance of the town than its people. Commissioning a hundred-thousand-pound statue of Francis Drake and last year spending thousands on planting flowers in six-foot-high letters that spell out "Apple Hill Bay" on a hillside that almost no one can see.'

Michelle nodded. 'Granted, the flowers were not my finest decision.'

'You've forgotten where you came from. Do you remember sharing my lunch most days at school because your parents could never afford to send you in with anything? My mum started putting more sandwiches into my lunchbox because she knew you didn't have anything. ReLoved is all about providing opportunities for the poorer people, the ones that always get overlooked.'

'Bringing tourism and people to the town will bring money to the shops, restaurants, pubs – and let's not forget the hotels,' Michelle said, pointedly.

'And that brings me to my next point. I'd have been quite happy putting out a stand offering free tea and cake and letting people look around all the new beach huts at their leisure, but you were the one who wanted to do the big funfair-type launch with fireworks, and you're paying for half of that when that money could be better spent on ReLoved. Most of my bookings are going to come from internet marketing or word of mouth or people staying there and sharing posts on Instagram or TikTok, not a big party that will mostly be attended by locals who will never stay there. I'm tempted to cancel the whole thing just so you can keep the money.'

Michelle's face fell. 'You can't do that. The launch is going to be one of the biggest events in our social calendar this year.'

Carrie sighed. 'Fortunately for you, I can't cancel the funfair as it's already been paid for and they don't do refunds – believe me, I asked. I suspect the fireworks company will be the same, too. But the town council need to do better about how they spend their money, not buy something flash and expensive at the sake of the projects that need it more.'

'OK, I get what you're saying. We actually have a budget meeting tomorrow, so I'll discuss ReLoved with my team then.'

'Good.' Carrie got up. 'Cowbag.'

'Squawker.'

Carrie laughed. 'That's a good one.'

'I've been brushing up on my insults for our meetings.'

'Then I'll have to do better.' Carrie gave her a wave and left.

~

Fern sat outside Councillor Bishop's office, waiting to go in, wondering what she could say to make her change her mind and reminding herself that she had to go in there and be polite, professional and calm.

'Councillor Bishop will see you now,' June, the councillor's assistant, said.

Fern stood up, dusted herself down and walked in.

'Good afternoon Fern, I presume you're here about the bus stops, do you have some designs for me already?'

'I'm here about ReLoved,' Fern said, sitting down opposite her.

'Ah, you're the fourth person to come and see me about that today. The intention was never to fund ReLoved indefinitely, the community funding was to help them get off the ground. They've had funding for the last two years and it was our hope that they would be self-sufficient by now.'

'None of that was communicated to Fletcher. He used some of that money to rent out bigger premises so he could mentor more people and now he'll have to go back to the shed. And just how exactly do you propose that they become self-sufficient? Is that what you tell the local schools, that they need to become self-sufficient too?'

'Well, that's different.' Councillor Bishop looked awkward.

'How is it different, both of them are teaching establishments? Do you propose that Fletcher should charge the apprentices that come to him?'

'Well, that's one way.' Councillor Bishop grabbed hold of the lifeline Fern was offering.

'The homeless people, the kids from poorer backgrounds, the retired that barely have enough money to heat their homes, they should all pay for the privilege of being taught?'

'Well, no, not them,' Councillor Bishop said.

'But that's who ReLoved is for, it's for the people who would never have had this opportunity if it wasn't for Fletcher and the other mentors giving their time and skills.'

'We have other areas of the community that need our time and money,' Councillor Bishop said, trying another approach.

'Like the hundred-thousand-pound statue of Francis Drake?'

'Why is everyone so against this statue? We should be proud of our heritage.'

'You and I both know the only possible link to Francis Drake is that scrawled name in the pub's guest ledger which could be anyone. And even if by some remote chance it was him, he hasn't done anything for our town or had any other link to here other than he stayed here for one night. Why would you want to spend a hundred thousand pounds celebrating that?'

'Well, it's all part of our town development plan. We want to make our town a wonderful place to be, encourage tourists, get them talking, sharing photos of our beautiful little village. Just like the bus stops you're going to paint for us, that will attract a lot of attention but there will be some that will say, "What will painted bus stops do for the town? Why spend money on that?"'

'Which is an excellent point. I'd like to give back my cheque for eight thousand pounds and for the funds to go to ReLoved. I cannot, in good conscience, take that from the council knowing that ReLoved is going to close from lack of funds.'

Councillor Bishop's face fell. 'You don't want to do the bus stops?'

'I'd love to, but not at the cost of ReLoved, it's too important.'

Councillor Bishop sighed. 'Look, I know you and Fletcher—'

'This has nothing to do with Fletcher and everything to do with people like George, Mo, Connor and Mary who are the mentors at ReLoved, the ones that used to be living on the streets and are now making a life for themselves. It has everything to do with people like Arthur, a retired, widowed man who was incredibly lonely before he came to ReLoved, people like Leo who was always getting in trouble with the teachers and the police and is now a successful artist, people like Coral who had PTSD and finds working with her hands a useful therapy, people like Donna who after losing her husband never left her house for over a year, people like—'

'OK, OK, I get the message,' Councillor Bishop sighed. 'I'll speak to my colleagues, maybe we can redistribute some funds. But even if we could, it would never be a permanent thing. Maybe we could extend it for another year but they need to find a way to pay for this themselves.'

'Then you need to help them do that too. These are not business men or women, or people experienced in marketing. You can't build them up and then kick the ladder out from under them. If there's a way you can think of for them to be self-sufficient then I'm sure they would love to hear it.'

Councillor Bishop nodded. 'I'll talk it over with my team but I'm not making any promises.'

Fern stood up. 'Thank you for seeing me.'

She walked out into the reception area to see Fletcher pacing nervously and rather sexily, wearing a gorgeous suit that clung to all his muscles in the right way.

He looked over at her and his face lit up. 'What are you doing here?'

'Take one guess.' She moved over to him and straightened his tie. 'You're wearing a suit, you said suits were only ever to be worn at weddings and funerals.'

'Well, I thought this was quite important too.'

'You look good.' She brushed a bit of sawdust off his shoulder. 'Really good. You know, I always wondered what you'd wear to our wedding, whether you'd be there in shorts and t-shirt which I see you in every day or whether you'd wear a suit. Not that I would have cared, you could have been wearing a dinosaur costume and I'd still be over the moon that you were there, ready to marry me.'

He looked down at her, his eyes soft. 'I'd have worn a suit for you.'

She stared up at him. 'To the wedding you never wanted.'

His eyes didn't waver from hers. 'I'd be lying if I said I never imagined what you would wear on our wedding day too.'

She frowned in confusion. 'You've thought about that?'

He nodded, reaching out to stroke a finger through a tendril of her hair. 'And whether you would wear your hair up or down, whether under the dress you'd still be wearing your beloved Converse.'

She swallowed a lump in her throat. 'I don't understand.'

'I know.'

Just then her phone rang in her pocket. She quickly grabbed it. 'Sorry, I need to get this. Shay is looking after Bones and I told him to call me if he dropped down below seven to give me a chance to get back.'

'Mr Harrison, Councillor Bishop will see you now,' the assistant said.

'OK, thanks,' Fletcher said, watching Fern in concern.

'Go and be fabulous,' Fern said and answered the phone.

'Fern,' Shay said, over the phone. 'Bones seems absolutely fine, we've just been playing with his tennis ball, but I've just checked his levels and he's gone down to five point one.'

'Oh my god, I'm on my way back now,' Fern said.

'Don't panic, if he drops any lower, I have a whole packet of digestive biscuits here and, as I said, he seems absolutely fine.'

She quickly hung up. 'Bones is at five point one,' Fern said, feeling like she was talking in some kind of code. 'Shay said he seems fine and they've just been playing with his ball. But the vet said he should be between five and fifteen and that if he drops below five we're to give him a biscuit or some kind of carby snack. And if he drops below four it's considered a hypo and we're to rub honey on the gums and give him another biscuit. Five point one is a bit too close to all that.'

'Agreed, let's go,' Fletcher said.

'No, you have your meeting, that's important.'

'You and Bones are the most important thing in the world to me.' He looked over at June. 'I'm sorry, I'll have to reschedule.'

He took Fern's hand and ran out of the office.

Fern's phone had rung twice from her bag on the back seat and Fletcher couldn't help thinking the worst as he drove them back to The Little Beach Hut Hotel. Fern didn't want to waste time stopping the car to retrieve her phone so he'd just kept driving. He pulled up in the car park as close as he could possibly get to Puffin Hut and they ran along the path towards it. Fletcher was quite surprised to see Shay sitting calmly next to Bones on the grass as Bones happily chewed on his ball.

'Is he OK?' Fern said, throwing herself onto her knees next to Bones.

'He's absolutely fine, I did try to call you. About a minute after we'd hung up, he went back up to seven and then nine a few minutes later. It must have been the fact that he was playing that caused him to drop.'

'Did you feed him?'

Shay shook his head. 'There was no need. You said we only need to intervene and feed him if he dropped below five and that didn't happen.'

Fern grabbed Shay's phone to check Bones's blood glucose level and Fletcher could see that he was already at ten point two.

'See, no need to worry,' Shay said, cheerily.

Clearly he didn't know that Fern had gone into full-blown panic mode and that Fletcher wasn't that far behind her. Was this what it would be like if he and Fern had children together, would they be constantly worrying over every bump and graze, every sniffle, every headache? Fletcher had always felt he was a laid-back man but Bones's diagnosis had proved his feathers could very easily get ruffled.

Fern buried her face into the top of Bones's head. 'You silly mutt, are you trying to give your mum a heart attack?'

Fletcher ruffled his ears and Bones licked his hand, wagging his tail and looking up at him with his big goofy smile that took up all of his face.

'Oh Fletcher, I'm so sorry I ruined your meeting for this silly great furball,' Fern said.

'It's not a problem. I'll head back over now and see if she can fit me in this afternoon.'

'But that meeting was important,' Fern said.

'You and the silly furball are important.'

She smiled at him. 'You're a wonderful dog dad, I'm sorry if it sounded like I didn't think that when I said you had to take responsibility for him.'

Shay cleared his throat awkwardly. 'I'm going to go and paint something.'

He got up and went back inside the hut.

'No, you were right, Bones is as much my responsibility as he is yours. No matter what happens between me and you, I'll always be there for Bones.'

She stood up and smiled sadly. 'There was a time you'd have said that about me.'

He felt that like a punch to the stomach. 'I'll always be there for you too, just not in a—'

Fern held her hand up. 'It's OK, I don't need to hear you say it again. It was painful enough the first time.'

Fletcher reached out for her. 'Fern—'

'Go and see Councillor Bishop. I'll see you later.'

With that she disappeared inside the beach hut too.

Fletcher looked down at Bones and sighed, stroking his massive velvety head. He was tired of trying to do the right thing, it hurt too damn much.

~

Fern had arranged to meet Orla and Ettie for a coffee after work although she was in no mood for socialising. She was tired from all the worry over Bones, she was exhausted from all the stress with Fletcher and she just felt so damned emotional all the time.

She walked into Seahorses with Bones and looked around. There was an elderly couple sitting in the corner sharing a cream tea, but the café was empty apart from them. Orla and Ettie were waiting for her in one of the booths. She slid into the chair opposite them, smiling at the oversized hot chocolate that was waiting for her with squirty cream and marshmallows on top.

'I thought you needed sustenance,' Orla said as Bones went to greet her friends.

Fern took a big sip. 'Thank you, I really needed that.'

'I'm so sorry to hear about Bones's diagnosis,' Ettie said, stroking his great big fluffy head.

'Thank you. It feels so scary and there's so much information to take on board. Fletcher has been helping me with it, which has been great, but I feel like I'm going to be worrying about Bones for the rest of his life.'

'It can't be easy but if you need anything, you can always rely on us,' Orla said.

Ettie nodded.

'Thank you.' Fern took another sip of the gorgeously creamy hot chocolate.

'How are things between you and Fletcher?' Ettie said.

'Lovely and awful at the same time. He has been so supportive with the whole Bones thing. We spent the night together last night on his boat just because he wanted to be there for me and Bones. But it's the strangest feeling of missing him so much and he's right there. It's obvious he loves me, which just makes the whole thing so infuriating. And then today he said something weird. ReLoved have had their funding cut so I went to talk to Councillor Bishop about it. Fletcher was there wearing a suit, so I talked about how I'd imagined him wearing a suit for our wedding day and he said he'd imagined what I would wear, what I'd do with my hair, what shoes I'd be wearing. Why is he imagining what I would wear to a wedding he never wants?'

'I'd imagine that, since this whole topic has come up, getting married to you has been uppermost in his mind, even if it's something he feels he can't offer,' Ettie said.

'I feel like there's something holding him back from taking that step with you,' Orla said.

'I agree. I think he's scared,' Ettie said. 'This came up the other day for an article I'm writing for the magazine: gamophobia is a fear of marriage most likely caused by a traumatic event.'

'I've heard of this too,' Orla said, a bit too quickly. 'Maybe Fletcher has suffered a traumatic event.'

Fern looked between the two of them with narrowed eyes. 'Do you two know something I don't?'

'Of course not,' Ettie said. 'We're just saying there is something going on here that is way beyond not wanting to get married. Have you spoken to him about why he's so anti-marriage?'

'I asked him this morning and he just said he doesn't believe in it.'

Ettie rolled her eyes. 'Ask him outright if he has a fear of marriage and see what he says.'

'I'm not sure knowing the whys will help. But I'm willing to try anything.'

CHAPTER TWENTY-ONE

Fletcher was just locking up ReLoved when he realised someone was behind him. He turned to see Theo standing there. Fletcher had been waiting for him to show up, knowing how unhappy he'd been when he and Fern got together in the first place. He was going to be pissed off now that Fletcher had broken Fern's heart.

'Have you come to beat me up for hurting your little sister?'

'I've considered it.'

'There's nothing you could do that would make me hurt more than I'm already hurting.'

Theo sighed. 'You're my friend and if I knew you'd broken up with someone you were completely head over heels in love with, I'd be round like a shot to see if you were OK. You breaking up with my little sister has made it a bit awkward for me.'

'I'm sorry about that,' Fletcher said, pointing to the picnic table. They both sat down opposite each other.

'I just meant that if I came to check on you after you

broke Fern's heart it would be disloyal to her. She also wouldn't thank me for interfering so I've been trying to keep out of it. I was also angry and I didn't want that anger to come between us. I came to see her last night and she wasn't there so I assumed you two had made up and she'd spent the night with you. And then I heard about Bones today and that you were helping her with him and a lot of that anger went away.'

'We did spend the night together, I held her in my arms as she was upset about Bones.'

Theo sighed. 'And there goes the rest of it. Despite my reservations when you two started dating you're the best thing to ever happen to her. The fact that you broke up with her because you thought, ultimately, she would be happier without you was actually a really decent thing to do, even if it was misguided. You're both hurting over this and I don't have any pearls of wisdom to share but if there's anything I can do to help you two get back together, then please let me know.'

Fletcher shook his head. 'I appreciate that but I just need to talk to her, explain everything and then take it from there. I'm going round to Fern's shortly to help her with Bones's injection and then we will talk.'

'OK, good. I'm still holding out hope that I get to give her away at your wedding.'

'I don't know if that will ever happen but there's a part of me that hopes for that too.'

~

Carrie had just finished making some cakes for her permanently hungry sons, and Fern of course, when there was a knock on the door. She smiled, knowing it was Antonio.

'Come in,' Carrie called as she took the cakes out of the oven.

'Mmm, they smell great,' Antonio said as he let himself in.

'They're too hot to eat right now but if you don't complain about anything today, I might just let you take one home.'

'That sounds like a good deal.' Antonio sat down. 'But actually, I came to see if you were OK after yesterday.'

'I am.' Carrie started making two cups of tea. 'I feel... cautiously optimistic about Fern and Fletcher. Her dog has sadly been diagnosed with diabetes and he's helping her with all the injections and everything. It's obvious he still loves her. How did it go when you spoke to him?'

'When I arrived I watched him for a while before he saw me, I have never seen a man so utterly broken before. He does love her very much, that was obvious. We had a chat and I put all the blame on you, I said that Fern felt like she had to go along with it.'

'That's good.'

'Yeah. He said something interesting though. He said he couldn't get married and, when I asked why, he said he's scared of letting her down.'

'Oh.' Carrie thought about this as she sat down, placing Antonio's mug in front of him. 'It sounds like the boy has some skeletons.'

'Don't we all, but some of us are better at keeping them locked away than others.'

'He needs to be brave enough to face his fears and he needs to talk to Fern about them so she can understand where he is coming from.'

'Well, I planted some seeds and now we have to see if they will grow,' Antonio said.

She held up her mug to chink against Antonio's. 'Cheers to that.'

～

Fern put Bones's food down on the floor for him and he snaffled it straight up. He seemed to be enjoying this new diabetic dog food just as much as his normal food but then Bones was always food motivated. Arthur had suggested waiting ten minutes after Bones ate before administering the injection just in case Bones was sick. Apparently injecting on an empty stomach was not a good thing so it was very important that Bones had eaten and kept it down. Ordinarily, Bones was never sick, but Fern didn't want to take any chances with this new diagnosis.

She checked on the petition for ReLoved while she was waiting. She'd set it up that morning and then shared it on the town forum's Facebook page. There had been lots of supportive comments on the Facebook post but that didn't necessarily mean those comments would result in a signature on the petition. She had to show Councillor Bishop that ReLoved was important to the town, much more so than a stupid statue or a painted bus stop.

She was delighted to see that the petition to keep the funding for ReLoved had already reached over six thousand signatures. That was more than the population of the town but she knew that it wasn't just the locals who used ReLoved, the impact of it stretched far and wide.

There was a knock on the door and Bones went

barrelling to it to greet whoever it was, though Fern knew it was probably Fletcher.

She opened the door and Bones burst out to greet the love of his life as if he hadn't seen Fletcher in months, not just a few hours.

Fletcher gave Bones lots of fuss and then turned his attention to Fern. 'Hey, I brought pizza.' He offered up the box and Fern smiled because without looking at it, she knew he would have brought her favourite, Hawaiian.

She also noticed he was carrying a small holdall and she wondered if he intended to spend the night with her again. Even platonically, she'd take it.

'Thanks,' she grabbed his hand excitedly, 'I have something to show you.' She tugged him inside and Bones bounced around them both. She pointed at the screen. 'Look.'

Fletcher bent over to look at her laptop. 'What's this?'

'It's a petition to save ReLoved. I set it up this morning and, look, it has over six thousand signatures already. You doubted that people would understand the importance of the work you and the other mentors do, but everyone can see your worth. These people want to save ReLoved as much as we do.'

Fletcher stared at it in wonder. 'That's... incredible.'

She watched him. '*You're* incredible.' He turned to face her. 'You're the most amazing man I've ever met and what you do for these people is wonderful. Clearly, I'm not the only person who thinks that.'

He stared at her. 'You see things in me I don't even see in myself.'

'Then it's about time you did. When we met, I didn't want

a relationship with anyone and then you came along and you were so kind, so sweet, so utterly lovely that I knew I would break all my rules for you. In the last few weeks we've been together, you exceeded every expectation I ever had for a loving relationship. You not only met the impossibly high bar I set for myself if I ever was to date someone, but you smashed through it. I felt so very lucky to have you in my life.'

He shook his head. 'No, I was the lucky one. You were so warm, so generous, you shone a light on my life so bright it was like a lighthouse in the storm. I love your passion and creativity, and your bravery and determination to leave your past behind you and make a life for yourself is an inspiration. I love you so much I feel my heart is full of you.'

She stared at him and swallowed the lump in her throat. 'And yet, here we are.'

He looked down, pushing his hand through his hair.

'Anyway.' Fern forced her voice to be bright. 'Let's have that pizza before it gets cold and then we can give Bones his injection.' She opened the box, enjoying the cheesy waft that immediately drifted out. She picked up a slice and took a big bite so she wouldn't have to speak.

Fletcher took a bite too then gestured to the laptop. 'Thank you for doing this for me.'

'It's no problem.'

Bones sat down between them, licking his lips as he looked adoringly at the pizza.

Her heart ached. 'God, this is so hard, I would always let Bones have the pizza crusts.'

'I was looking up what treats we could give him that won't affect his blood glucose levels. Cucumber is supposed to be good now and again and that fat-free Greek yoghurt we use for his licky mat, we could give him some of that.'

286

Fern grabbed a teaspoon and scooped a tiny bit of yoghurt on the end of the spoon and offered it out to Bones. He lapped it up but Fern still couldn't help feeling a little guilty that he wasn't getting pizza.

'Did you get to see Councillor Bishop?' Fern said, as she tucked into a second slice.

'Tomorrow morning,' Fletcher said.

'Well you can show her the petition. When she sees the number of people who want to support you, that will help you massively.'

'I hope so, I did see her briefly as she was running out to another meeting at the school. She said we need to find a way to be self-sufficient and I just don't know how we can do that. It's a lot of money to raise, the rent alone is huge.'

'You need something that brings you a steady regular income, but I—' She stopped as she looked around at the beach hut, an idea suddenly forming in her head. Could it work? Would Carrie even agree to it?

'What?'

'I don't know, an idea maybe.'

'Tell me.'

She shook her head. 'It's an unpopped kernel of popcorn right now, it needs some heat and time to… grow.'

'OK, can I help… with the heating or popping?'

'No, it might be nothing, give me a few days to figure it out.'

He nodded. 'OK.'

She tossed the uneaten crust back into the box. 'Right, let's do this injection.'

They persuaded Bones to lie down and she got the needle ready. Fletcher put the licky mat down in front of Bones and he started licking away at the yoghurt.

Fern took a big breath and injected him but, this time, Bones let out a little whimper of pain as the insulin went in.

'Oh god, I hurt him,' Fern said, pulling the needle out the second she had finished. Bones glanced round at her and the look he gave her was so doleful, as if he'd been punished, that the tears she had been suppressing all day poured down her cheeks. 'I'm so sorry, Bones.' She shuffled closer to him, stroking him and kissing him, soaking his fur with her tears.

'Hey, come on,' Fletcher said, pulling her against him for a hug. 'It's OK, it's only a little prick, like when he has his vaccinations. It was probably just a bit of a shock for him.'

'I hate this so much. I feel so sorry for him and I can't explain any of it to him. What must he be thinking?'

'He'll get used to it, it's just different for him. But it can't have hurt him that much. Maybe you just hit a sensitive spot.'

'Or maybe I did it wrong.'

'You definitely didn't do anything wrong, this isn't your fault, you're trying your best.'

Fern sat up and tried to wipe away her tears as Bones was already nudging her hand, concerned that she was clearly upset, but more tears just replaced them because it wasn't just Bones making her cry, this whole stupid situation with Fletcher was torture. 'You know, whenever I had a bad day, we would take a shower together and you would just hold me, and for some reason it made everything feel so much better and now we can't even do that.'

'Fern, I'm trying to do what's right for you.'

'This doesn't feel right. I still can't believe we're never going to kiss again, never going to make love, never going to walk hand in hand along Blackberry Beach, never have the children we both wanted so much.' She wiped away the tears again. 'I feel like I'm grieving and it's the worst feeling in the world. And now with Bones...' she shook her head. 'Maybe you shouldn't come round any more. My life hasn't been a bed of roses but getting over you is going to be the hardest thing I've ever done. I can't even begin to move on when you're always here, being so bloody lovely. So take the next few days off. I'll be fine on my own. I had thirteen years on my own, so I can do it again. I'll drop Bones round to you on Saturday so you can spend some time with him then.'

Fletcher reached out for her. 'Fern, let me explain—'

'I don't want to hear why we can't be together. I'm going for a shower. Please be gone by the time I come out.'

She went upstairs, undressed and walked into the shower, turning on the spray so it pounded over her head, letting her tears fall and get washed away. She shampooed her hair and was just rinsing it out when there was a noise behind her. She turned and there was Fletcher standing just in his shorts. They stared at each other for a while and then, without a word, he walked under the shower head with her and wrapped his arms around her. She stood frozen for a second and then slid her arms around him, leaning her head against his chest. The tears that had stopped bubbled to the surface again and she cried against him. He stroked her head. This was everything she needed right now. It wasn't sexual – whenever they'd done this in the past, it had very rarely led to sex – but it was much more intimate than that. It was mediative and restorative and a tangible representation of the deep bond they shared. She knew she would never have this with anyone else.

After they had stood there for a while, long enough for the tears to have stopped and probably long enough for their fingers to go all pruney, she looked up at him.

He pushed the hair from her face and gave her the

briefest of kisses on her lips. It was nothing more than a peck and she certainly didn't think it was going to lead to something more, but then he frowned and she immediately recognised that look. Her heart leapt as he cupped her face, his mouth hovering over hers.

'I'm not a saint Fern, Christ I wish I was,' Fletcher said, then he kissed her hard, as if she was the air he needed to breathe.

She kissed him back with a desperate need. She didn't know what this meant, whether he wanted to get back together or if it was just a blip, but she didn't care, she ached for him. She ran her hands over his back and when he slid his hands over her breasts she let out a noise that was primal. He moved his hand between her legs and she quickly pushed his shorts off his hips, wrapping a hand around him and gasping at how much he clearly needed her. It was only a matter of moments before she was crying out, clinging to him, her legs shaking so much that if he hadn't been holding her she would have crumpled to the floor. Before she could even catch her breath, he lifted her and, as she clasped her arms and legs around him, he was inside her a second later. She let out a sob, desperate to feel this connection between them. He kissed her hard as he moved deep inside her, he wrapped an arm around her bum supporting her, holding her tighter against him, while his other hand tangled in her hair. She was aware of that feeling bubbling up again, her whole body alive with love so that it lit her up, igniting her from the inside. She pulled back slightly to look at him, tracing her thumb across his lips, staring into his eyes as he took her higher and higher until she soared over the edge, shouting out his name, clinging to him as that feeling ripped through her so hard, she could hardly breathe.

She was aware of him turning the water off, grabbing a towel and wrapping it around her as he carried her through to the bedroom and laid her on the bed. And then he was over her, inside her, kissing her, consuming her, so her only thought was him and how he was touching her, making her heart sing.

Impossibly, that feeling started building again, filling her veins, filling every part of her with a blissful warmth, and as he pulled back to look at her, she stroked his face.

'I love you,' Fern said.

He kissed her hard and then he was falling over the edge and taking her with him.

CHAPTER TWENTY-TWO

Fern woke to an empty bed but could hear Fletcher clattering around in the kitchen. There was no sign of Bones either. She grabbed one of Fletcher's shirts hanging in the wardrobe and pulled it on, doing up a few cursory buttons. She caught her reflection in the mirror on the way out the bedroom: her hair was a wild bush, her lips were swollen and her eyes were bright; she looked like she'd been ravaged. She went down the stairs and had the satisfaction of seeing Fletcher pause with his mug halfway to his mouth as he stared at her.

'You're wearing my shirt,' he said, his voice rough.

'I am, but if you don't like it, I can take it off,' Fern said, innocently, undoing one of the buttons.

'No, I don't have the time to deal with the incredible fall-out of what will happen once you're standing naked in front of me. I have my meeting with Councillor Bishop in half an hour.'

'Oh god, no you can't miss that again,' Fern said, noticing he was wearing his suit trousers and a shirt. 'Give me a few minutes and I can come with you. I can show her the petition.'

'OK. I've fed and injected Bones.'

She looked at her watch. 'God, you should have woken me.'

'It's OK, I figured you needed the sleep,' he said, a smirk playing on his lips.

'You're looking very satisfied with yourself this morning,' Fern said.

'I had no intention of ending the evening that way when I stepped in the shower with you, but Christ I'm glad that it did.' He downed the rest of his coffee. 'Listen, we need to talk about last night, about—'

'Insanely hot shower sex?'

'Yes, that.'

'About how you took me like a crazed wild animal?'

His eyes widened. 'Was I that bad?'

'You were that good. It was hot as hell. And for the record I have no regrets.'

He stared at her. 'Well, we need to talk about all that, about us, about why I've been so reluctant to get married, the wedding dress—' he gestured to the dress still hanging on the banister. She hadn't had the heart to return it yet.

'We don't need to talk about the wedding dress, we can put that down to a moment of madness,' Fern said.

'We do need to talk about it, about all of it, and I have some things I need to tell you but not now. Will you have lunch with me today? We can meet at Blackberry Beach around one? I'll bring those crab sandwiches from Claws that you like so much.'

'OK.' She watched him, standing on the other side of the kitchen to her. She wanted to cross the gap and kiss him but she had no idea where she stood. 'I'll, umm... go and get changed.'

She went back upstairs, had a quick wash and threw on some more appropriate clothes, then went back downstairs to find Fletcher now sporting a tie and shrugging on his suit jacket.

'What do you want to do about Bones?' Fletcher asked.

Fern quickly checked the dog's glucose levels on her phone. 'I'll leave him here for now and text Shay to come and get him, he'll be arriving shortly anyway to finish painting Puffin Hut.'

They gave Bones an abundance of fuss and had started walking down towards the town when suddenly a woman stepped out of one of the shops in front of them. Her eyes widened as she stared at Fletcher.

'Fletcher?'

Fletcher stopped dead and Fern watched as the colour drained from his face.

Fletcher finally found his voice. 'Lauren?'

'Yeah, hi.'

'What are you doing here?'

'My aunt died so I'm here for her funeral.'

'Oh god, I'm so sorry.'

Lauren shrugged. 'We were never that close but as the woman did raise me for most of my life, I thought I'd better pay my respects.'

Fletcher looked at Fern as if he wanted to be anywhere else but here. He turned back to Lauren. 'I can't believe you're here. It's been years. How are you?'

'Good, things are good. Better than they were anyway.'

Fletcher nodded. 'That's good.'

Fern cringed at how painfully awkward this was. She had

no idea who this woman was but it felt like Lauren and Fletcher were the last people that they each wanted to see.

Fletcher clearly decided it was time to do the introductions, which Fern was grateful for; she was feeling a little like a spare part right now.

'Umm... This is Fern, my ... friend.'

Fern winced. After what they had shared the night before, to hear herself described as only a friend hurt a lot more than it should.

'This is Lauren.'

But who Lauren was to him was clearly deliberately left unsaid. Even Lauren, it seemed, was waiting for Fletcher to explain their connection. When he didn't she was happy to fill in the gaps.

'I'm his ex-wife.'

Fern felt as if she had been punched in the stomach, the air leaving her lungs in one harsh breath. Fletcher closed his eyes as if in pain at those words.

'Your ex-wife?' Fern croaked.

'I can explain,' Fletcher said. 'I was going to tell you.'

'It's true? How can it be true? How can you not have told me you'd been married before?'

'It was very short-lived,' Lauren said.

Fern stared at her in horror and then turned back to Fletcher, disappointment, anger, sadness all vying for control. She needed to get out of here.

'I should go,' she said. 'I have stuff to do.'

'No, wait,' Fletcher started.

'No, I'm sure you have lots to catch up on with your *ex-wife*.'

Fern turned and moved away.

'So who's that?' she heard Lauren say.

295

'Just the love of my life,' Fletcher said, which ordinarily would have made her feel warm inside but now it felt like a lie. How could they love each other and not know everything about each other?

She hurried off down the hill, feeling her heart breaking inside.

~

Lauren had disappeared almost as quickly as Fern had and Fletcher was left watching the threads of his life unravel faster than he could hold them together. The frustrating thing was that he had been planning to tell Fern everything the night before, but then Fern had got upset and comforting her had turned into amazing sex and there hadn't been the time to slip it into the conversation. He'd hoped to tell her everything at lunch, but now it looked like meeting Lauren had forced his hand.

He wanted to go after Fern, explain everything, but he knew she'd be too angry to listen right now. He just hoped she'd show up for lunch as planned and then he could talk to her.

With his head in turmoil, he made his way to the council offices but as he rounded the corner he could see a giant elephant sculpture in front of the entrance. He immediately recognised it as one of Leo's. As he got closer he realised Leo was handcuffed to it, holding a placard saying, 'Save ReLoved'. Another placard strapped to the side of the sculpture declared, 'We shall not be moved'.

It certainly made a statement.

'Leo, what are you doing?'

'I'm protesting,' Leo said, a big grin on his face that said he was loving every minute of it.

'Well, I can see that. Aren't you supposed to be at the exhibition in Plymouth?'

'The gallery is closed Tuesdays, so thought I'd make use of my day off today. Although don't tell anyone in there, I've promised them I'm staying until they agree to save ReLoved even if it takes all week. I'm hoping it will be resolved this afternoon. I've called the local news station, they're going to send a camera crew down here later to film my protest and try to get a statement from Councillor Bishop.'

'Wow Leo, how did you even get this here?' The elephant was at least twelve-foot high.

'I have my means.'

Fletcher looked up at the council building to see a few faces staring at Leo pressed against the windows. Councillor Bishop was not going to like this, especially having Apple Hill Bay appearing on the news in any kind of negative light. But could it influence her decision or could it end up working against them?

'I really appreciate this but I'm not sure this is a good idea,' Fletcher said.

'We have to be loud otherwise they won't hear us.'

'Fair point. I have my meeting now with Councillor Bishop,' Fletcher said.

'Good luck, give her my regards,' Leo smiled sweetly.

'I will.'

Fletcher went inside, hoping the councillor wouldn't hold this against him.

Fern hadn't been able to face going to see Councillor Bishop knowing that Fletcher was going to be there too. She decided she'd email the councillor with a link to the petition instead. So she stopped off at Orla's café to get some croissants for her and Shay. Her head was buzzing. How could Fletcher have been married and never mentioned it to her? And was this the reason he was so anti-marriage? Or was it that he'd loved Lauren and nothing would compare to that?

The café was thankfully quiet, the morning rush of dog-walkers and hikers hadn't arrived yet. There was only one elderly man sitting in the corner with his dog as Orla laid out all the cakes and pastries in the glass cabinets.

'Hey, can I have two croissants please?' Fern said. She wasn't sure if she wanted to talk about what had just happened, because she couldn't even begin to get her head around it.

'Sure, is this for you and Shay?'

'Yes, I'm starting work on a new hut but Shay will still be hard at work finishing off Puffin Hut so I doubt he'll make it here today.'

Fern couldn't help noticing that Orla looked a little disappointed at this. She'd long thought that Shay had a little crush on her best friend but she hadn't realised those feelings were reciprocated.

'Well, take him two then, my treat,' Orla said, adding a third croissant to the bag.

This had suddenly got interesting.

'Are you OK, you seem a bit... pissed off?' Orla said.

Fern sighed. 'I am pissed off. I've just found out Fletcher was married before he met me.'

'What?' Orla abandoned the bag of croissants and moved back to where Fern was standing. 'When?'

'I don't know. I guess several years ago.'

'Did he tell you?'

'No, we just met his ex-wife,' Fern said.

'Oh my god, that's how you found out?'

'Yeah. I just can't believe he would keep something that big from me. I know we haven't been dating for long but how did it never come up? Why wouldn't he tell me?'

'I don't know, that feels a bit...'

'Duplicitous, deceitful.'

'It just doesn't feel like something Fletcher would do,' Orla said. 'I guess he had his reasons. And I guess we shouldn't judge until we know all the facts. What were the circumstances of the marriage: how long were they together, why did they split up?'

'I don't know. I stormed off as soon as I found out.' Fern rubbed her face. 'And I was rude to her, I barely even acknowledged her, and it's not her fault Fletcher never told me.'

'It's kind of understandable. But you should probably talk to him,' Orla said, gently.

'Urgh, why are you so sensible and level-headed?'

Orla laughed. 'I am the water to your fire. That's why you love me.'

Fern grunted her disapproval though she knew Orla was right.

'I didn't come in here for practical advice, I was hoping you would shout and swear at him with me.'

'Well, it is a bit of a dick move.'

'Is that the best you've got?'

Orla shrugged. 'Sorry. I don't have it in me. And Fletcher is too nice.'

Fern sighed. 'We're supposed to be meeting for lunch. I guess I could go and talk to him then.'

'I think he owes you an explanation. Then you can decide whether you still need to be angry at him.'

'Fine. You better give me one of those chocolate chip muffins too and I'll decide whether he deserves it or not.'

'That's the kind of revenge I can get on board with. Take it out the bag to show him what he could have won. And if you still think he's an arse, put it back in the bag again and take it with you.'

'Now that is cruel.'

Carrie had just got off the phone from taking a booking from a customer. Word was spreading already and they hadn't had the official opening yet.

She turned round to see Antonio walking up her garden path so she immediately went and put the kettle on, then waved him in before he had a chance to knock.

'I have no complaints today,' Antonio said, sitting down.

'Really, none?'

'Nope.'

'Then you have to try harder.'

He grinned. 'I was in the area so I thought I'd pop by and you could give me a tour of the finished huts.'

She looked at him suspiciously. 'Why?'

'Well, because I'm running out of things to complain about so I thought a tour would give me more ammunition.'

She laughed and plonked a mug of tea down in front of him. 'You'll have lots to complain about after the opening on

Saturday, the noise and rubbish for one. Maybe you should go out of town that night.'

'I wouldn't miss it for the world.'

They stared at each other and Antonio cleared his throat awkwardly, focussing on the tea. He took a sip and frowned. 'No sugar.'

'You don't like sugar in your tea. I only put it in to annoy you.'

'Is that so? Well, maybe our little meetings have given me a taste for it.'

Just then the door was flung open and Fern walked in, stopping as soon as she saw Antonio. 'God, I'm so sorry. I didn't mean to interrupt anything. I can come back later.'

'No need, I was just going anyway, the tea here is substandard,' Antonio said.

Carrie laughed and he gave her a wink as he walked out the door.

Fern watched him go. 'Sorry, I didn't realise you had anyone here.'

'It's not a problem. I'm sure he'll be back tomorrow.'

Fern studied her. 'Is there something going on between you two?'

Carrie paused. 'You know, I'm not entirely sure. What can I do for you anyway? You came in here like a woman on a mission.'

'Well, as you know, we've been talking to Councillor Bishop about ReLoved and although she thinks she might be able to rejig the town council funding so ReLoved can continue to be funded for another year, she keeps harping on about them being self-sufficient and that's not easy for the nature of the business. So, I had an idea. It involves you and The Little Beach Hut Hotel so feel free to tell me where to stick it, or if you wanted to take some time to think about it that's fine too, but I don't want you to feel any pressure to say yes. I've not even mentioned it to Fletcher yet so if it's a no, that's fine.'

'Come on, out with it,' Carrie said with a laugh, gesturing for Fern to sit down.

Fern took a seat. 'I had the idea that Fletcher and the mentors could each design and build their own beach hut here at The Little Beach Hut Hotel. The huts will be in keeping with the ReLoved theme of using recycled materials and furniture so each one would be completely different while still keeping the basic footprint of your beach hut designs. And then the money made from renting each one could go towards ReLoved. Obviously we would have to arrange a fee to go to you to cover ground rent or utilities, or say a twenty-five percent cut, but this way they have created something that will give a regular income.'

Carrie thought about it for a moment, weighing out the pros and cons as she drank her tea. 'It's a clever idea. I've got planning permission for fifty huts on top of the ten I built last year but I decided to only build thirty to start and then I could decide on the best place for the other twenty based on the feedback from the guests. We could easily add another five huts now – well, after the launch – and being made from recycled furniture will give them a unique selling point. And yes, we can work out a fee to cover the bills but I don't need to take a cut. I like it. It will help people who work at ReLoved on the road to self-sufficiency and it means they can concentrate on what makes ReLoved so wonderful. I'm happy to go ahead. Do you want to tell Fletcher or shall I?'

Fern pulled a face. 'I think, as this is a business transaction between you and him, you should tell him, then you can stipulate any conditions you feel necessary without my relationship with him getting in the way.'

'OK, I can do that. How are things going between you two?'

Fern sighed. 'Your guess is as good as mine. We... spent the night together last night, intimately, and he wanted to meet for lunch so we could discuss... us, but then we were walking through town together this morning and ran into his ex-wife.'

Carrie choked on her tea. 'His what?'

'Yes, you heard right. Apparently Fletcher was married in the past, something he never mentioned to me, and now I just... don't know where we stand.'

Carrie stared at Fern in shock. 'Christ, in all of this I never saw that coming.'

'Me neither. I need to talk to him.'

'Well.' Carrie let out a heavy breath. 'I'm having second thoughts about this offer for ReLoved now.'

Fern shook her head. 'Don't. This has nothing to do with that. This town, the people, it needs ReLoved. Regardless of what happens between me and Fletcher, it doesn't take anything away from what he and his team do up there.'

Carrie nodded. 'You're right. I will go and talk to him on a professional basis.'

'Thank you. Right, I better go, I have a lot of painting to do.'

'Yes, no slacking.'

Fern stood up and gave her a hug. 'See you later.'

Carrie watched her go and sighed. She needed to put her professional hat on and talk to Fletcher – and somehow not interfere in her daughter's relationship.

CHAPTER TWENTY-THREE

Fletcher paced at the bottom of the steps to Blackberry Beach, wondering if Fern would come or if he needed to go and find her. He didn't want her to turn up at the beach and him not to be there because he really needed to talk to her. If she didn't show in five minutes he would go and look for her. He should have told her about his marriage before now; by hiding it from her he had made it a much bigger thing than it needed to be.

But bang on one o'clock Fern appeared at the end of the tunnel. She looked at him warily as she reached the last few steps. He offered out his hand but she refused to take it.

'I didn't know if you'd come,' Fletcher said.

'I didn't know if I'd come either. I can't believe you wouldn't tell me about this.'

He gestured to the picnic blanket and she sat down. He sat down next to her feeling like he was suddenly on the verge of losing everything. He offered the sandwich he'd bought for her but she shook her head.

'My stomach has been churning all day thinking about

you hiding this from me and why. I'm not sure I could eat anything right now.'

'I was going to tell you last night but... things got in the way, so I planned to tell you at lunch today. I know my hand has been forced because we bumped into Lauren but that's what I meant when I said I had things to tell you this morning. I should have told you a long time ago and I'm so sorry I didn't. When we first started dating, I never told you because I didn't want you to hate me. Everything was so perfect with us that I didn't want to ruin it with my baggage. When I realised how much I loved you, I was scared I would lose you if you knew, and it became harder and harder to bring it up as the weeks passed. I was a coward and I convinced myself that as it didn't impact on us then maybe you didn't need to know. But of course it impacted on us. Every time I thought about marrying you, my marriage to Lauren came back to haunt me and I couldn't do it. You deserve to know why and I'm going to tell you everything.'

'Why would I hate you? I don't care that you've been married in your past. We all have baggage, god I have a ton of it. But I do care that you kept it from me.'

'I didn't tell you because... I was an awful husband and a terrible person. There is nothing I can say about that part of my life that won't make me sound like a complete dick.'

'I think you better tell me something. Finding out that the man who never wanted marriage was married before is raising all kind of questions in my head. Like, perhaps you loved her more than you love me.'

'I never loved Lauren, not for one second. Christ, I was seventeen when I met her and a complete twat. The only thing I thought about was sex and getting drunk. There was always a big group of us that would hang out in the parks or try to get served in the pubs and clubs. My mate started dating this girl called Olive and Lauren was her best friend so she became part of our group too. I didn't really know her or take the time to get to know her, she was just there and we'd chat now and again about nothing. My eighteenth birthday was the day before hers and on her birthday she had a big party in her house and decided we should both celebrate together. She was flirting with me all night, making it very obvious she wanted to sleep with me. And thinking with my dick, I was happy to oblige. It was just a drunken shag, it meant absolutely nothing and I thought she felt the same. It was no secret she was sleeping with a different boy every week. But after she... cried. She said she'd never had someone be so kind to her during sex before. Every other man had been a quick shag and left. I took my time with her and she thought that meant I loved her. She said she always knew I liked her, but she didn't realise I liked her that much.'

'Did you like her?' Fern said.

'No, and I know that makes me sound like scum, but I had no interest in her at all. It was just sex. I was a complete arsehole at that age. My actions when I slept with her certainly weren't out of love. I was just... She was drunk, we both were, and I just wanted to make sure she was OK, that I wasn't taking advantage of her, so I kept things nice and slow, kept checking to see if she was happy with what I was doing.'

Fern gave a sad little smile. 'You were respectful and considerate, just like you were the first time we made love.'

He frowned. 'What you and I shared that first time was nothing like it was with any other woman I'd been with before. I was completely in love with you, though I don't think I knew it at the time. But I thought you were incredible, still do actually. I wanted you to feel what I felt for you when we made love. I might have been respectful when I was with Lauren but that was only because I know how big I am and I never ever want a woman to feel threatened or intimidated when she's with me. She saw it as something else and told everyone we were dating. She became really clingy. But I wasn't interested in having a relationship with anyone at that point and her clinginess made me want to get even further away from her. God, I was such a shitbag.'

He sighed, pushing his hand through his hair.

'I used protection when we slept together – I might have been a drunken, eighteen-year-old fuck-up, but I know I used a condom – but a few weeks later, she's knocking on my door telling me she's pregnant. Being a selfish prick, all I could think about was how this was going to ruin my life. I had plans and being a dad wasn't part of them. She wanted us to get married and her aunt was pushing me to do the right thing. My parents were telling me not to be so stupid and throw my life away but I knew I had to be responsible for her and my baby. Not even a week after we got married she lost the baby and I felt... relieved. It was all over, I could go back to my own life. How shitty is that? I felt bad for Lauren because she'd been really upset when she lost the baby but I soon realised it wasn't because of the baby but because she knew I would leave her. She'd had a difficult childhood. Her dad had walked out on her eighth birthday, her mum hated her because of it, and she'd ended up living with her aunt who was less than thrilled. And—'

'For the first time in her life someone had been kind to her and she clung onto that with both hands,' Fern said. 'I know how that feels.'

'Yeah, and then I let her down too. She thought we'd be

together forever, she wanted to try again for another baby. She said that this time the baby would definitely be mine.'

'What?'

'Yeah, I was shocked by that too. Apparently she had slept with another guy the night before she slept with me, and another man a few days before that. Lots of her friends had teased her about how she knew who the father was, but she said she knew it was mine. It had to be. I felt like I'd been conned. I moved out and told her I wanted a divorce. She told me she would never divorce me but my parents were good friends with a lawyer and she said there was a good chance I could get the marriage annulled as we had never consummated it after the marriage, and because it was likely Lauren was pregnant with another man's child at the time we had got married. With an annulment we didn't have to wait a year before we started divorce proceedings. We started going through the annulment process but Lauren would phone me ten, twenty times a day, she'd come round to my house every day, beg me to take her back. She'd turn up at my work. She was even arrested trying to break into my house. When my cousin, who was working out in Tenerife, offered me a job, I jumped at the chance to get away from it all.'

'For her to see a future in a relationship that was pretty much non-existent, she must have been so desperate,' Fern said.

Fletcher rubbed his hand across his face. 'She was going through hell. I didn't see it, I didn't want to see it. I just thought once I'd gone, she'd move on. We'd never had any real relationship, we'd barely even seen each other in the weeks leading up to the wedding. I didn't realise how badly she was coping with the loss of this perfect happy future she'd planned out in her head. I was having the time of my life in Tenerife but after I had been out there for five or six weeks, my mum called me to say that Lauren had tried to kill herself, she'd taken an overdose...' The guilt clawed at his insides.

'Oh shit, Fletcher.'

'I know, I felt like scum. I'd made this all about me and what I wanted and needed, and I never stopped to see what Lauren needed. Maybe I should have tried harder to make our marriage work. I'd made a commitment to her and that was something to take seriously. But I abandoned her just like everyone else in her life. Although I found out later this hadn't been the first attempt on her life, she'd tried a few years before we'd even met, so she'd obviously been struggling with her mental health for a while. But it gutted me that I was the trigger for that time.'

'It wasn't your fault.'

'Of course it was. She was standing on the bridge ready to jump and I drove straight past, pretended it wasn't my problem. I should have been there to support her, instead I was getting drunk every night in a completely different country. I ran away.'

'You didn't know, you can't blame yourself.'

Fletcher shook his head. He had lived with the guilt of what had happened for the last twelve years.

'I flew straight home. I went to the hospital and Lauren was basically being kept alive by machines. The image of her hooked up to all those tubes and wires still haunts me to this day. They didn't think she was going to make it. It was touch and go for about a week before she finally started to get better. Her aunt gave me hell, she said I was the worst thing that ever happened to Lauren and I knew she was right.

Apparently she had been drinking herself into a stupor pretty much every day.'

He sighed heavily.

'When she was finally fit enough to leave the hospital, we got her some counselling but then her aunt said I needed to leave her alone otherwise she'd get attached again and it would be worse when I inevitably left her when the annulment finally came through. But I'd already walked away from her once, I wasn't going to do that again. I told her that although nothing was ever going to happen between us I would always be there for her as a friend. We stayed in touch for a few months. I met with her a few times a week. She seemed to be doing OK and she accepted that we were friends, she wasn't flirty or clingy any more, we were just mates. She seemed... less, though. Not the same Lauren as she was before.'

He fiddled with the sleeve of his shirt. 'As soon as the annulment came through she moved abroad and broke contact with me after that. Her aunt said she was fine and needed to be left alone. She refused to give me any contact details and I never saw her again. But I did hear a few years ago that she was married so I hope that she found some happiness. I was hoping to chat to her today just to see if she was OK but she ran off almost as quickly as you did.'

Fern stared at him for the longest time. 'Is that why you don't want to get married?'

He swallowed. 'I was a terrible husband, I wasn't there to support Lauren when she needed it the most. I ran away at the first sign of trouble. Why would you want to marry me after hearing that? I was a self-centred prick. I broke her.'

Fern shook her head. 'You were a boy and mental health is not something they ever teach in schools, what to look for

310

or how to help someone. And it was never a real marriage, you married out of duty not out of love.'

'What difference does that make? I made a commitment to her, to look after her in sickness and in health, and I walked away from that in less than a week. What kind of husband would I be for you?'

'An incredible one. Because when you love someone you move heaven and earth to be there for them. Something I've seen these past few days with Bones. I'm not saying you couldn't have done more to help her, but most boys your age would not have married Lauren in the first place. Most boys would not have come back from living the highlife in sunny Tenerife to help her. Most boys would not have stood by her as a friend while she received counselling. And most boys would not have carried this guilt around with them for the last twelve years for something that really wasn't your fault.'

Fletcher stared at her in confusion. He'd just told her what a shitty husband he'd been and Fern was still staring at him as if he was some kind of hero.

'I think, with me, your rose-tinted glasses are firmly on.'

She reached across the mat and took his hand. 'Fortunately for you, I'm in love with the man you are now, not the boy you were twelve years ago. I think it's time you let go of the guilt. If you don't want to get married, then don't, but don't let this burden of your past hold you back from embracing your future.'

She handed him a paper bag but held onto it as he went to take it. 'Any more secrets or skeletons in cupboards I should know about?'

'God no, a secret ex-wife was more than enough,' Fletcher said.

'Then you can have this.'

He opened up the bag to see one of Orla's double chocolate chip muffins. He looked at Fern in confusion.

'I was only going to give you that if I was happy with your answer.'

He felt like he was in some weird twilight zone. He had been holding onto this secret for so long, so afraid that Fern would hate him for the way he'd treated Lauren, but not only was she telling him she still loved him but she'd given him a cake.

She stood up. 'I have to go. Carrie will probably unadopt me if I don't finish these huts in time for the big opening. I'll take my sandwich though, I'm not wasting that.'

He handed her the bag. 'What happens now?'

'That's entirely up to you. I love you, I still want that future with you. If you feel you want that future with me, marriage or not, you know where I am.'

She leaned down and kissed him on the cheek and hope bloomed in his heart.

She moved away but he snagged her hand. 'Come to mine tonight, if you want. I'll cook and I can help you with the injection.'

'OK.'

'And… you could stay, if you want. Makes it easier to inject Bones together tomorrow if you stay.'

She frowned. 'Let's be clear what this is. If you mean stay where I spend the whole night looking at your back so you don't have to look at me then no, I'd rather sleep alone. If you're inviting me to stay so you can ravage me again, then hell yes, I'll stay.'

He stood up and put his hands on her shoulders. 'Then let's be really clear. If you come to mine tonight we will chat about us and our future and that wedding dress I'm so desperate to see.'

He heard her breath hitch.

'And after I will take you to bed and make love to you in a way that will leave no doubt at all about how I feel for you.'

She stared at him in shock and then nodded. 'Then I'll see you tonight.'

She took a step back and then another and he was so desperate to kiss her, to hold her close, but they needed to talk first and there wasn't time to do that now.

She waved and disappeared up the steps. He watched her go and couldn't help the huge smile that spread across his face. He grabbed the blanket and his cake and quickly made his way back to ReLoved. He had work to do.

Fletcher had just finished showing Lana how to create a dovetail joint when he looked up to see Carrie standing in the doorway.

'Will you be OK here for a bit?' he said to Lana. 'George is over there if you need any help.'

'Sure, I'm fine.'

Fletcher went over to greet Carrie. 'Hi, is everything all right?'

'Yes, I'd like a word with you, if you can spare the time,' Carrie said, but there was an undertone to her words that made him think he was in trouble. Carrie was always so lovely to him, but he supposed he deserved her wrath after this week.

'Is this about Fern?'

'I'm not here to talk about you and Fern, even though I'd

like to give you a good shaking. I'm here in a professional capacity.'

This threw Fletcher. 'Oh well, shall we chat outside?'

He guided her to the picnic bench outside and they sat down.

'I was concerned to hear that ReLoved might be in trouble,' Carrie said.

'We all are. I spoke to Councillor Bishop this morning and she doesn't know if they can extend the funding for us. They are having a meeting later today to discuss it but she said it may be that they only cover the rent for the barn and some of the bills, not the salaries of the mentors, we will have to be self-sufficient to cover those. I'm not sure what we can do.'

'Well, that's what I'm here about. Fern came to me this morning with a rather clever idea. She has suggested that you and the other mentors each design and build a beach hut for The Little Beach Hut Hotel, so five huts in total. You can use old bits of furniture or reclaimed materials but it has to be in keeping, size-wise, with the design specifications of the other huts as that's what I have planning permission for. Any income that then comes from renting those huts out will belong to ReLoved.'

Fletcher stared at her, excitement blooming in his chest as he thought about this. 'Are you serious? This is a wonderful opportunity. The mentors will love doing this and the apprentices can help them too.'

'It's got to look pretty, it can't be thrown together.'

'No absolutely not, everyone here at ReLoved takes great pride in their work.'

Carrie nodded. 'Eventually, when the huts are up and

running, we'll have to discuss a fee to cover the utilities and a few other expenses.'

'Yes of course.'

'I charge fifty-five pounds a night or three hundred and fifty pounds a week. So far the huts that are in use are pretty much booked out for the whole year and I expect the same for the new ones, but there are quieter periods. You'll probably be looking at an income of around fifteen to eighteen thousand a year for each hut.'

'That's amazing, that'll more than cover the salaries for the mentors.'

'If the huts prove popular, there may be the option to add a couple more huts in a few years too,' Carrie said.

'This is really generous and it gives us all a wonderful project to work on, too.'

'Your huts will have a unique selling point as they will look quirky and different to the others. When people stay here, it will be a focal point too. But this is a big project and it needs to be done right, I can't have leaky roofs for the sake of something artistic.'

'No of course not, I'll oversee each of the huts myself. Thank you for this, it's really kind—'

Carrie held up a hand to stop him. 'It's Fern's idea because, despite your relationship problems this week, she put ReLoved above all of that. She's a kind, generous and wonderful woman.'

'She absolutely is all of those things, that's why I love her.'

'I promised myself I wouldn't interfere but you'll be making the biggest mistake of your life if you let her go.'

Fletcher nodded. 'I know. I was trying to do the right thing for her but it wasn't my decision to make. I cocked up spectacularly when I broke up with her and you have no idea how much I regret hurting her in that way. I'm seeing her tonight and I'm...' he paused, changing what he was going to say. He didn't want to mention what he'd been doing that afternoon. 'We're going to talk about our future.'

Carrie gave a little smile, then it vanished. 'Finding out you had a secret ex-wife is quite an obstacle to overcome. But if she can forgive you for that, I'd say there's still hope for you two yet.'

Fletcher nodded. He had hope now, whereas before he had none. He just hoped that with all of his mistakes this past week, Fern was now on the same page.

CHAPTER TWENTY-FOUR

Bones's injection had been a success, Fletcher's lovingly cooked meal had been eaten and Fern was sitting on his deck looking out over the water.

Fletcher had the local news playing on his laptop as he sat next to Fern. He hadn't heard anything from Councillor Bishop to indicate whether they'd agreed to extend the funding but a news crew had turned up at ReLoved earlier in the afternoon, interviewed him and some of the others and then gone down to the council buildings to film Leo's protest. Leo had texted him a few hours before saying Councillor Bishop had made a statement to the news crew just after five thirty and that Fletcher needed to watch the news.

The newscaster introduced the story and then passed over to a reporter standing outside ReLoved as she explained the story, which sounded a lot more dramatic than perhaps it was.

Fern took his hand as she watched it and he loved that she wanted this for ReLoved as much as he did.

Fletcher appeared on the screen and he cringed, hoping he came across well when he'd had no time to prepare.

'That was really good,' Fern said as the report showed interviews with other mentors and apprentices. 'It was very honest, heartfelt and succinct.'

The report cut to Leo handcuffed to his brilliant sculpture as he chatted about how ReLoved had changed his life. Finally the report showed Councillor Bishop coming out the main entrance to make a statement. She looked like she had been born to stand in front of a news crew and Fletcher suspected that she was enjoying her ten seconds of fame, despite the circumstances.

'ReLoved is a very important and much loved part of our community,' Councillor Bishop started. 'It has been completely invaluable in providing skills and opportunities to hundreds of people since we set it up two years ago.'

'We?' Fern said, indignantly.

'She can take all the credit she wants if she extends the funding,' Fletcher said.

Fern grunted her disapproval. 'Everyone in Apple Hill Bay knows where it started anyway.'

Councillor Bishop continued talking. 'The original funding was for two years but it was never our intention to close ReLoved down and it was a priority item to discuss in our budget meeting today.'

'I bet it was after Leo invited the news crew down there,' Fern muttered.

'I'm pleased to announce that funding for this brilliant project has now been confirmed for another two years and we will be working with other community partners to help ReLoved become self-sufficient too.'

'Is she really taking credit for your collaboration with The Little Beach Hut Hotel too?' Fern said, aghast.

'It looks that way but I honestly I don't care which way she wants to spin it. This is a huge relief.'

The reporter handed back to the studio and Fletcher turned off the laptop.

'You did it,' Fern said, giving him a hug.

'We did it. You organised the petition, that had to have some bearing on the case too. Thank you for that. And I can't thank you enough for your brilliant suggestion about building the huts for The Little Beach Hut Hotel. Everyone will enjoy doing it but it also means we get a regular income too.'

'It was something worth fighting for... Just like our relationship.'

He pulled back to look at her and he knew now was the time to talk. The sun was just starting its descent across the sky and they'd chatted about the beach huts and ReLoved but somehow they'd avoided talking about the most important subject of all.

He wanted a future with her. He wanted her as his wife but, despite her magnanimity earlier, he still couldn't let go of the guilt surrounding his behaviour towards Lauren. One of the reasons his parents had fought was because his dad was never there, he would go from work to the pub and always come home late. At weekends, he'd be playing golf or tinkering down at the allotment or going out for day-long cycle rides and his mum had felt like she was raising Fletcher and his sister alone. She never felt like she was a priority. Fletcher had never been there for Lauren either. He couldn't let go of this fear that he would be a complete failure as a husband to Fern too.

He had to be brave, he knew that. As Antonio said, he had to give it his best shot and he knew he would put his heart and soul into that future with Fern.

He stood up and took Fern's hand.

'Fletcher.'

Fletcher looked up to see Lauren standing on the towpath.

'Hi. Are you OK?'

'Yeah. I'm sorry to interrupt, I just thought maybe we could have a quick chat. I fly back to Spain tomorrow morning and I feel like we have some things to talk about.'

What he really wanted was to take Fern to bed and show her how much he loved her, how she would always be his priority, but he had turned his back on Lauren before and he wasn't going to do it again.

'Sure, we can do that.' He glanced over to Fern hoping she would give her approval, especially as she now knew about his past with Lauren.

Fern smiled at him and nodded. 'I should probably go and have an early night anyway, I didn't get a lot of sleep last night.'

Fletcher suppressed a smirk.

Fern stood up and whistled for Bones but Fletcher snagged her hand.

'You don't need to go.'

'Yeah I do.' She squeezed his hand. 'I'll see you later. Nice to see you again, Lauren.'

He helped her step over the edge of the boat, Bones jumping onto the towpath to join her. Then as she started walking away he offered his hand out to help Lauren aboard, immediately feeling as if he was being unfaithful.

'Sorry I keep turning up at the most inopportune moments. I just thought we need to clear the air.'

'No need to apologise and I don't think there's any need to clear the air,' Fletcher said.

Lauren sighed and sat down. 'We haven't spoken since our annulment came through. I feel like we do have things to talk about.'

'To be fair you moved to Spain and I had no way of contacting you. I did say that we could be friends but I do understand why you didn't want anything more to do with me.'

'You see, that right there is what we need to talk about. You looked horrified to see me this morning. And as Fern is someone who you claim is the love of your life I'm very surprised you never told her about us.'

'I didn't want her to hate me.'

'Why would she hate you? You didn't do anything wrong.'

This surprised Fletcher; he'd been a terrible husband to Lauren. It was one thing for Fern to forgive him so easily, quite another to hear Lauren say it. 'Oh sure, our marriage was a whole bed of sunshine and roses.'

'Our marriage was a sham, you and I both know that. We should never have got married. Our relationship was based on one night of drunken sex and a pregnancy which probably wasn't even yours. You were the only one of the men I slept with who used protection. I didn't want to piss off the others by asking them to wear a condom. I was a people pleaser and I thought that the only way I could get men to like me was by sleeping with them. You were utterly lovely when we slept together. No one had ever been that kind to me before in my life. Suddenly I could see my whole life in front of me, married to this perfect, kind guy. I thought you

321

were my only chance at happiness, so I clung onto you. I told you I was pregnant with your child and instead of telling me to sling my hook like every other man would have, you married me. So when I lost the baby I knew that my beautiful bright future had gone with it. And then I acted like some weird stalker, begging you not to leave, following you, trying to break into your house. I'm not surprised you ran.'

'I should have been there for you.'

'You didn't owe me anything, you have nothing to feel guilty about. I wasn't in a good place, I hadn't been for several years before we met, actually. And when I tried to take my life, you came back from a dream job to be with me, helped me get counselling. You were there for me after, kept ringing me to check on me, you'd meet with me for lunch. You didn't have to do any of that. You went above and beyond and you shouldn't be ashamed about that. You were a good friend.'

'But when our annulment came through, you left, you didn't even say goodbye, you just cut me out of your life. I was worried about you. Your aunt said it was for the best that I let you make a clean break. She said I was the worst thing that ever happened to you so I figured your life would probably be better without me in it.'

'I left because I was embarrassed of what I had put you through: the pregnancy, the marriage, the stalking, ruining your job in Tenerife. I figured you would be better off without me.'

He shook his head. 'I look back at that time and I feel sick that... that you tried to... end your life because of me, because of what I did.'

'It was not because of you and you must never think that. I had a messed-up childhood, you know that. And what would our lives have been like if you had done the noble and righteous thing and stayed married to me? We didn't love each other, hell we didn't even know each other. We would have argued, and eventually we would have hated each other. That's not a positive environment for either of us or any children if we'd had any more. And you didn't ruin my life. Meeting you was the best thing that happened to me. You gave me that bar to aim for. Before you, men treated me like shit and I allowed it, thinking that was all I deserved. You showed me what to aim for when looking for a man, someone who treated me with respect and kindness. I'm married now, he's a really good man, he makes me happy, and I don't think I would have ever found him if it hadn't been for you.'

Fletcher stared at her. 'I'm so pleased you've found happiness. I'm not sure I can take any of the credit. Maybe I showed you how not to do a marriage and hopefully you aimed a lot higher than that.'

She reached across the table and took his hand. 'You need to let go of your guilt now. If you want forgiveness, I forgive you, but I promise you, there is nothing to forgive.'

He let out a heavy breath. He had carried this burden around with him for twelve years but hearing Lauren say he hadn't ruined her life, that it wasn't his fault, he felt some of the weight of it slip away.

'Also, I've been in this town five minutes and I know more about you from the locals than I did in the week we were married. I know that you and Fern are this perfectly happy couple, that she wants to get married and you broke up with her because you felt you couldn't give her that. You can't let our past ruin your future. I had no qualms at all about getting married again. I was in love, real love, not the weird stalkery kind I had with you. And not to damage your ego, but what we shared didn't even enter my mind when I said yes, when I walked down the aisle, when I said I do. I moved on a very long time ago so I hate that you haven't, that you've carried this with you ever since. I look back at that period of my life and recognise it as my darkest days, but I absolutely never blamed you for any of it. And, judging from how you looked after me when you came back from Tenerife, the little I knew of you before we got married, and from hearing the people of the town talk about you, I know you would make an amazing husband. Do you love her?'

'Yes, more than anything. She's my entire world.'

'And do you see yourself spending the rest of your life with her?'

'Yes, absolutely.'

'Then why are you sitting here with me?'

He smiled. 'I will always be here for you Lauren, if you need me.'

'You're a good man, but it's time you were there for the woman you love.'

Lauren stood up and he stood up too.

'Take care of yourself Fletcher, I wish you a life of unending happiness.'

'Thank you, I wish that for you too.'

'I already have it, now it's your turn.'

He helped her ashore and she gave him a wave before disappearing down the towpath. He looked around the boat feeling lighter than he'd done in years. He knew what he had to do.

∿

Fern was sitting out on her decking, admiring the sun sinking into the waves, when she saw Fletcher hurrying along the path towards her.

'Hey, how was your chat with Lauren, is she OK?' Fern said, secretly pleased the chat had been so quick and that he'd come to her straight after.

'She set me straight on a few things. I have something I need to say to you.'

'I have something I need to say to you too,' Fern said, gesturing for him to sit down next to her.

He shook his head. 'Mine is pretty important.'

'Mine is too.'

He paused then nodded for her to go ahead.

'When I was young, I was so caught up with the idea of getting married – the dress, the cake, what the bridesmaids would wear, the candles, the flowers, the big party – that I never really gave much thought to the marriage,' Fern said. 'Of course, part of the getting married dream was that I would be with a man that loved me so much that he wanted forever with me and that in itself was something I found very difficult to believe in given my upbringing. But for all my dreams of the big day, I didn't really have a clear picture in my head of what a marriage was. But I know now. Being married to someone is a beautiful adventure – children, jobs, holidays, a new house, a big troublesome dog – but it's also a partnership, being part of a team, it's being there for each other through all the wonderful ups and terrifying downs that life throws at you. It's holding each other's hand through the good times and the bad. We have all of that. We had that from the beginning. I could not have got through the last few days if you hadn't been there for me and I cannot imagine going through the journey of life without you by my side. I want to share the joys and tears with you. You *are* my husband and I don't need a piece of paper or a big party to prove that.'

Fletcher stared at her. 'I want that life with you too, more than anything, but... it would be a shame to waste that dress.'

Her heart leapt. 'What are you saying?'

'I'm saying that I was so hung up on the past that I let it ruin my future. I was so scared of making the same mistakes and losing you that I pushed you away. I want you as my wife, in every sense of the word.'

Fern paused. 'I don't want you to do something you don't want to do. I'm yours, we don't need a wedding to confirm that. We were meant to be together.'

Fletcher shook his head. 'I thought about marrying you many times and what our wedding would look like, what you would wear and what our beautiful future together would be like. Ettie was right, she did see me looking at engagement rings. But I was never brave enough to take that step after what happened with Lauren. I told myself we didn't need it, that we were fine as we were.'

'We are.'

'Stop trying to talk me out of it. I love you. You have changed my life so completely and utterly and I can't wait to start the rest of our lives together, as husband and wife.'

Fern let out a little gasp as he got down on one knee and offered out a ring. It was a carved wooden ring and she knew immediately it had come from the beautiful bookcase as he'd clearly saved one of the tiny wooden flowers as the centre-piece for the ring.

'Fern Lucas, will you marry me?'

She threw herself at him, kissing him hard, and he

wrapped his arms around her as they fell back onto the grass. Bones barked excitedly as he leapt around them.

Fletcher eventually pulled back. 'Is that a yes?'

'Let me see this ring again,' Fern said.

He held it up so she could see it. 'I made it for you this afternoon using remnants from that bookcase you loved so much. We can get you a proper ring with a diamond in it—'

His words were lost as she kissed him again. 'I love it,' she said against his lips. 'And I love you so so much and I want to get married to you as soon as possible.'

He kissed her hard and then pulled away. 'I want to do this wedding right.'

'It doesn't need to be a big affair.'

'No, I like the idea of marrying you on Blackberry Beach, something simple. But I also think we need to take the time to get to know each other properly – the good, the bad, the ugly and everything in between – before we commit to the rest of our lives. So how about, if you still want to marry me after four months of living with me on my boat, of seeing me, warts and all, we get married at the end of September?'

'I would love that. September is still warm enough but not too hot, a lot of the tourists will have gone so we might have the beach to ourselves and Councillor Bishop might even agree to close it for the evening. And as for living with you on your boat, I can't think of anywhere better to start our engagement.'

'You can even paint the inside if you want, with dinosaurs.'

Fern laughed. 'I might hold you to that.'

Carrie watched the funfair from her back door, a huge smile on her face. The grand opening had gone without a hitch. Michelle had even come along and set up a red ribbon to cut to declare it officially open, which seemed a bit pretentious but the crowd had cheered, loving the pomp and ceremony of it all. Carrie, Fern, Fletcher, Theo and Shay had spent the afternoon giving tours of all the beach huts and everyone had loved the little huts and especially how beautifully they had been painted with all the different animals. Now everyone was enjoying the funfair, she could hear the squeals of delight as people had fun on the rides.

A movement caught her eye and she saw Antonio walking towards her.

'Have you come to complain about the noise?' she asked.

He laughed and offered out a bottle of champagne. 'I brought you this.'

'Oh that's lovely, thank you.'

'I thought we could share it tomorrow night after I've taken you out to dinner to celebrate the opening.'

She felt her eyebrows shoot up. 'You want to take me to dinner?'

'Yes I do.'

'And then you want to come back here and continue celebrating with champagne?'

He moved closer. 'Yes.'

'Are you trying to get me into bed?'

He smiled. 'Straight to the point. This is whatever you want it to be. It can just be dinner and you can share the champagne with your family, or it can be dinner and champagne and conversation or... it can be dinner, champagne and sex. It's entirely up to you.'

The thought of making love to Antonio made her

328

nervous and excited all at once. She looked at the bottle of champagne. 'Well, it kind of seems a shame.'

'What does?'

'You're here now, the champagne is here. It seems a shame to wait until tomorrow.'

He grinned. 'You've always been a woman that goes after what she wants. I like that.'

'Well fortunately for you, I want you, I have done for a while. But if you complain about the sex after, this will be the shortest relationship you've ever had.'

'I promise that won't happen. The complaints were merely an excuse to keep coming to see you.'

'Yeah, I finally figured that out too.'

Carrie leaned up and kissed him and he wrapped his arms around her, kissing her hard before shuffling her backwards into the house.

Fern walked through the fair eating an ice cream and smiled at everyone enjoying themselves. It seemed like the whole of the town and lots of other local villages had come out to support the opening of The Little Beach Hut Hotel. She couldn't be happier for Carrie that everything had gone so well for her.

She looked down at her hand wrapped in Fletcher's, and she couldn't help but smile at the beautiful engagement ring, the shine of the wood glinting in the lights from the fair. She still couldn't quite believe she was engaged. For a while that had felt like an impossible dream and now she had the rest of her life with Fletcher as husband and wife. She had moved out of her little beach hut this week and onto Fletcher's boat.

And it just worked, the two of them together, just as it had always done. They clicked together perfectly and, for some reason, everything felt that tiny bit better. Maybe it was still the excitement of being engaged, but she kept looking at him as they ate, or as he read a book, and her face ached from smiling so much. When he made love to her, he looked at her with such complete adoration that it made her heart feel so full.

Although they'd spoken about starting a family before they'd broken up, they hadn't discussed it since getting engaged and, while she was happy to wait until after the wedding or even until they got a house, she kept imagining herself walking around the boat with a baby and adapting the boat to encompass a nursery.

'What are you thinking?' Fletcher said.

'How much I love you and how happy you make me.'

'That's funny, that's just what I was thinking.'

She smiled then frowned.

'Actually that's not entirely true,' Fern said.

He looked down at her with concern. 'You're not happy?'

'I am deliriously happy.' She stopped and turned to look at him. 'But that's not exactly what I was just thinking about. I know we've got four months until our wedding and I'm more than happy to wait until then, but I was wondering how you felt about trying for a baby straight after. I know we spoke about this before and I know you kind of wanted to wait until we got a house but—'

Her words were lost as he cupped her face and kissed her.

He looped an arm round her shoulders and started walking again. Fishing his phone out of his pocket, he swiped the screen a few times and then passed it to her.

'These are my saved items in my Amazon account.'

She smiled when she saw a cot, a pushchair, a car seat, and various other bits of baby paraphernalia.

'I think raising a baby on a boat is not the most ideal environment,' Fletcher said. 'But with two parents and a dog that will love it so completely and utterly, I know we can make it work.'

She turned to face him again. 'So we're going to do this?'

'I think we should go home and start practising right now.'

She laughed. 'I need to come off the pill and then we probably need to wait a few weeks for that to come out of my system and then we need to work out when I'm ovulating and—'

He bent his head and kissed her again. 'Or we don't worry about any of that and just have a lot of fun trying.'

She smiled against his lips. 'I like the sound of that.'

EPILOGUE

Four months later

Fern fastened the beautiful blue moonstone necklace Fletcher had given her for her birthday round her neck. Rather than always looking at it and being reminded of the night she didn't get her proposal, she would always look at it now and smile because it was the necklace she got married in. It also matched her engagement ring so it seemed fitting to wear it today.

She stood back to admire how she looked in her perfect wedding dress. It was beautiful, the flowers glittering in the sunlight pouring through the bedroom window. She couldn't wait to see Fletcher's face when he saw her. He was waiting for her in the lounge as they'd decided to arrive at the wedding together. She was so excited she was finally going to marry Fletcher that her body was practically buzzing.

She walked out the bedroom and admired Fletcher standing in his suit as he stood in the doorway staring out over the river.

He turned to look at her and his whole face lit up in wonder. He quickly moved towards her.

'You look magnificent,' he whispered, his eyes raking down the dress and back up. But when he met her gaze again she could see he was a little emotional.

She stepped up to him and held his face. 'Hey, you can't cry on our wedding day.'

He laughed. 'I think there might be a few more tears today. You're making me the happiest man alive today by becoming my wife. I felt for so long that I don't deserve it but now I couldn't be happier to be taking this step with you.'

She reached up to kiss him. He moved his arms around her, holding her close so his fingers grazed the bare flesh above the back of the dress, making goosebumps erupt across her skin. He pulled back slightly. 'This dress is incredible, later I'm going to make love to you while you're wearing it and then I'm going to take it off and make love to you again.'

Her heart leapt with desire. 'Stop it, or we're never getting out of here today.'

'Ordinarily, I'd say that was great, a day spent with you in bed is never a waste, but we have something far more important to do today.'

She trailed her finger down his chest. 'We have to come back in two hours to feed and inject Bones, so maybe you can show me what newlywed sex looks like then.'

He grinned. 'I absolutely can do that.'

'I cannot wait to make love to you as my husband, I hear it's ten times better once you're married.'

He laughed. 'Oh, it will rock your world. Before we go, I bought you a gift.' He nudged a large, wrapped box towards her. 'I wanted to make all your dreams come true.'

She frowned in confusion. 'You're marrying me, that's the greatest gift you could ever give me.'

'Just open it."

She unwrapped the paper and laughed to see a Mr Frosty ice-drink maker.

'This is brilliant, thank you.'

'Come on, we have a wedding to go to.'

She slipped on a pair of white sparkly Converse she'd found in a charity shop – she definitely preferred comfort over style on a day like this – and then whistled for Bones who was busy chewing on the doggy top hat they'd tried to put on him earlier. Fortunately the bow tie around his collar was still intact.

Fletcher offered out the bouquet of wildflowers she knew he'd handpicked for her this morning and she accepted it, admiring the colours before taking his hand as they stepped outside.

They walked along the towpath towards the car park and Fern froze as she saw a splendid-looking shire horse waiting patiently with flowers plaited into its mane, harnessed up to a little pony trap, decorated in white and yellow flowers.

'Oh my god, Fletcher, this is amazing, I had no idea you'd arranged this.'

'Well, Carrie said you'd always dreamed of arriving in a horse-drawn carriage. I know the pony trap isn't quite a carriage but—'

'It's perfect,' Fern said and ran forward to stroke the velvety soft nose of the horse. Bones came to greet the new visitor too, but, once he was satisfied it wasn't a dog that needed playing with, he lolloped off.

'Her name is Loveheart,' Fletcher said, stroking the horse's neck.

'Really?'

'Yes, it seemed appropriate.'

He offered out a hand and helped her up onto the seat then sat next to her and took the reins, clicking the horse into a walk. Bones bounced around at the side of them.

Fern leaned her head against Fletcher's shoulder as they plodded along. 'My heart is so full with happiness I think it might actually burst. I love you so much.'

He kissed her on the forehead. 'I love you too.'

He smiled as they moved along; he looked so at peace, so happy, that she knew all his earlier worries about them marrying had now gone.

The wedding itself had been fairly easy to organise. After Carrie had spoken to Councillor Bishop, she'd agreed to close Blackberry Beach after five so they could hold an evening wedding. It was going to be a simple affair and Fern thought that it couldn't be more perfect. They were doing the legal bits at a registrar office in a few days but that was just a box-ticking exercise, this was her proper wedding.

They reached the tunnel that led to Blackberry Beach and Blake, one of Fletcher's apprentices, was there to take control of Loveheart.

'Thanks Blake,' Fletcher said.

'Yes, thank you and thank you, Loveheart,' Fern said as they climbed down.

They walked through the tunnel towards the beach. She smiled to see the paintings that had brought her and Fletcher together. It was a fitting place to get married. This had been their beginning and now this was where they started their happy ever after.

They got to the end of the tunnel where Shay and Theo were waiting to escort her up the aisle. Ettie and Orla, looking gorgeous in their sunshine-yellow dresses, were poised to follow them.

Fletcher gave Fern a kiss on the cheek. 'I'll see you up there.'

'You can count on it.'

He walked off and took his place at the end of the aisle.

Fern paused a moment to take a breath. The sea was a beautiful sapphire, sparkling in the late afternoon sun as it lapped onto pure white sands. And there were all their friends and family waiting for them.

The music started, Ellie Goulding's, 'How Long Will I Love You'. Fern linked arms with Theo and Shay and started walking forwards towards her future.

ALSO BY HOLLY MARTIN

Sunshine and Secrets at Blackberry Beach

❧

The Wishing Wood Series

The Blossom Tree Cottage

The Wisteria Tree Cottage

The Christmas Tree Cottage

❧

Jewel Island Series

Sunrise over Sapphire Bay

Autumn Skies over Ruby Falls

Ice Creams at Emerald Cove

Sunlight over Crystal Sands

Mistletoe at Moonstone Lake

❧

The Happiness Series

The Little Village of Happiness

The Gift of Happiness

❧

The Summer of Chasing Dreams

❧

Sandcastle Bay Series
The Holiday Cottage by the Sea
The Cottage on Sunshine Beach
Coming Home to Maple Cottage

❧

Hope Island Series
Spring at Blueberry Bay
Summer at Buttercup Beach
Christmas at Mistletoe Cove

❧

Juniper Island Series
Christmas Under a Cranberry Sky
A Town Called Christmas

❧

White Cliff Bay Series
Christmas at Lilac Cottage
Snowflakes on Silver Cove
Summer at Rose Island

❧

Standalone Stories

The Secrets of Clover Castle (Previously published as Fairytale Beginnings)

The Guestbook at Willow Cottage

One Hundred Proposals

One Hundred Christmas Proposals

Tied Up With Love

A Home on Bramble Hill (Previously published as Beneath the Moon and Stars

For Young Adults

The Sentinel Series

The Sentinel (Book 1 of the Sentinel Series)

The Prophecies (Book 2 of the Sentinel Series)

The Revenge (Book 3 of the Sentinel Series)

The Reckoning (Book 4 of the Sentinel Series)

STAY IN TOUCH...

To keep up to date with the latest news on my releases, just go to the link below to sign up for a newsletter. You'll also get two FREE short stories, get sneak peeks, booky news and be able to take part in exclusive giveaways. Your email will never be shared with anyone else and you can unsubscribe at any time
https://www.subscribepage.com/hollymartinsignup

Website: https://hollymartin-author.com/
Email: holly@hollymartin-author.com
Twitter: @HollyMAuthor

A LETTER FROM HOLLY

Thank you so much for reading *Sunshine and Secrets at Blackberry Beach,* I had so much fun creating this story and creating a wonderful new location in Apple Hill Bay. I hope you enjoyed reading it as much as I enjoyed writing it.

One of the best parts of writing comes from seeing the reaction from readers. Did it make you smile or laugh, did it make you cry, hopefully happy tears? Did you fall in love with Fern, Fletcher and Bones as much as I did? Did you like the little treehouses in Wishing Wood? If you enjoyed the story, I would absolutely love it if you could leave a short review on Amazon. Getting feedback from readers is amazing and it also helps to persuade other readers to pick up one of my books for the first time.

If you enjoyed this story, my next book, out in October, is called The Midnight Village. It's still the small town romance you would expect from me but this one has a slightly magical twist.

Thank you for reading.

Love Holly x

ACKNOWLEDGEMENTS

To my family, my mom, my biggest fan, who reads every word I've written a hundred times over and loves it every single time, my dad, my brother Lee and my sister-in-law Julie, for your support, love, encouragement and endless excitement for my stories.

For my twinnie, the gorgeous Aven Ellis for just being my wonderful friend, for your endless support, for cheering me on, for reading my stories and telling me what works and what doesn't and for keeping me entertained with wonderful stories. I love you dearly.

To my lovely friends Julie, Natalie, Jac, Verity and Jodie, thanks for all the support.

To the Devon contingent, Paw and Order, Belinda, Lisa, Phil, Bodie, Kodi and Skipper. Thanks for keeping me entertained and always being there.

To everyone at Bookcamp, you gorgeous, fabulous bunch, thank you for your wonderful support on this venture.

Thanks to my fabulous editors, Celine Kelly and Rhian McKay.

To all the wonderful bloggers for your tweets, retweets, facebook posts, tireless promotions, support, encouragement and endless enthusiasm. You guys are amazing and I couldn't do this journey without you.

Thanks to Mrs Murals, a fabulous mural artist, who patiently answered all my questions about painting murals.

To anyone who has read my book and taken the time to tell me you've enjoyed it or wrote a review, thank you so much.

Thank you, I love you all.

Cover design by Emma Rogers

Printed in Great Britain
by Amazon

25531665R00199